THE COUNTERFEIT MAN

PHILIP GRANT

Yellow Brick Publishers

First published in Paperback 1993.

YELLOW BRICK PUBLISHERS
2 LONSDALE ROAD
QUEENS PARK
LONDON NW6 6RD

British Library Cataloguing in Publication Data
A catalogue record for this book is available from the British Library.

ISBN: 0-9520560-4-6

Printed and bound in Great Britain by
Cox & Wyman Ltd, Reading, Berkshire

Dedication

To Norma - My Wife

Foreword

The origins of this story lie in a visit I made to the Octoberfest at Rudeshelm some years ago. I would like to thank the good people of that town for the warmth of their welcome and the quality of their wine.

Later the idea was refined during the time I spent in the hot-house atmosphere of the Middle East. Some of those one meets there are not always what they seem!

I must emphasise, however, that all the events and all the people depicted in this novel are entirely imaginary (with the exception that a R.A.F. raid was made against the Germania monument in late 1944).

I would like to thank all those who have helped to bring this work from conception to delivery. I think you will enjoy the result.

The Author, London, 1993.

CHAPTER 1

Saturday — October 13th, 1973

Hugo Lansing stabbed his finger at the doorbell for the second time. He listened intently when it stopped ringing but could hear no sound inside. A frown cast itself over his handsome features, his pale cerulean eyes narrowing in the process.

She had been out at eight - understandable enough. But - he looked at his quartz watch - ten past twelve was different. He cursed himself for not letting her know he was coming. But if he had stopped to phone from Washington he might have missed the plane. Dammit, he thought, he should not need to announce his arrival. But why had she been cool recently - yes, distinctly cool since that last night together? The memory of it brushed away the frown and he smiled to himself. It had been good.

He poked his finger towards the bellpush again but stopped in mid-air. What was the use? She obviously was not in. He walked along the landing to the flat next door. From within he could hear what sounded like the midnight movie blaring away. He hesitated, thought better of it and retraced his steps past her flat and down the staircase. At the bottom he turned sharp right and set off across the lawn to the private road at the back of the flats where he had left his car.

A sudden chill surrounded him and he shivered. As the mist swirled round his legs an uneasy feeling descended over him and he slowed down. Could she possibly...? No, absurd, impossible.

Ahead of him the thick damp air cleared a little and he saw, at the kerb in front of his Buick, an NYPD patrol car. A large black policeman got out and stood on the sidewalk facing him.

'Can I help you, mister?' The words sounded conciliatory, but the tone was not.

'No thanks, officer. Just looking for someone who isn't at home.' He walked towards his car, but the patrolman barred his way.

'Mind identifying yourself, sir?'

Hugo put his hand in the flight bag hanging at his shoulder. The man in front of him tensed visibly and from his left a voice said 'Just put the bag down slowly and step away from it!'

He turned to find the other member of the patrolling team holding a regulation Smith and Wesson thirty-eight in both hands, pointing at his chest.

'Steady on, officer,' he said with an awkward smile as he spread his hands and lowered the bag gingerly by its shoulder strap. He dutifully stepped away from his bag towards his car. The first cop went over to it and opened it to look inside while the one with the gun, whom Hugo took to be a Puerto Rican, made him put his hands on the roof of his car, and frisked him.

'He's clean, Bailey. What's in the bag?'

'Papers mostly. Some tapes.'

'Is there any need for all this?' Hugo asked with

a touch of steel in his voice. The Puerto Rican gave him a look for an answer.

'ID?' asked Bailey.

'In the side pocket of the bag you'll find my official ID and my UN pass,' Hugo replied curtly.

Bailey was already thumbing through it. His partner had joined him and they examined it by their car's interior light.

'Whatya doing here at this time?'

For a moment Hugo hesitated, considering whether to answer.

'Just visiting, as I said '

'Who?' asked the Puerto Rican.

'Miss Tasker, twenty-nine C.'

'You was here earlier tonight,' Bailey said accusingly.

'Yes, she wasn't in then. I came back but she still isn't at home.'

'You know her well?' There was a touch of sarcasm in the Puerto Rican's voice.

'She works for me. I had some important stuff to go over before going to a conference in Washington on Monday morning.'

The patrol car's radio spluttered out a call sign and the Puerto Rican took out the handset and held a conversation with HQ. Hugo strained to hear what was said but could catch only an odd word here and there.

'Riverdale west twenty-ninth ... prowler suspect ... some UN guy ... missing woman ...'

The policeman put back the radio, turned towards Hugo.

'You mind coming down to the precinct house

and clearin' this up?'

'I don't see what it's ... Do I have a choice?' Hugo asked resignedly. The two patrolmen shook their heads in unison.

It was an hour before Sergeant Barty Hampton gave Hugo his attention, an hour during which he made two fruitless calls to Elizabeth Tasker's flat. The thought came to him again after the second one. At first it seemed too ridiculous to contemplate. After all, he assured himself, nobody else in all of twenty-eight years had suspected, except maybe the General. Then again, she had seemed cool recently - since that last night. But surely if ...

'Sorry to keep you waiting sir, but this place is none too quiet on a Saturday night, as you can see.'

Hampton sounded like a salesman in a shoe shop or a liquor store. No sign of menace. Hugo laughed at his own suspicions.

'I hope you've checked me out and found everything satisfactory! I realise you have a job to do, but ...'

'Good of you to say so, sir. You certainly don't seem to be our prowler!' Hampton paused. 'Now about this missing woman?'

'I'm not sure if that's an accurate way of describing the situation,' Hugo said.

'But she is missing, isn't she? - you've been looking for her and phoning her for, eh, six hours or so. Isn't that so?'

'Yes it is but ...' Hugo replied with less confidence.

'Where do you think she is?'

' I don't know exactly, but surely ...'

' Isn't your job with the UN?'

'Yes.'

'You're security rated aren't you?'

'Yes '

'And her?'

'Well, yes.' Hugo began to feel distinctly uneasy. This was certainly not the way he wanted the conversation to go. Again that dark little suspicion flitted across his mind. He realised Sergeant Hampton was waiting for him to say something. He could think of nothing clever.

'What would you say if I was to tell you that she packed up and left her flat tonight?' Hampton asked suddenly.

'You mean ... packed up and left?' Hugo tried hard to hide his surprise.

'That's what I said.' Hampton sounded a trifle less casual.

'Where did she go?' Hugo struggled to appear less worried than he was rapidly becoming.

'That we don't know ... as yet.' Hampton added the last two words with the air of someone who soon would know.

'Has she ever done this before - gone away, I mean - without telling you?' Hampton asked.

'There will, I'm sure, be a perfectly innocent explanation for it all,' Hugo said, deliberately ignoring the sergeant's'question. Barty Hampton was not put off so easily.

'I asked if this is the first time she's gone away

like this?' he demanded, putting his arms on the table and leaning across towards Hugo. Hugo struggled to control himself and to think clearly. He pondered whether to lie and say that she had done something similar in the past but decided to stick as far as possible to the truth.

'I think it is, yes. But are we not perhaps reading too much into a simple matter of a secretary going away somewhere on a Saturday night?' he asked, a trifle superciliously.

'I'm not reading too much into it, sir. Are you?' responded the policeman.

'No, of course not, sergeant,' Hugo countered blandly.

Hampton stood up. 'I doubt if there's anything more we can do tonight. As you say, sir, the whole thing may be an innocent escapade. We'll keep you informed and I trust you'll do the same. If you hear anything let us know.' The interview seemed to be at an end.

'Thank you, sergeant.' Hugo shook the policeman's hand.

'Goodnight, sir.' Barty Hampton remained behind his desk as Hugo Lansing left. The telephone rang as the door closed behind him.

'Hello, yeah ... You guys are on to this damn quick, aren't you? ... Well, I dunno - maybe nuthin' in it .. and yet her boss does seem kinda uptight. Well, I thought I caught some tense vibes. For a minute there I sorta got the feeling he was a bit less than frank. Maybe they're more than just colleagues. Something smells a teeny bit like seafood.'

Back in his flat Hugo Lansing was worried. He tried to convince himself that there was no need, that the phone would ring and she would tell him where she was and that everything was all right. But underneath he could not escape the thought that something was wrong. He was unable to figure out what it could be. She could not possibly know the truth, but something had made her run. She would not have gone in such a way if it were simply a matter of her feelings for him ebbing away. No, it had to be more than that. But what? Had she conceivably found out? Impossible. Only one person might have guessed the truth - or something akin to it, and that was the General, and he did not count any more.

He never had. He had only been a means to an end. The old fool. The mother now, she was different. The only woman I've ever feared, Hugo thought to himself. Fear tinged with respect - affection even. He soon gave up waiting by the phone and went to bed. Sleep took a long time coming and when it did he had his recurrent dream - the one in which he is grown up, but is extremely small, in the corner of a huge room. At the far end a little old woman who seems about ten feet tall is talking to him in tones of admonition, but in a foreign language. He is wracked by humiliation and finds that he has no trousers on. The door bell rings and she tells him to answer it, but he looks down at his bare legs ...

The telephone had rung several times before Hugo picked it up.

'Mr. Lansing?'

'Yes.'

'Bart Hampton here. Have you heard anything from Miss Tasker?'

'No. Nothing. Haven't you ... found out anything?'

'Yes, as a matter of fact, we have. She took a taxi to Kennedy Airport last night. Any idea where she could be headed?'

'No, none. She wasn't planning to go anywhere as far as I am aware,' Hugo replied, 'or to meet anyone.'

'I thought not. Okay, we'll keep looking. If she gets in touch, let us know.'

'Yes, yes I will. Thank you for calling sergeant. So long.'

He put the phone down and looked at the time. It was nine forty-two a.m. Whilst having a shower he pondered what to do next. He thought of her that last time - in the shower and after. He had wondered whether he was in love with her. Now he knew he was not. During this crisis he was worrying about himself, not her.

Had he ever been in love, he wondered? With Greta - had it been love with Greta? No, not love. Passion maybe. Then why? Enlightened self interest, Borsakov had called it. Married to a Senator's sister. For all the good it had done him ... except of course for ACME ... The water suddenly turned colder, interrupting his reverie. He turned it off and wrapped himself in a large towel, one of hers he noted with a wry smile, and lay on his bed. He lit a long, dark cigarette and drew its smog into his lungs. He would have to make contact. He knew that now. But give it a few hours.

At two o'clock he could wait no longer. He went to the phone. It rang before he reached it.

'Hello.'

'Is that Hugo Lansing?'

'Yes.'

'52nd Precinct here. We have some news of Miss Tasker.'

'Yes, what? Where is she?'

'You knew she had gone to Kennedy Airport?'

'Yes, I knew.'

'Well, from there she appears to have flown to Frankfurt. Mean anything to you?'

Hugo's sharp intake of breath was not heard by the man at the other end of the phone.

'No,' he answered barely audibly. 'No, nothing.'

'Oh. Well, that's all we've got so far.'

'Thank you. Goodbye.'

Hugo put the phone down slowly and lit a cigarette. He was frowning again.

CHAPTER 2

The phone rang, naggingly, insistently. At about the fifth ring I awoke and for an instant experienced that weird feeling of not knowing who, what or where I was. Then it came to me, and I stretched my arm across Sandy's torso - why did I always end up on the wrong side of the bed? - towards the phone. I looked at the compelling nakedness of the body beside me and my hand stopped halfway, tempted to linger again in that passionate countryside. Far better than answering the stupid, unfeeling telephone with all the trouble it might have in store. If only I had known how much!

It rang again and I knew that whoever wanted me would let it go on ringing, and I did not relish the thought of trying to make love against such a background. Apart from which Sandy still had not woken up - and there are limits.

'Hlo,' I mumbled, trying to make it as sleepy a response as possible.

'Fox here,' came the reply.

'Who's that?' Sandy asked, waking up as the phone bumped into her left breast.

'FOX I told you,' the voice came louder, 'are you bloody well asleep, Lockhart?'

'Yes,' I replied, putting a hand over Sandy's mouth. She proceeded to eat my fingers.

'Stop trying to be the wit of the century and listen to me. I've gotta job for you. I want you to find a woman.'

I bit my lip to prevent myself making a crack about having found one and being very satisfied, thank you. Instead, I extricated my hand from Sandy's mouth, caressed her breast and mimed drinking from a cup while Fox droned on. Sandy's bum wiggled so enticingly as she made for the kitchen that I nearly threw down the phone and ...

'She was reported missing a few hours ago. Her name is Elizabeth Tasker - you know her - she's secretary to the Director of U.N.P.A.'

I certainly did remember her. Rather an aloof broad - but Fox interrupted my thoughts again in his characteristic monotone.

'In fact it was he who reported it. Seems he went round during the evening with some work for her ...'

'Yeah, sure, work!' I butted in.

'You think it could've been somethin' else?'

'You kidding?' I asked.

'We don't <u>all</u> spend our spare time humping, Lockhart.'

'No, sure,' I said with conviction, remembering the one glance I had had of Mrs. Fox.

'Well, shut your smart mouth for just a few seconds, will you?'

I was as silent as the grave.

'You still there Lockhart?'

'Yep.' Being told to keep mum always did make me want to sound like Gary Cooper.

'Right. Few hours ago she goes missing. Her boss reports it to N.Y.P.D. They check his ID and see he's gotta security rating. So they let us know. Further enquiries establish that she packed and took a taxi to Kennedy Airport. Flew to Frankfurt. Funny thing is HE doesn't seem to know a goddam thing about this flight, yet he's her boss. He went to her flat expecting to go over some work with her before a big conference on Monday, or so he claims.'

'Is that all we've got?'

'So far, yes.'

'And you want me to look into it?'

'More than that, Lockhart. I want you to go find her!'

'What, me? All the way to Germany?'

'Yes please, Lockhart, if you will be so kind.'

'But that ain't my beat. I'm strictly a desk johnnie, you know that. It's years since I ...'

'You gotta valid passport?'

'Yeah,' I mumbled, knowing there was no way out.

'Then get packed and be at Kennedy in two hours. I'll have someone meet you with tickets and some background, a photo and so on. And Lockhart?'

'Yeah?'

'I've no-one else. You know how short the department is and you know this dame, which may be a help. All you have to do is find her, find out if there's any good reason, or maybe I should say BAD reason why she flew the coop, then bring her back here. O.K?'

'O.K. boss,' I said, looking at Sandy as she returned and wondering whether there was time for ...

CHAPTER 3

It did not take Hugo Lansing long to conclude that there were two alternatives available to him. He could either go after Elizabeth himself and find out just how much she knew ... then what? Or he could seek help. That would involve getting in touch with Borsakov and, of course, admitting the possibility that he had somehow given himself away.

But had he? Why else had she flown to Frankfurt? It had to be because she suspected something, something she wanted to check on, in Rudesheim. There could be no other explanation for her sudden, unannounced flight to there, of all places.

Try as he might, he could not think what it was that must have led her to suspect. Maybe that night when she had told him so much about her childhood and he had felt obliged to reciprocate. Even then, he had stuck rigidly to what he knew must be true. Unless ..

Speculation would not help. He would have to do something. He donned his crombie overcoat and left the flat, turning north towards where he reckoned the nearest phone kiosk to be. As he set off, a lanky individual with rather bushy hair and a pock-marked face got out of a Plymouth coupe and followed him.

In Memorial Park Hugo Lansing skirted the

little lake and climbed the path to the top of the hill. A thick set man with closely cropped hair and rimless glasses went on feeding the ducks, throwing them odds and ends from the pocket of his pale grey topcoat. Hugo entered the cafe and served himself a coffee and two doughnuts, paid for them and went over to a corner seat overlooking the park.

Five minutes later the thick set man came in, ordered the same and went over to the corner where he sat down with his back to Hugo. They were the only people in the cafe, apart from an old man at the other end who seemed to have gone to sleep with a Coke.

'Still dunking your doughnuts, my friend?' asked the man.

'Only those without jam,' answered Hugo, smiling almost imperceptibly at the stubbly neck in front of him.

'As you can see I got your message. What's the problem?' the man asked, barely audibly.

'My secretary has taken off. Gone to Frankfurt.'

'So?'

'That's the nearest point to Rudesheim. My birthplace!'

'Ah, yes, your birthplace,' Borsakov smiled as he watched a chunk of his doughnut disintegrate in the coffee.

'When was this?' he asked sharply.

'Last night.'

'Does anyone else know?'

Hugo paused briefly before saying, 'The police.'

'Oh. That is most unfortunate. How much does

she know?'

'I'm not certain. Very little I should think, but it must be enough to make her suspect.'

'Tell me all, my friend.' Borsakov made it sound like an order. Hugo related the whole episode from the time he had called on Elizabeth the previous evening.

'You must follow her. Somehow you must allay her suspicions. Or else .. We will be able to give you some assistance. Someone will contact you after you arrive in Frankfurt.

It is imperative that she is prevented from passing on what she knows, or suspects, to them. If that can be achieved - one way or another - without undue suspicion falling on you, it may be possible to retain your value. It has been very limited up to now, but I had high hopes that in the years to come you would attain such positions that would enable you to ... but that may never come to pass now.' Borsakov sounded genuinely sorry.

Hugo said nothing. He wanted to argue, he wanted to mention ACME, but he said nothing.

'It is the only way, my friend,' Borsakov went on quietly, 'you must go now, tonight, before you are prevented.'

'Do you think that is likely - so soon?' Hugo asked.

'It is what I would do.' Borsakov nodded to himself.

The old man in the corner nearly fell off his chair and the Coke bottle smashed on the floor. A tall cleaner with a lot of hair ambled over and swept up the pieces. Hugo got up and left, giving Borsakov a surreptitious squeeze on the arm as he passed.

Back at his flat he took only ten minutes to pack his flight bag, stuff his UN passport into his coat and leave. He hailed a taxi as it disgorged a passenger on the other side of the road, near a Plymouth coupe.

'Kennedy Airport, quick as you can!' he said to the driver.

CHAPTER 4

Theo Franklin's office was a mess, piled high with folders and books and maps, the desk littered with notes and memoranda and doodled scraps of variously coloured paper. Its disarray was matched by his own. His dessicated hair jutted out from his druffy scalp in every possible direction like an untidy coconut, above a face which bore the marks of a lifetime of eczema. His sea island cotton shirt had given up the fight against neglect and lay open at the neck to allow his stubby fingers to battle against the eternal itch above his collar bone.

The door opened and Miss Stebbing scurried in with a file, laid it down in front of him and went out without a word. A large red 'B' adorned its front cover. He grunted and opened it, rifling quickly through its few pages. Pausing at one of them he stabbed a podgy finger at the top line and followed the text down like a child in second grade trying to read. The finger left the page and prodded the intercom.

'Get me Fox, code three,' he said in a youthful tenor voice which belied his middle age.

'Mr Fox on the blue line, go ahead' squeaked Miss Stebbing.

'This Lansing thing - what's the score?' Franklin asked.

'I'm not sure, Theo, could be a no-no. His secretary takes off without warning, flies to Frankfurt. He reports her missing to N.Y.P.D. - that was Saturday night. Sunday he goes for a walk in the park, back to his flat, then HE takes off for London. Could be he's just chasing after her to make up a lover's tiff.'

'He's screwin' her, is he?'

'Seems so, Theo.'

'Then why report her missing?'

'Maybe he figured it was the quickest way to find out where she's gone. If he is into something funny, seems unlikely he'd go to the cops.'

'Maybe,' Theo sounded doubtful. 'You say he just went for a walk in the park?'

'Hang on, Theo, I've got our guy here with me now.'

Franklin turned to the file again, concentrating his attention on the first page.

'Theo,' Fox sounded apologetic, 'Apparently he stopped on the way to make a call at a phone booth.'

'Who did?'

'Lansing, on his way to the park.'

'Oh no!' Franklin moaned.

''Fraid so.'

'Who did he meet in the park?'

'He didn't meet anyone, but he did stop in a cafe for coffee.'

'Anyone else there?'

'Another guy did go in and have a coffee but didn't seem to talk to Lansing or pass anything on.'

'Your man was there?'

'Yeah.'

'Ask him how near they sat.'

There was a pause before Fox said, 'Pretty close but this other guy had his back to Lansing. One other thing - they both ordered the same - coffee and two doughnuts.'

Theo Franklin closed his eyes and delved into the depths of his memory.

'What did the other guy look like?' he asked.

'Thick set, short hair, rimless specs,' Fox replied, after a brief pause.

'That's Borsakov!'

'Oh Christ!' was all Fox could say.

'Exactly. This IS something. Your guy's a bit wet behind the ears isn't he? Meeting in the park - oldest bloody trick in the book!'

'Sorry Theo. He's new, he'll learn.'

'Better bloody well learn or he can go back to being a college drop-out or whatever he was! So Lansing got away to London. What about the woman?'

'We put Lockhart on to her. He followed to Frankfurt yesterday.'

'That's where Lansing's going too, sure as hell. According to his dossier he was born near there.'

'Yes,' said Fox slowly, 'Must be something in his past.'

'No goddam percentage in speculating. This Lockhart - he's reliable, is he?'

'Well,' Fox sounded doubtful.

'Oh God, not another kid is he?' Franklin rubbed his watery eyes.

'No, Theo, but he ain't used to this sorta thing,

exactly. He's more of a desk guy. He was all I had - and it was only to chase a secretary that had probably taken a sudden holiday. There was nothing to suggest ...'

'Okay, okay,' Theo interrupted, 'Have you anyone over there?'

'Yeah, a German - Klaus Holtz. He's a tough cookie, I believe.'

'He'll maybe need to be.'

'How should we play it now, Theo?'

'Just string them along. We've nothing to hold this guy Lansing for. Get your man Lockhart to find the girl and see what she knows - which is probably precious little. When Lansing arrives there the German can keep an eye on him. They may just come back and then we can really cover this Lansing guy. He's obviously due for a number seven job if he's been talking to Borsakov. Sounds like the girl's clean - unless she's gone ahead to ... There I go speculating when I said it was pointless.'

'I'll keep you posted,' Fox said.

'You do that,' Franklin replied, bringing the conversation to an end. His attention returned to the file and he rifled through its pages again.

'UN Personnel. I wonder ...' he murmured to himself.

'Polly,' he spoke into the intercom, 'Bring me the dead file on Patel, that Indian guy that wasted himself not so long ago. Then get me Larry Osborne at the FBI office in Phoenix.'

He pushed aside some papers to make a place for another file on his desk and went back to scratching his neck.

CHAPTER 5

Larry Osborne's Oldsmobile threw up a dust cloud that could be seen for miles as it crossed the dry Arizona plain towards the mountains. He could see ahead of him the little town of Jackson Stop, the home of General John C. Lansing, U.S.A.F. Retired. He was not used to interviewing Generals and was not looking forward to the prospect. This was especially the case as he was not at all sure what he was supposed to be looking for, except information about the General's adopted son, Hugo. He did not like jobs he did not fully understand.

He stopped at the first gas station in the town - in actual fact the only one - and asked the way. The toothless old man grinned his reply. 'Keep right on agoin' up Main Street, fork left at the end and yurr there.'

Sure enough, just beyond the end of town stood a bungalow on the left. On the porch in a large chair, his lower half covered by a large plaid blanket, sat a thin old man. He stared straight ahead, a dribble of saliva stretching from the left corner of his mouth almost to his lap.

'Excuse me, sir, I'm looking for General Lansing. Can you help me, please?'

There was no response but the old man's head turned slowly. He gave a grunt. The sound of hooves made Osborne turn round, and a girl on horseback, whom he had passed earlier, came up to his car.

'You won't get nothing out of the General. He's been like that for years now.'

'HE is General Lansing!' Osborne had not been expecting this.

'That's right. Who are you - from State Capital?'

'No. I'm looking for information and I rather hoped the General could help me.'

'What do you want to know?'

'It's nothing you would know anything about. It concerns years ago, when he was in the war.'

'Oh, well, it'll be Aunt Ellie you want. She knows everything about everyone round here. AUNT ELLIE!' the girl called out, with her hand to her mouth.

The screen door behind the old man opened outwards and a woman of about sixty, wiping her hands on her apron, emerged.

'What can I do for you?' she asked in a voice softer than her lined features.

'He wants to ask about the General,' the girl said in a loud whisper.

'You be off home, Candy, your Uncle Lester's looking for you. He phoned ten minutes ago. You know what he'll do if you're late again. And button up your shirt.' The girl looked at Osborne as she did up the top button which pulled her denim shirt tightly across the front of her chest. She seemed to take a long time to complete the manoeuvre, then turned her pony and kicked it into a canter back down the road.

'She'll come to no good, that one,' the woman

muttered as she watched the girl's departure. She turned to Osborne.

'How can I help you, young man?'

'I was hoping to talk to General Lansing, but ...' his voice trailed off as he nodded towards the still figure. She walked over to the chair and wiped the corner of the old man's mouth with her apron. She pushed back a strand of hair which had fallen across his brow.

'This young man's come to see you, John,' she said to him. The General's head turned, but away from Osborne. He grunted. The woman turned back to the door and held it open.

'Best come on in, I'll see if I can help you.'

Larry Osborne was surprised by the interior of the bungalow, which was somehow much larger than appeared from the outside. It was sumptuously furnished in a European style with much mahogany and velvet.

'I'm afraid my husband will not be able to assist you. He suffered a stroke four years ago and another nine months back. He was quite a different man before that.'

She looked at him inquiringly.

'I'm Larry Osborne. I'm with the FBI.' He showed her his identity card.

'Sit down. Can I get you a drink? You must be dry if you've driven across the plain.'

'Thank you. I'll have a beer if I may.'

When she had brought him the drink she sat down and looked at him expectantly.

'My inquiries concern Hugo Lansing - your adopted son, I believe.'

'Ah, Hugo, I see. He is not our son, adopted or otherwise. What do you want to know about him?'

Osborne suddenly had a wild idea, and asked, 'He's not here, is he?'

'Here? He hasn't been here for three years or more. What is this all about?'

'I can't tell you that.' (I don't know myself, he thought.) 'I would just like you to tell me as much as you know about Hugo Lansing, his origins and so on.'

'As far back as that? We were not married then, you know, at the end of the war. That was when my husband... he has not always been like that. Did you know he was decorated personally by Eisenhower?' She smiled at the memory. 'If you want to understand about Hugo I'll have to tell you my husband's story, from the beginning.' She looked across at Osborne, who took his cue.

'Please do, tell me about your husband the General.'

She leaned back in her chair and spoke.

'The Lansings came to the States from Germany along with millions of others last century, about 1880, I think it was. His father was only a boy then. They travelled west to Arizona and then the family split up, some going on to California. I believe a cousin went into movies when they started.'

'Excuse me interrupting, but do you know what part of Germany the Lansings came from?'

'Yes. A place called Rudesheim. John never forgot that because his brother was actually called Rudy. They make wine there, you know. When we were in Washington in the fifties we always used to get wine for the table from there, that is wine that was made there. We used to entertain a lot then. Senators, diplomats... Where was I? Oh, yes, with the first ones to come over.' She gave an almost imperceptible shake of the head and went on.

'It was always said that John's grandfather left Germany because of some disreputable incident, but we were never sure. Anyway, he started a store where many of those travelling west used to stock up with provisions. The business did not do so well after the turn of the century, but John's father went into it and carried on. His mother, whom he adored, came over from Germany later, about 1903, I think. At first she was with her parents in Omaha but for some reason decided to go west. She met John's father in the store - that was in Prescott - and she stayed there instead of going on. They were married the following year, then when she was pregnant she visited her parents in Omaha. John was born there, three weeks premature.'

She rose from her armchair and went out to the veranda. The old man did not show any sign of recognition. She grasped the handle at the back of his chair and squeezed the switch. With a muffled whirring the chair took off down the veranda. At the other end she turned him to face the sun and tucked him inside the large blanket. Osborne watched from the door as he held it open for her to re-enter.

'It's all he does now, sit out there. It's a crying shame for a man who's been so active all his life.' She stood for a moment watching her husband through the window then turned back to Osborne, a single tear trickling down the deep wrinkle at the side of her mouth. She smiled self-consciously at the young man. He shuffled awkwardly.

'I'm sure sorry to distress you like this, ' he said.

'It's not you, Mister Osborne, it's just life.'

'But I'm sorry to make you rake over it all like this.'

'Don't you worry about that, I enjoy talking about John and his family. I'm extremely proud of him.' She gave an almost imperceptible sniff. 'Where was I now?'

'General Lansing was born in Omaha, you had told me.'

'Ah, yes. Well, of course, his mother brought him home and then two years later, that would be in 1909, his brother Rudy was born. They called him that after Rudesheim where the family came from. I told you that, didn't I?

Unfortunately the store did not do so well after that. Then when the first war came there was some prejudice because of their German origins. John's grandparents still conversed in German and this was not liked, of course. The business never picked up after that. During the war his grandmother died, then in 1919 his grandfather took Rudy up Baldy Peak and they got lost and died of exposure. His father never recovered from these blows and in fact got tuberculosis the following year. Apparently it was so rare out here in those days - still is, I suppose - that the medics didn't cotton onto it in time. He died in 1920 when he was fifty. John and his mother were left alone there. She took him to Omaha, to her family.

He joined the army as a boy just three years later and served our flag for forty-four years. He once told me that he thought maybe he had joined the army to prove how American he was after what folks had said about them during the war. I doubt it. I think he simply knew what he could do best by instinct.' She looked up at Osborne.

'Can you tell me anything about Hugo, how did your husband meet him?'

'You know, I had almost forgot it was Hugo you came about and you let me go on so.'

'I'm sorry, I didn't mean to imply...'

'That's all right young man,' she interrupted, 'You're quite right to bring me back to the point. The fact is - I can't tell you too much about what happened because it was all during the war, over in Germany, before I met him. What I do know is that when he came back from Europe he had this boy in tow. There was a bit of a rumpus about it in official circles, mind you. In fact I was told years later by someone whose name you would certainly know, that it was the only blot on his entire record and that only his reputation saved the boy from being sent back.

My husband had always been upset at losing his family the way I've told you, and being aware of his German background, he apparently got this idea that he could try to help some German child from Rudesheim after the war. He was in Frankfurt just after the surrender. That's quite near Rudesheim. Well, imagine his surprise when he meets not just any German kid, but a Lansing. So he gets the crazy idea of adopting the lad. Well, there was no way he could do that over in Germany - or over here for that matter, but he did not realise that. You see, he was unmarried and nobody would let him adopt a child of sixteen.'

'He was sixteen, then, when he came over here?' Osborne was getting impatient.

'Yes, that he was. John thought that if he brought the boy over to the States he would be allowed to stay. He was right, too.'

'How did he get the boy into the country?'

'He simply flew him across the Atlantic! He was a colonel in the US Air Force by then, you see. It wasn't very difficult for him to do that. When he got the lad stateside he took him to his mother in Omaha. She could still speak German and kept him for about two years, I think. By then his English was fluent and he had proved to be a brilliant young man, years ahead of his contemporaries, in spite of having come through the war in Germany. He remained with John's mother - John was soon back in Europe - until he got into MIT.'

'He was at MIT?'

'Yes, he was. Graduated summe cum lauda.'

'When did you meet him, Mrs. Lansing?'

'Not till years later. My husband and I met in Europe. He stayed on there for years after the war. He was involved in the Berlin air-lift and was promoted to General when NATO was established. I worked in various American establishments as an interpreter - I spoke fluent Russian in those days, and that was much in demand. We met in London originally, then later on in France, and finally got married in 1949. He was forty-two and I was, well, a bit younger. By the time I came back to Omaha with John, Hugo had left for Massachusetts. It was three years later that I met him.'

'What did you think of him?'

'In what way?'

'In any way, just, what did you think of him?'

'To tell you the truth, I never liked him. I never have. He gave me the impression then, and it holds to this day, though I don't know why, that he was somehow laughing at John, that he had no real affection for him. In fact I don't think he ever had affection for anyone. There was the girl at... but that's all past.'

'No, tell me please,' Osborne insisted.

'There was a rumour that he got a girl into trouble ... you know?'

'What happened?'

'She is supposed to have died having an abortion. Nothing ever happened in the way of a solid accusation or anything. I remember the night John came home after seeing Hugo about it. He was very upset, but would never tell me what had transpired. I've always thought that Hugo as good as admitted it. John's mother knew Hugo better than anyone. I once asked her what she thought of him.'

'What did she say?' Osborned leaned forward.

'She said a very strange thing. She said she was afraid of him. When I asked her what she meant she replied in German, something about him not coming from our world. My German is not very good and that was the nearest I could get to what she was trying to say. She refused to elaborate and I never broached the subject again. What happened to Hugo after that is on the record. You will know all about his brilliant career at the UN, his marriage, and so on.'

Although in fact he did not know all the rest, Osborne thought it best to let on that he did. He nodded.

'Can you tell me nothing more about your husband's first contact with Hugo?'

'No, I'm afraid not. But there's someone else who can.'

'Who's that?'

'Hank Carlile. He was my husband's Staff Sergeant throughout the war. They went everywhere together. Hank came back here with us and runs the place now.'

Osborne looked at her inquiringly.

'This place, Jackson Stop. You see, one of my husband's mother's family settled out here even before she came over to Omaha. She inherited ten thousand acres here and it passed to John when she died. The name comes from her German family but was anglicised to Jackson, and he stopped here!' She smiled.

'Is Mister Carlile around now, do you know?'

'He's not here today, he's gone to Phoenix on business.'

'When will he be back?'

'Tomorrow, I should think.' She rose once more and looked through the window.

The General sat, just as before.

'Have you any family, Mrs. Lansing?'

'Why do you ask?'

'Idle curiosity, I suppose.'

'No, it isn't. You're wondering whether all this goes to Hugo, aren't you?'

'It had occurred to me, I must confess.'

'A natural enough question. The answer is 'no.' Hugo doesn't know it, but John changed his will after the first stroke. Up to then Hugo WAS the beneficiary, neither of us having any other family.'

'What made him change his will, do you know?'

'Hugo did, funnily enough. He came out here after John's first stroke. Something he said upset John terribly. What it was he would never tell me.'

'You mean they had a row?'

'No, no, nothing like that. Hugo was quite pleasant, very sorry about the General and so on. No, there was something else. It must have been something Hugo let slip without realising it. I remember quite well, it was after dinner one evening. We left the table, Hugo excused himself and I pushed John out to the verandah. You must understand that although partially paralysed he was still in full command of his faculties, unlike...' her voice faded and her face saddened. She shook away her grief and went on, 'I pushed him out, and when I asked him if he wanted a drink, I saw the look on his face. It was very strange, a mixture of puzzlement and anger is the nearest I can get to it.'

'What had you been talking about, can you recall?'

'They had done most of the talking. They hadn't seen each other for quite some time and they were talking about Germany, I think, and when they had met and so on. Oh, and yes, I remember the subject of Rudy came up. It's coming back to me now, maybe because I've been telling you all about it. Yes, John mentioned Rudy and something Hugo said made him go very quiet. It was just after that we went outside.'

'What did he say?'

'Who, Hugo?'

'Yes.'

'I can't remember. Might it be important?'

'Perhaps. Was anyone else there?'

'No.'

'Did you ask the General what had upset him?'

'Yes, but he wouldn't say. He said he had something to think about. I left him alone on the verandah. It was a few days later he sent for his lawyer and changed his will.'

'In favour of?'

'Well, me firstly, but when I go Hank gets everything.'

'Hank Carlile?' Osborne sounded mildly surprised.

'Why not? He's done everything for years round here. He has a lovely wife who's still only in her forties and they have three fine children - well, two fine and one just a little bit lacking. That's her spoke to you when you arrived - Candy she's called. Hank and his kin will appreciate this place far more than Hugo ever would.'

'Does Hugo know that the General changed his will?'

'I doubt it. He hasn't been back since then.'

'Not even when your husband had his second stroke?'

'No, although he did have a good reason then.

He was away on some UN mission.'

'But he never came back later?'

'No.'

'Isn't that rather odd?'

'Yes it is, but don't forget they were never very close. John met him over there then brought him home and left him in Omaha. After that they only saw each other occasionally, although of course the General always took a close interest in Hugo's progress.'

'I think I've upset you enough Mrs. Lansing. It's been very good of you to answer all my questions so thoroughly.' He rose and shook her hand. 'One last thing, can you tell me where I can contact Hank Carlile?'

'I think he always stays at the Holiday Inn in Phoenix. I'm sure he will be there until tomorrow. I'll see you out.' She opened the door for him, but he waved her out first. She went over to the crumpled figure in the chair.

'Mr. Osborne's going now, John.' The old man's head moved and he frowned lopsidedly. Osborne did not know what to do in the way of shaking hands, so gave an informal salute, turned away and walked to his car.

CHAPTER 6

Hank Carlile looked past the bell-hop's outstretched finger to where the house phone stood on a window-ledge of the Rodeo Bar in the Holiday Inn, Phoenix. He went over and picked up the handset.

'Hello, Hank Carlile here.'

'Hello, my name's Larry Osborne, Mister Carlile. I wonder if I might have a few minutes of your time to ... '

'What's your business, son?'

'I've come from Mrs. Lansing ...'

'Nothing happened, has it?' Hank Carlile interrupted quickly, anxiously.

'No, no, the General's fine ... leastways as fine as ...' Osborne's voice trailed off with some embarrassment.

'Oh, you didn't know about the General's health then?'

'No, I'm sorry.'

'That's okay, son. Now what can I do for you?'

'I'm here in the hotel, Mister Carlile, and I just want to ask a few questions, about the General as a matter of fact - won't take long. But we can't talk like this over the phone - where are you now?'

'In the Rodeo Bar,' Hank replied slowly, not sure what to make of it all.

'I'll be there in seconds,' said Larry, and hung up.

'Sit down, have a drink,' invited Hank as soon

they had shaken hands. He waved to a passing waiter as they settled into a large corner seat in the almost empty bar.

'Thanks, I'll have a beer,' Osborne replied, as he pulled out his FBI card and showed it to Carlile.

'Well, I'm impressed,' was the response. 'What can I do for you?' This time Hank refrained from addressing the other as 'Son'...

'As I think I said, I've just come from visiting General Lansing. I had hoped to find out one or two things from him, but ...'

'So you spoke to Mrs Lansing,' Hank finished what the other was trying to say.

'Yes. She suggested I speak to you. You have known the General for a long time, I believe.'

'Yeah...' Hank concurred. 'But, say, what is this all about?'

Larry smiled, guessing that Hank's loyalty would make it well nigh impossible to get him to say anything to the General's discredit, if such had been his intention.

'It's not about the General, at least not directly. It's about Hugo Lansing that I want to know.'

'Oh, him,' Hank Carlile's voice sounded very negative.

'You were with the General when he first, eh, found Hugo and brought him Stateside, weren't you?' Osborne asked.

'I sure was. With the old man all through the war and after.'

'What can you tell me about the boy - as he was then?'

'What exactly do you want to know?'

'Well, everything I guess, just as much as you can tell. Start from when you first met Hugo if you like.'

Just then their drinks arrived and Hank remained silent until he had made inroads into his beer. Then he settled back in his chair, half closed his eyes and spoke.

'If you want the whole story...' Hank started.

Osborne nodded and took out his notebook.

'... It began in London, strange to tell, just before the war ended - leastways the war in Europe, that is... The General - he was a colonel then - was drinking in one of them clubs that officers used to use, when he gets talking to some of the RAF guys. Appears that they had been on a sortie over Germany a few months previous - that would have been, say, Christmas 1944 or just before. Don't suppose the General was paying them too much heed - them guys was always talking about their flying deeds. But doesn't the name Rudesheim come up. Seems these chappies was sent over specially to knock hell outta some German monument that nobody's ever heard of - leastways nobody outside Germany. This thing is perched up on a mountain overlooking the Rhine and was built last century as some kinda symbol of German might and all that crap. They never give up, do they?

Anyhow, these guys were sent over in the hope that they would destroy this 'ere monument - I suppose with the idea that it would strike a blow at the enemy's morale. There certainly wasn't no strategic value in the place! But as I said they mentioned Rudesheim and this caught the Old Man's attention, seeing as how his people originally came from there. Did you know about the General's German forebears?'

Larry Osborne nodded. 'Mrs. Lansing told me all about that side of it.'

'Fine,' continued Hank, pausing long enough to savour his beer. 'Well, as I said, the Rudesheim thing kinda made the Colonel sit up and take notice. He wanted to know all about it. Mind you, there was precious little they could tell him about the place, seeing as how they'd only flown over it once - and at night.'

'Wasn't he sorta upset that they'd been bombing the place?'

'I dunno - he never ever said. The funny part of it was, they never hit the goldarned statue thing. Every goddammed bomb missed. Sure wasn't no tribute to the RAF!' Hank chuckled and swallowed the last of his beer.

Osborne ordered more, and waited for the other to resume his tale.

'He told me about it the next day,' Hank went on. "You know Hank" he says to me next morning, "I had a brother Rudy named after that place Rudesheim. I'm gonna go and visit it if I gets the chance." It were the first I'd heard of this German thing in his family, but in the next few months he told me the whole story - which you got from his dear wife. I reckon he'd kept mum about it up until then 'cos we was at war and he didn't reckon it too clever to advertise the fact. Course, he wurn't alone - there was plenty of guys with folks as 'ad come from Germany or Italy - and even Japan -

durin' the war.

Any road, upshot was, he began looking for a reason to git to this 'ere place. Pretended he wasn't, at first, but I knew. Then in the early fall - about three or four months after the war ended - his chance came. Lots of the guys were keen to get back home, naturally enough - I was myself - so he got the chance to take a post in Frankfurt.

I remember looking at the map when I first heard and findin' this Rudesheim spot just a few inches away. He looked at me and gave a little smile, but said nuthin'.'

As a matter of fact, he said nuthin' at all 'til we'd been in Frankfurt about six weeks, then he says, "Hank, we've worked bloody hard since we come here, I reckon we deserve a furlough. We're goin' away for the weekend." Then I cottoned on to what were in his mind. It were my turn to smile.

We got there in the late afternoon of a lovely fall day. It were.as pretty as any picture from National Geographic. A little old-fashioned town right on the Rhine river, with mountains risin' up behind and all the way up there was terraces of grapes growin'. Just think - they'd been growin' them things all through the war. I reckon the land were no good for nuthin' else, anyways.

We found an old Inn place to put us up - they was only too glad to get their hands on a few dollars, I reckon - and we spent a coupla days just walkin' and drivin' round the place. The locals were pretty surly to begin with, but once they got used to the sight of us they was none too unfriendly, I suppose.

I kept wondrin' if he were gonna ask about his ancestors, but he never.'

'What about the statue - didn't you see it?' Osborne asked.

'Uh huh,' Hank grunted as he drank more beer. 'Not that first time,' he added.

'So you went back?'

'Course we did. You see that first time we heard that they was gonna have a wine celebration thing a few weeks later, the first they'd had since the war.'

'The Oktoberfest,' Osborne interjected.

'That's right - that's what they called it. Well, they didn't exactly ask us to it, but they didn't keep it no secret either, so the Old Man decided to pay another visit when it was on. About four weeks later, it was. "Hank, we're due fur another weekend, don'tya think?" he asks, and I knew where we was goin'. It sure was some weekend. As I said, they hadn't celebrated like it all through the war, and they was mighty keen to make up lost ground. They had all sorts to drink - beer by the gallon, wine by the barrel and some local made brandy that was strong stuff. We even had some of their own champagne.'

'Sounds like you were getting quite friendly by then!' Osborne interposed with a chuckle.

'Yeah, I guess so. Gettin' drunk together kinda - breaks down barriers I guess.'

Hank, as though matching his actions to his thoughts, drained the remainder of his beer. Larry obliged with a fresh order and when it arrived Hank was already talking, his head resting against the plush seat-back, his eyes half-closed.

'The Old Man got quite friendly with the town mayor, matter of fact. He was a pretty old fellow - after all, all the young ones had long gone to fight for Hitler - with thick white hair and a glass eye. That first night they was high as kites. Next day the Colonel had come to about three in the afternoon and we was walking down to the river where we'd heard you could get a sail on the Rhine, when this old guy - the Mayor - comes outta the Town Hall - you know they calls it the Rat House! He greets us like long lost cousins which wasn't surprising 'cos that's just what he tells us we were, leastways the Colonel, and I guess he kinda wrapped us two together in his mind.'

Hank took a long breath and an equally long pull at his beer before going on.

'You see the night before, while I was, well ... gettin' to know some of the local talent if'n you see what I mean - the Old Man had been tryin' out some of the German he knew and explaining about his family connections with Roodyshime.' Hank slurred the name even more than before. 'Apparently, the old Mayor fella had recognised the name as soon as John introduced himself. Probably explains why we was treated so darned friendly.' A smile spread across Hank's face. He sipped his beer slowly savouring the memory. '"Conqueror's privilege" she called it ...' his voice tailed off.

'Pardon?' Larry asked.

'Eh? Oh, nuthin', Hank replied, shaking himself back to the present. 'Where was I?'

'The Mayor guy sees you and the Colonel outside the Town Hall.'

'Yeah, that's right. Said he had been lookin' up the records but everything had been put away in the cellars 'cos of the war and he couldn't find nuthin.' However, he promised to look out what he could and show the Old Man the next time we visited.'

'And did he?' Osborne asked.

'We never seen him again.' Hank emptied his glass as though to emphasise the finality of his statement.

'What happened? Did you get posted?'

'No - the old guy did!'

'Huh?'

'When we got back to the base at Frankfurt there was a flap on about security - some missin' stores. That wur nothin' very outta the ornery, but some guys from the Auditor General's office had paid a surprise visit and didn't like what they found. Anyway it wur several weeks before we could get back to Roodyshime. By then it was gettin' near to Christmas and we set off loaded with presents. When we got there it was to find that the Mayor had died.'

'Mmmmmmm' was all Osborne could say.

'Yeah, dead he was. A coupla weeks after we'd been there he'd had a stroke or somethin'.' Hank paused.

'So what about the records?'

'Well, the Old Man tried to ask but the Mayor had been the only guy left who knew much about them. You see there had been very little to record durin' the war, precious few births or marriages, I suppose, and few enough local deaths, so he had done the record-keeping himself. When he died there seemed to be no-one could make much of them. As I told you, they wus all stashed away in the Town Hall cellars. Result was we never got to see any.'

'When did the boy come into it?' Osborne asked.

'Ah, that was at Christmas. You see, the weekend we went was about two weeks before but we took presents, as I said. Well, with the old man's death we weren't in much of a festive mood, so we took them back to base with us. But with time to think we decided that they ought to have them anyway so we went back again right at Christmas. That's when we met the lad for the first time, although I remembered seein' him the weekend we learned of the Mayor's death. We was drivin' away down the main street when I saw this young fellow standing on the town hall steps lookin' at us kinda intently.'

'But you actually spoke to him the next time, at Christmas?'

'Yeah. We had a few days furlough and, of course, there was nowhere else the Old Man wanted to go - nor me neither come to that! So Roodyshime it was. We had a helluva time! They was celebratin' THEIR first peace-time Christmas too, after all. Some of their menfolk had gotten back as well.

We got there Christmas Eve in the mornin'. That night we was in a beer hall place with a band playin' and everyone makin' merry when this young guy comes up. It wur difficult to hear him, but I could just make out him sayin' "Lansing." Uf course, I thought he wur addressin' the Colonel, and so did he 'cos he says, "Yes, I am Colonel Lansing." Then the boy explains that it's HIS name too. Well, of course, the Old Man was cock-a-hoop at findin' another Lansing. So after a spell he takes the boy back to where we was stayin' - while I was otherwise engaged, as you might say.

After that they were well-nigh inseparable. Between us we had a helluva good Christmas considerin' we was so far from home.'

'When did you next see him?'

'A coupla days after we gets back to camp the Colonel says to me quite sudden-like, "That boy is almost certainly a cousin of mine." "You don't say!" says I, "Too goddam true, Hank," he says, then goes quiet. I didn't say no more, knowin' he'd tell me what he wanted me to know in his own good time.'

'What was the boy like to look at and so on?' Osborne asked.

'He was tall, very fair and good lookin', but kinda old for his years. I'd seen a few lads like that before - boys that 'ud been in the fightin' before they shoulda been, if you see what I mean. Very serious he wur, hardly ever smiled - kinda nervous, I suppose. Couldn'ta been easy for him. But later when we gotta know him he would smile a little and his eyes light up - then he wur real handsome. I remember thinkin' as how the girls'd be chasin' him pretty soon - if'n they wurn't already.

Then, quite sudden-like, he turns up at the base

in Frankfurt. Unknown to me the Old Man had invited him to call if he were ever our way, and the lad had got himself a lift in a truck bringin' some booze to the base.

Of course we had our own whiskey, but the Colonel had arranged for them to let us have some wine and beer - in return for dollars. At first the MPs was none too pleased, but when they heard he was likely related to the C.O. they let the boy in. In any case, with the war over they were hardly worried about the 'enemy' no more.

By this time too, word was from home that we was to start gettin' reconciled to the Germans to rehabilitate them, help them rebuild the country, especially as the East was in the grip of the Ruskies. So, apart from them that were real Nazis, we was trying to be friendly. I remember one kid driftin' round the base, a thin little runt he was...'

'This was another boy?' Osborne interposed, realising that Hank was getting off the subject.

'Yeah, sorry, I kinda drifted away from what I was tellin' you. Anyway, this Lanzig boy - that wur the German way of spelling the name L-A-N-Z-I-G- turns up at Frankfurt. I don't think the Old Man had thought it through properly 'cos he didn't know rightly what to do with the kid. It were OK for a coupla days, but then he had to decide what to do with him. So he decides to get him some work. We was beginning to have some dealings with the locals and he sets the lad onto some translatin' work, but that didn't work out for some reason. Then the Colonel was called away to Paris for a few days and he asked me to keep an eye on the boy.'

'What did he do on the base all day long?'

'Spent most of his time readin' as far as I can recall.'

'German books?'

'Naw - we hadn't any German books. English stuff, anythin' lyin' round. His English was pretty good, you know, but I guess he wanted to improve it. Anyway that didn't last so long 'cos he kinda disappeared. One day he just didn't turn up at the base.'

'But I thought he was IN the base.'

'Not sleepin' he weren't. In spite of our friendliness to the locals, we couldn't have one actually livin' on the base, so he stayed with some friends of his in town. Then, as I say, he just didn't come in one day. The Old Man were none too pleased when he returned from Paris. He sent some MPs to look for the kid, but they couldn't find him. About three weeks later he turns up again, just like that!'

'Where had he been?' Osborne asked.

'Dunno. Don't think the Old Man knew either - not for sure. Seems the boy told him he had some word of a relative or somethin' in another part of the country and had to go. Things was like that then, remember - the whole place a might chaotic.'

'When did the Colonel get the idea of taking him back to the States?'

'Right outta the blue he says to me one day, "Hank, I'm gonna take young Hugo home."Well, I thought he meant to Roodyshime. I thought maybe he was just gonna leave the boy there before goin' home himself. Then he says, "He's acomin' to the

States with us." You could'a' knocked me down with a feather! I seen he was gettin' real friendly to the kid, but not that friendly.

'"What are you gonna do with him?" I asks. "Adopt him if I can," he says. Well a feather wasn't in it for knockin' me over, I'll tell you! I told him I didn't see how that would be possible, him not bein' married even. But that didn't seem to put him off. He said he had made up his mind, he was gonna fly him back home and take him to his mother to live. She still spoke German, he said, and would make the boy feel at home!'

'What was the boy's reaction?'

'At first he seemed kinda doubtful, I think. Then he began readin' lotsa stuff about the States, and after a few weeks he was talkin' about lookin' forward to it.

Meanwhile the Old Man was pullin' strings like billyo, but there didn't seem any way he could adopt the boy over there. So in the end he just took 'im.'

'Took him?'

'Yeah. A few weeks later we was able to go. The base was runnin' pretty smooth by then and he says it were time for us to get back home. When we was ready we simply took the boy on board the B45 and flew him back to the States.'

'Wasn't there any fuss, I mean about taking him with you?'

'Well, yeah, but the Old Man was the CO and the kid was willin' enough. Some of us tried to tell him it was a crazy notion, but he wouldn't listen.'

'What about when you got Stateside?' Osborne

asked, mindful of past dealings with the US Immigration Service.

'Well, there was some guys askin' questions of course, but don't forget we was a bit like returnin' heroes. The Colonel had a chestful of medals, you know.'

'But what about papers?'

'Oh, they was on our side. They took pictures of the Old Man with his arm round his German cousin.'

'Sorry, I meant ID papers for the boy.'

'Ah, them papers. I think he had a birth certificate, yeah, I feel sure he had one of them, but that was all.'

'Did you ever see it?'

'Yeah, reckon I must've, but I don't recall.'

'What happened then?'

'The Colonel took the kid to his mother in Omaha. I went home for my leave, of course. When next I seen him he told me everything was OK and the boy was goin' to stay with his mother.'

'Did you ever see Hugo Lansing again?'

'Hardly at all. Two, three times maybe. You see as long as we was still in the Air Force I spent my home leaves with my family, not with the Old Man. Then later when he asked me to come and run Jackson Stop, well, Hugo was hardly ever there.'

'What was your impression of him, later, when he had grown up?'

'Quiet fella, always thinkin'. Behind them eyes you could tell his mind was always workin'. Clever, of course, mighty clever. But kinda cold, I reckon. But them Germans is.'

'When did you last see him?' Osborne asked.

'Must've been after the General's stroke he came out.'

'Did you talk to him much?'

'Not a lot. He was only here a coupla days.' Hank paused. 'Funny thing ...'

'What?' Osborne leaned closer.

'Well, first day he asks me to show him over the place, and we arrange it for the next day. That afternoon and evening he spends with the General. Comes next mornin' and he says not to bother. There was a funny sorta look on his face - almost a smile Then he left.'

'What do you think was on his mind?' Osborne asked.

'Dunno rightly. He didn't seem in no great hurry to go that day, just didn't have no more interest in seein' over the place.'

'But you don't know why?'

Hank Carlile merely shook his head.

'Do you know if Hugo Lansing has any family?'

'Divorced I think - no kids as I know of.'

Larry Osborne concluded that there was nothing more to learn. He rose and extended his hand.

'Thank you very much Mr. Carlile, you've been most helpful.'

'Been a pleasure talking to you, son.' Hank burped and smiled with embarrassment.

CHAPTER 7

Hugo Lansing looked along the wing of the Tristar and into the clouds below. He knew he must be near his destination. He wondered what there would be to meet him down there. Had Elizabeth gone to Frankfurt because she knew something, or simply to check on a suspicion of some sort? It must be the latter, he decided, otherwise she would either have confronted him or gone to the security people - there was that guy Lockhart who had had the damned cheek to flirt with her right there in the office.

She could not know the truth - the REAL truth. Even the General had not guessed that, and he had been most likely to, being in at the beginning as he was. The start of it all, twenty-eight years ago... down there, in Rudesheim.

He stood on the steps of the Town Hall watching the car drive past. The driver saw him and he stared back, trying to look suitably diffident and curious at the same time. So these were the Americans who had been asking questions about the Lanzig family. How fortunate he had been able to get to the old Mayor first. Otherwise they might have got hold of the town records with the pages of Lanzigs intact. The pages that would have told the truth.

The old man had resisted for quite a while - kicking and struggling under the pillow. It had to be done. He was the only person there at the time who could remember all the family. With him gone and those pages safely tucked away it should prove possible to keep up the deception for long enough to gain the confidence of these naive Americans.

The next move was to introduce himself to them directly. Christmas gave him the opportunity to do that. A very suitable time! The Colonel's face when he had announced himself as a Lanzig - or rather Lansing!! That was a good move - doing it when the other man's attention was taken up with the local crumpet. After that it had been easy, almost too easy. The Colonel was only too anxious to believe in a boy who had lost his parents in the war, a boy from his very own family. How ironical - he had not even bothered to check the register.

Insinuating his way into the US base in Frankfurt had been so easy under the Colonel's protection.

Then had come the bombshell.

'How would you like to come back to the United States with me?' the Colonel asked, right out of the blue!

For once he had not needed to hide his true feelings. He was genuinely surprised and confused by the suggestion. He needed time to think about it and had said so. He also needed to get in touch with the one person who could tell him what to do. It had been difficult to see how he could manage that, bearing in mind the Colonel's almost constant attention. Then when Lansing had gone to Paris, his chance had come. After waiting a few days to avoid it seeming too much like cause and effect, he had gone back to report to the Major.

'Like something to drink, sir?' The air hostess' question interrupted his reminiscing.

'Mmmmm? Ah, yes please, a whisky.'

Whisky - the first time he had drunk that was in Frankfurt, all those years ago. He remembered the bottle he had smuggled out of the base that time he went back to report. He remembered the Major's face.

'He suggested what?' was the astonished question.

'Yes, sir, he has asked me if I would like to go back to America with him.' He stood to attention, looking straight ahead.

'My God, what an idea! You have done well, very, very well.' The Major laughed and took a long pull at the whisky.

'And what did you reply?' he asked, a trickle of whisky on his chin.

'I said I needed time to think about it.'

'You certainly do. So do I!' The Major pushed the bottle towards him.

'Sit down and have yourself a drink while I think this out.'

For five minutes the Major paced up and down. However, he had known all along what he would be asked to do.

'You realise what this will mean, don't you? You will have to go back with kind, gullible Colonel Lansing to the United States of America and live there permanently. Become an American in effect. Up to now you have been playing a part for a few weeks to see what there might be of value to find out. But this. This will mean a lifetime of playing a part. How old are you?'

'Twenty-two, sir.'

'Your parents both dead?'

'Yes, sir, at Stalingrad.'

'As a sixteen year-old you should prove quite a bright lad! If you could get to college over there, then university, there's no telling where you might end up!' The Major passed him the whisky again.

So he had spent the next three weeks immersing himself in the identity of Hugo Lanzig, sixteen year-old German war orphan. Up to then his preparation had been sketchy, enough to get by for a few weeks only. But to be able to keep up the deception for ever he needed to be steeped in his new persona, to think, act and react like the Hugo Lanzig who never was. He also had to avoid returning to Rudesheim lest he inadvertently give himself away - especially as a genuine Lanzig might turn up there with the country returning to normal. So he was coached in German and learned all about the town of his birth from a captain in the Russian army.

'Remember,' the Major had said, 'Your German must be perfect, you may come across some German-speaking Americans over there.'

How right he had been. Grandma Lansing in Omaha liked to speak German a lot of the time and had never been happy with his plea that he wanted to speak only the language of his adopted country. He had got away with it, however, except once when she had used some quaint phrase which she told him he ought to know as it was peculiar to that area round the bend in the Rhine at Rudesheim.

Fortunately she had ascribed his lapse to the ignorance the young always have for the ways of their elders. Even so, she had always seemed to him just a little suspicious after that, and he had been glad when the time came to leave her and go to college.

It had been pretty well plain sailing after that. He was way ahead of those kids there. As the Major had said, it was easy to be a very bright sixteen year-old when one was actually twenty-two.

There had been only two scares. The time he twisted his ankle and had to avoid being x-rayed. The doctor whom the Major had consulted had said that was the only real way he could be caught out. Something to do with bone age showing up on an x-ray. He had jerked his foot at the last minute to blur the picture, and so annoyed the radiographer that she told him to clear off if he could not keep still.

Then there had been Mary. She had been the first girl he had come across who seemed to want it as much as he did, which was probably why she had become pregnant.

That had been a nasty scare - her dying having an abortion. Good thing she did like it so much and had more than one guy sweating over who had been responsible! If only he had known that sooner there would have been no need to tell the

Old Man about it. Anyway, he had gotten away with it.

The Colonel had been married by then. Of all the dames to choose he had found himself one that spoke Russian! Not that it mattered much by then. He hardly ever saw them and by that time had ceased to think in his mother tongue, far less speak it.

Even on the few occasions he made contact with his controller he had never used it. The first time had been when he asked advice about whether to go to the Harvard Law School or MIT.

'Not Harvard,' he had been told, 'We already have someone doing well there. Go to MIT and take business studies. We think there's a future in that.' Then they had told him to make no further contact unless it was imperative for his safety, or until he had some real stuff to give them.

So he had gone to MIT, getting his US citizenship in the process. And then had come his interview for the UN job.

'Why do you want to work for the United Nations?' the pasty-faced old guy had asked him.

'Maybe because I was born in Germany and now I'm American. I just believe in the UN concept,' he had replied, making it sound as spontaneous as possible. Sure enough, it had got him the job.

Not that administration, even in the UN, had taken him near enough to the corridors of power to be of much use. On the other hand, it had been surprising how much he could deduce from what little he did know, and he was aware that if he could get higher he would gain the confidence of so many who did know things. Little things maybe, but put alongside hard facts, these little things meant something to the right people.

For five years he had sifted such information, making deductions which took him nearer to a knowledge of who made the important decisions and how they could be influenced in the right direction. Then had come the opportunity he had been awaiting: the feasibility study prior to the introduction of U.N.P.A.

He had taken the chance with both hands. In the one, the chance to make his mark among his peers, and in the other the opportunity to get much nearer to the centre of things. Three weeks he had spent, day and night, making quite certain that the study would prove his ability, and that the concept of a central register of U.N. personnel was a valid goal and a real possibility.

Later he learned that his had not been the only study of the subject, but it had been the most profound and, perhaps more importantly, the one which had most clearly pointed in the direction that coincided with the inclinations of those who had initiated the idea.

Not surprisingly, he was offered a job in the new set-up. How he had wanted to tell someone of his achievement! That the years of preparation were about to bear fruit ... but he knew he must remain silent, confident that his progress was being noted in Moscow as much as in Manhattan.

Once he had had an almost overwhelming desire to make contact. Walking along a corridor of the UN building, he had seen the Major, now a General and member of a top-ranking Soviet mission, coming towards him. For an instant he had hesitated, considering whether to make some kind of secret sign, but had pushed the idea from his head. As they passed the Major looked right through him - but was that not a tiny smile of recognition that he had detected?

Five years he had spent as third assistant on the project, when quite unexpectedly he was called for an interview.

'We've been watching you, Lansing.'

A miniscule shiver ran up his spine.

'And we think you are TOP MAN material.'

'Thank you, sir,' was all he thought he ought to say.

'How would you like to have the job of Assistant Director?'

The smile he allowed to suffuse his face was genuine enough to impress. He swallowed obviously, knowing that that, too, would give the right impression.

'Gee, that's great, there's nothing I would like better, sir.'

'Then that's settled - except for security clearance.'

The shiver was somewhat more obvious this time.

'As you know, Hugo,' a broad grin now for a new member of the establishment who could be addressed by his first name, 'A guy in your present grade has no access to classified stuff at all. But the Assistant Director, now that's another cookie, eh? You'll have to let these security types run the rule over you. However, I don't suppose that's gonna get in the way. We know you ain't a born American, but just because you was originally a Krau... that is, a German, don't matter. Not as if you was a commie or anything like that, eh?' A guttural laugh followed the attempt at wit.

He had to delve into his memory, back to the three weeks of coaching to establish his persona. Once or twice he had lapsed a little, but such was the subtlety of his inquisitors, that these were taken for proof of his identity. To have had it off pat might have aroused suspicion.

As Assistant Director, he had access to all the Agency's files. Moscow, for political reasons, had gone cold on the idea and none of their people participated in the project. They had carried the Eastern bloc along by their coat-tails of course, but nearly all the other UN members played an active part, so that the Agency had on file the names and curricula vitae of hundreds of experts in different fields. Included in many of these were annotations from various sources. Usually in the form of work references, these gave an insight into the character of the subjects, and sometimes their weaknesses.

It did not take him long to single out the most likely subjects for further vigilance and possible use.

In the final analysis only two or three had proved to be vulnerable, but once they had been 'turned' they were useful members of the Kremlin's worldwide network of informers, spies and traitors. There was to be one notable failure - Patel the Parsee who, years later, jumped out of the sixteenth floor of the Chrysler building, just after Borsakov had put the screws on. But at least he had not lived long enough to give the game away and the very thing that made him vulnerable to blackmail was reason enough for him to commit suicide, or so the official inquiry concluded.

CHAPTER 8

In 1966 an Argentinian was appointed Director of UNPA. While capable enough, he was not brilliant, and owed his position to political pressure more than anything. In Hugo's eyes he did not have much going for him, except a very attractive wife.

Shortly after taking over, Angel de Luz invited Hugo down to his ranch and introduced her. Pilar and Hugo hit it off as soon as they met.

He had studiously avoided entanglements with women since the episode with Mary, and had been surprised how little this had bothered him. Now, on meeting Pilar, all that was a thing of the past. He wanted her - badly. That she wanted him was not immediately obvious, but she put out enough subtle signs of encouragement to ensure his continued desire.

After their first meeting he did not see her for about six months. During this time he threw himself into his job with abandon. He had two reasons for this. One, he wanted to make damned sure he made a big impression, and two, he wanted to get something on his boss. He wanted something that he could use to oust Angel de Luz from the Director's chair and that would serve as insurance against Angel's discovery of his affair with Pilar. For he had already decided to have her.

She arrived in New York that summer, and forty-eight hours later Hugo contrived to bump into her in Macy's.

He bought her some French perfume, making it seem like a spontaneous gesture.

'Wear it for me sometime,' he said as he handed it to her.

'Perhaps I shall,' she replied, her generous nut-brown eyes fixing his in a tantalising smile.

Ten days later the Argentinian had to go to Washington on business. Hugo had modestly declined the trip, explaining that it was too important for a mere Assistant Director.

She rang him that evening.

'Angel said to call you if there was anything I needed. And I'm wearing your perfume.'

When Hugo arrived she was wearing little else. Her generous eyes were as nothing compared to the generosity of her body. It had been a long time for him, but what he did not know was that it had been a long time for her, too. A few weeks later she told him why. Contented, they lay in front of the simulated log fire in her apartment.

'Do you remember that first time?' she asked dreamily.

'I'll never forget it. The night you wore my perfume.'

'You had it up like there was no tomorrow!'

'If I remember rightly, you were pretty eager yourself, darling!'

'I had good reason. That was the first time in

ages.'

Hugo looked keenly into her face.

'What do you mean, ages?'

He tried to recall how long she had been without her husband, but there had been several times when his boss had flown home for a few days. So how come ...?

'Angel hasn't shown much interest these last few months. And until you, there was no-one else.' She paused. 'I think he's turning ... queer.'

Hugo put his arms round her and drew her close, snuggling her face into his neck. That way he was able to conceal the grin he could not prevent spreading over his face. He had what he wanted - something on his boss - and from the man's own wife!

It took him a month or two of close observation and discreet delving to prove to himself her theory was correct. Little things that he would not otherwise have noted came to have a meaning. Angel was undoubtedly homosexual, latent, if not already active.

Hugo's dilemma was that, while he wanted to make use of his knowledge, it would almost certainly mean Angel's removal, and he would lose Pilar.

After three months of wondering what to do he met Greta Stanhope, and Pilar did not matter any more.

His mind made up, he went into Macy's one day, and on the ground floor found a sales counter covered in typewriters. With a quick glance around he assumed the air of a customer and inserted a scrap of paper into the nearest model. Using his gloved right hand he tapped out three lines rather untidily, removed the paper as the salesgirl approached and inserted a cheap envelope into the next one along. He tapped out an address, pulled it out of the typewriter and walked away, smiling at the girl as he went. Ten minutes later the letter was on its way.

Three weeks later Angel de Luz was allowed to retire to his ranch outside Buenos Aires and U.N.P.A. needed a new Director.

The nomination lay with the U.S.A. and their choice was between Hugo and someone from outside the Agency who had the advantage of being older than Hugo as well as being native-born American. The latter point was neatly countered at the meeting to choose the new incumbent by an old friend of General Lansing, who pointed out that if the U.S. could employ Von Braun on its missile programme, there could hardly be any harm in giving this job to a guy who was only a kid when he left Germany!

After that it was in the balance, but eventually went to the man who had just previously become engaged to the sister of the Senator from Wyoming - Greta Stanhope.

She was as different from Pilar de Luz as camambert is from stilton. She was tall and blonde with sculptured bones and grey eyes that smiled only when they wanted to. The first time she and Hugo met was at a dinner party in the penthouse of a new apartment block on East ninety-second Street. He was there only because a Dutchman he knew in the U.N. had had to take a rain check at the last minute, and had insisted on Hugo taking his place.

Ten days later they were in bed and three weeks after that in the 'Engaged' column of the New York Times. He had informed Borsakov at the same time as he had told him about how he had arranged for Security to take a special interest in Angel de Luz. The Russian was pleased about both revelations. To have their very own man head of one of the U.N. agencies and married to a Senator's sister - that was some achievement!

However, Greta, after her initial passion was assuaged, proved a rather cold woman. Maybe she needed to have a child. The fact that it turned out to be impossible she found hard to accept and insisted on a visit to the Mayo Clinic before being convinced that she was barren. After that she showed less and less interest in sex and spent many weeks back home in Wyoming on the ranch while Hugo worked in New York.

The prospect of being childless was viewed by Hugo with scant regret. He did not, however, wish to resume a celibate existence. Instead, he made use of one or two of the numerous young ladies who earn a good living 'entertaining' delegates to the U.N. and other international agencies housed in New York or Washington. He was able to repay them by dint of making sure they met all the right customers. This, in turn, gained him access to interesting personal information on quite a few subjects who became targets for Borsakov's attention.

This went on for about five years, during which he saw his wife from time to time in New York or Wyoming. It suited him to remain married while having the freedom of a bachelor - how often was he congratulated on achieving such a blissful state and for some reason Greta did not once bring up the subject of divorce. Then Elizabeth came on the scene. Elizabeth ... He smiled to himself. Then the smile faded at the thought of what lay ahead.

'Fasten your seat belt, sir,' the air hostess said, 'We'll soon be in Frankfurt.'

CHAPTER 9

I never did get time for any more with Sandy. In fact, I have not seen her from that day to this. I was barely able to drop her off at her place before catching the plane to Frankfurt as Fox had ordered. During the flight that Sunday morning I tried to catch up on some sleep, and from time to time looked at the picture they had given me of this Elizabeth Tasker. She was tall and slim with a finely-boned, rather aristocratic face - rather like some 'English Lady' in an ad. for Earl Grey tea.

I remembered meeting her in the UNPA office from time to time. She was very cool and, come to think of it, sounded just a bit English. I scanned the info. on the back of the photo. That figured - born in England 1945, emigrated to Canada 1961. Joined the outfit in Montreal 197O, transferred to N.Y. 1972, appointed Director's personal secretary, May 1973.

I wondered just how 'personal' she was. Couldn't be all that close, I surmised, if she went off without even letting him know, unless of course their very relationship was the reason for her flight. Yes, that could be it - a lover's tiff. If so, and she was tired of him maybe... Yeah, I might ... The thought bucked me up a bit, for the job seemed a pretty boring business otherwise.

Security work often is - compiling dossiers, searching through dusty files, quietly instructing

Immigration not to let this one in or, occasionally, escorting that one out. Rarely any real excitement, almost always behind a desk. Hadn't had to draw my shooter in years. Not since that time when I had been a bit slow.

I fingered the scar under my shirt, where my left kidney should have been. Lucky, I suppose, lucky to be still around, although life seemed empty sometimes. I stirred myself from such maudlin thoughts and called for another whisky, but was too late as we were beginning our descent to Frankfurt.

Klaus Holtz had his BMW on the tarmac. I had met him a couple of times before, at the UN and once when he had been in Willy Brandt's bodyguard on a visit to Washington. He was a big guy with a very engaging smile and an enormous capacity for beer, or whisky - or anything with alcohol in it, come to think of it!

It was not long before he had steered me through the usual formalities and we were seated in a small office he had borrowed from somebody.

'What is this about, this lady what is missing?'

'I know very little, Klaus, only that she's hopped it from New York where she works for the Director of the U.N. Personnel Agency.'

'You think she has vital information?'

'That's just what we don't know. The Agency, as you may know, is about people - all kinds of guys with different backgrounds from different countries who're supposed to help the Third World in whatever way is needed at the time. Not specially secret stuff, although I suppose she might know enough to put the screws on some poor mutt who's not kept his private life too private, if you see what I mean.'

'So if there are no secrets why are you...?'

'You know what it's like, Klaus. Every goddam-med thing's secret these days - how would we earn an honest buck otherwise?'

'But you do not think she has gone over to *them* with ...'

'I dunno what to think. It doesn't seem very likely that she has anything to go anywhere with. Maybe she just ran away for personal reasons. Whatever - we've gotta find her and make sure, and I've gotta take her back so's someone can spank her backside for bein' such a damn-fool nui-sance.'

'So where do we start?'

'I was kinda hopin' you could tell me. After all, this is your stompin' ground. I suppose it'll have to be good old-fashioned leg work.' I rose from the seat which was too soft and too low, and I felt tired. I needed a drink.

'Look Klaus, my German ain't no great shakes. Why don't you nose around a bit and see what you can see while I repair to yonder hostelry and moisten the parched membranes?'

He stared at me. 'Ah, ya, you want to drink. I am so sorry.' He picked up the phone to call for drinks, but I stopped him.

'No, please, I'd rather go to the regular bar. You never know what I might pick up.' Klaus did not appreciate the idiom.

The airport bar seemed different from those I

was used to. European - that was it.

It had been so long since Interpol, and even longer since London. 'Maybe if I have time,' I figured, 'I might flip over and look up a few of the old haunts. Yes, a good idea. If this dame doesn't need nursemaiding all the way back, I can stick her on a plane and have myself a few days.'

Klaus hove in sight and I abandoned my daydreaming.

'Any luck?' I asked.

'Ya, maybe so. I have found a passport man who thinks he has seen her. But no-one in customs remembers.' He shrugged, and to my surprise, waved away the idea of a drink. Mine had restored the circulation and gingered up the brain cells enough to get me back on the job.

'Come on, we'll check the airline, should have done it before.'

She was registered as arriving on that morning's flight from Kennedy, but no-one had seen her since the immigration guy. We went out to the taxi rank and asked there, but without luck. We tried the car hire places as well as the railway and coach stations and the desk where you can book into the local five-star hotels - all without luck.

'She seems to have disappeared, your lady.' Klaus observed.

'Which is rather suspicious. Any innocent traveller would have left some sort of trail, don't you think?' I asked.

'This is so, this is so,' Klaus replied sagely, nodding his head. But I felt he was not convinced. Neither was I.

I was beginning to think that we would have to make it an official inquiry and get the police to go round hotels and search for a trace of her passport. I wanted rather to keep it informal for the sake of speed and privacy, but without picking up her trail at the airport, I could not see how we would achieve that. We were making our way across the main airport concourse, through the crowds, when I thought I caught a glimpse of our missing woman about fifty yards in front. I gestured to Klaus and we pushed our way past a few dozen travellers, and came up to two women having an argument in English. The one who had caught my attention was speaking.

'Of course I'm part of the tour, why do you think I've got this?' she asked with a strong flavour of exasperation, as she waved a black and yellow striped plastic wallet under the nose of the other.

'But surely you were on the coach this morning,' replied the one wearing the blazer with a large black and yellow badge on the lapel bearing the legend 'Sunrise Tours'.

'No I was not. I've explained that. When I got off the plane I felt ill. You would have known that if you had not been late to meet us.'

'I'm sorry about that but ...' the courier broke off as she became aware of us taking an interest in the conversation. I had already decided that the complainant was not our woman. There was a superficial resemblance, however, and the argument intrigued me.

'What seems to be the trouble?' I asked, dredging up from my past my most impressive Scotland

Yard voice.

'Who are you?' the courier asked officiously. The other woman looked none too impressed either.

Kurt broke in with a stream of German. After a few answers he turned to me.

'This woman,' he indicated the tourist, 'arrived this morning on a package tour from Gatwick, England. The guide was late in meeting the plane because of traffic, and when she arrives this lady is not well and is in the medical room. But when the coach goes, nobody is missing. So the ill one is not ... not there.'

'You mean you had a full complement of passengers when you took off in your coach to the hotel?' I asked the courier.

'Yes, that's what's so strange. No-one was missing this morning. Then an hour ago when I went back to the office in town I got this message that we had left somebody behind at the airport. So here I am. And it looks as if she is right.'

I already had the photograph of the Tasker woman in my hand.

'Is this the other ... was this woman on your bus this morning?' I asked.

She looked at the picture with a slight frown.

'There was I think someone rather like that, but I can't recall seeing her when we reached the hotel.'

'Why, that's her!' exclaimed the lady tourist, eyeing the photo.

'Who?' I asked.

'The woman who was here this morning. She was quite nice when I was feeling ill. I didn't see her after she took me to the medical room '

I exchanged glances with Klaus.

'Which hotel did you take them to?' I asked, turning to the courier.

'The Krone, Rudesheim,' she replied. I looked at Klaus again.

'A small town along the Rhine - the centre of the Oktoberfest,' he explained. I turned away with him in my wake and we jostled our way to the car. The two women we left, arguing about how quickly the one could get the other to Rudesheim.

'Do you think this woman who made up the group to Rudesheim is our woman Tasker?' Klaus asked as we took the road out of Frankfurt.

'It looks very like it. That woman back there seemed quite sure.' I lapsed into silence while I thought about it.

I figured that what must have happened was that Elizabeth Tasker had arrived in Frankfurt looking over her shoulder. Seeking a none-too-obvious route to this Rudesheim place she had come across a woman in a tour group going to the very place. This woman is ill, the bus is late and in the confusion Tasker takes her place, boards the bus and gets a free ride to Rudesheim - in such a way that her destination might have gone undetected. Very neat. A cool nerve she has.

The only question is - why did she go *there*? We were soon in the car on our way to find out.

I felt we were making some progress, and promptly fell asleep. Klaus woke me up as we entered Rudeshiem.

The place was thronged with a capital TH. Not only were there tourists but, as it was Sunday, locals as well. They say the best wine in Germany is made there, where the river turns at right angles for a few miles to run due west so that the slopes above the town face south. On a given day in early October chosen by a committee of local wine makers, the grape harvest begins. Of course it is celebrated in thorough teutonic fashion and everyone gets drunk - usually on lager.

This is what we had happened upon!

The steep little main street - the Drosselgrasse - was awash with swaying, singing crowds, the so typical sound of the German brass band issued from almost every window, and the whole place was utter chaos. Our first stop was the Krone Hotel, but no-one there could recall a Miss Tasker, nor was she registered there, which was hardly surprising. None of the genuine Sunrise tourists were about either. Carrying out a systematic search for our quarry was clearly going to be damned near impossible, but we did what we could in the way of asking the usual questions in all the usual places. Without success.

After a while we split up. I continued looking while Klaus went off to try to find us rooms for the night. On the way back down to our rendezvous - the Oak Door Bierkeller - I noticed in front of me a man and a woman - and she had protruding from her handbag a black and yellow striped plastic pouch. I lengthened my stride to catch up with them, but before I could, they were confronted by a line of locals swaying from side to side, blocking the road. One of the least steady of them detached himself from the line and stepped up to the woman, quite clearly with the intention of kissing her, much to the amusement of his fellows.

Her husband was not amused. He waved what appeared to be a large sausage at the local drunk, but was too late to prevent him planting a squelchy kiss on the wife's cheek.

I reached them as she giggled away her embarrassment and husband fumed through a mouthful of sausage.

'Excuse me,' I began, taking out the picture, 'I believe this woman came here this morning on the coach from the airport. I wonder...' I got no further. Her husband pulled me roughly by the shoulder.

'Do you mind not molesting my wife. We don't know you, do we?'

He waved the ridiculous sausage in my face and propelled his wife away into the crowd before I could get any further. I followed them for a few minutes in the hope that I might get another chance to talk to her, but lost them in the crowds. By this time I was both tired and hungry - and made my way to our rendezvous to meet up with Klaus.

On the way an inviting smell assailed my nostrils, and I saw a stall selling the kind of sausage the offensive Englishman had waved at me. I bought one, and on the off-chance showed the stall-holder Elizabeth Tasker's picture.

He thought he could remember the face, but not the where or when! She seemed as elusive as ever, this woman who might be no more than a secretary on holiday. I cursed her roundly - and Fox for sending me on such a damnfool mission ... People were turning to look at me and I realised I was talking aloud.

I was letting the job get to me. Too long behind a desk. I consoled myself with the thought that I had told Fox I was not the man for the job, and bit deep into the sausage.

I found the Oak Door and pushed my way in through the crowd to where Klaus stood at the bar. He had found us a room in an Inn a few miles outside Rudesheim, but had had no more success in tracing our quarry than I. We decided to have a few drinks then visit the Krone Hotel again in the hope that some of the Sunrise people had returned for the night.

Four lagers later we arrived outside the hotel. At the kerb a large coach was parked. On the front was a yellow and black 'Sunrise' sticker, and from within we could hear the murmur of voices and see a flicker of light. There was a man standing on the steps into the coach, and as we watched he turned to face us. It was the Englishman I had crossed swords with earlier.

His eyebrows rose in recognition, and he gave a sickly grin.

'I say, I'm terribly sorry about being such a bore earlier on when you wanted to speak to Edith -

that's my wife, you know. But that Kraut-wallah kissing her fairly got my dander up, don't you know.'

'No matter, I understand,' I said, hoping he might prove helpful. Just then his wife pushed her way out of the coach.

'Found them, then?' he asked her.

'Yes,' she replied, and saw me. She held a pair of spectacles in her hand, and waved them at no-one in particular.

'Hallo,' she said, 'Sorry about earlier...'

'I've already apologised, dear,' the husband interrupted.

'What was it you were going to ask me?' she went on, oblivious of his contribution.

'I was going to ask if you had seen a young woman on the coach from the airport this morning.' I took out the picture and held it towards her. She waved the spectacles again and said,

'It would have been no use asking me earlier in any case - I left my reading specs on the coach and we couldn't find the driver to get in for them any sooner.' She put them on - revolting things with blue plastic rims studded with diamante.

'The light's very poor here, of course,' she simpered as she squinted at the photo.

'Come inside, old man. We'll see better there and I can buy you a drink by way of amends for my uncouth behaviour earlier,' said her husband taking hold of my arm.

I tensed a degree or two and disliked him a degree or three more. I hate being touched.

Klaus said, 'This is a good idea you have. If you

do not remember we must ask of the others on the party if they have been seeing her.'

I had to admit he was right, and led the way inside. I stopped at the reception desk where the light was good, but Klaus was already leading the others into the bar. He shrugged at me and grinned.

'Yes, I think that's her.' Edith opened hopefully, when I got round to showing her the photo again.

'Half a mo, I saw her on the bus this morning,' said her husband.

'Don't interrupt, Dear, I'm telling it,' she added, turning the wrath of her spectacles on him.

'You've seen her then,' I added, 'Where, when?'

'There's not a lot to tell, really,' she went on, with the air of someone about to embark on a long story.

'This morning, after we arrived, I was doing my best to sort out which room we had been given - you were outside helping with the luggage 'cos they'd lost some labels - weren't you, dear?'

I bit my lip.

'Well, she - that's the woman in your photo - was asking about a monument near here. Quite a famous landmark it must be.'

'Germania?' Klaus asked.

Edith turned the full force of her spectacles on him and went on, 'I believe that is its name. Anyway, she was asking the way there and the ... eh ... you know, Gerda ...'

'The receptionist, dear?'

'No, she's not the receptionist, is she? I thought the big dark girl was the receptionist. Surely Gerda is the ...'

I could contain myself no longer.

'Please,' I tried hard to ignore the specs, 'Tell us what happened.'

'Where was I? Oh yes, she was asking how to get there - to this monument, whatever it's called' a glare at Klaus, 'and Gerda explained that you can walk up to the lift thing and it takes you up the mountain. It sounds very lovely up there. We're going there tomorrow, I think.'

I gulped the last of my brandy and stood up.

'Thank you, that's been very helpful.'

'You're not going just yet, are you?' the husband asked, 'have another drink. You know they say this is the best brandy in the world, made right here in the town, it is. We've hardly had a chance to get to know each other.' I do not know whether he was referring to the brandy or me.

Edith tried to stand up but did not quite make it and plumped back down into the plush upholstery. The action forced a hiccough from her and she grinned sheepishly. She removed her spectacles and contrived to look quite human.

We bade them goodnight and made for reception where I asked for Gerda, but she was not on duty. Klaus spoke to the guy who was and turned to me.

'She asked about Germania and how to get there, but that is all, it seems. But now the funicular is closed.'

'Well, there's very little else we can do tonight,' I said, 'Nothing in fact. I suggest we get to bed and make an early start in the morning. First stop's got to be this Germania thing. I'll go up there myself, if you don't mind, while you check with your office - Fox said he would keep us informed of developments. Then perhaps you could return here and nose around a bit in case our lady did leave a trail in the town. You never know - you might even bump into her! God alone knows what precisely she's here for, so anything could happen.'

CHAPTER 1 O

On the Monday morning I set off to trace Elizabeth Tasker's footsteps and ascend the mountain by way of the cable car, exactly as she had done.

I am afraid that my parents did not incorporate in the genes they passed on to me one labelled 'head for heights.' I did not enjoy that journey in the flimsy (or so it seemed to me) swaying-out-in-space-with-nothing-beneath-you cage. I was never more happy than when it disgorged me (the devilish thing did not even stop) at the top.

In a few minutes I was worm's-eye viewing the monstrosity that this woman had come so far to visit. Germania is, I suppose, a marvellous monument - if you like that sort of thing. About a hundred and fifty feet of solid stone support a thirty-foot bronze Rhine maiden. Various aspects of the base are emblazoned with bas-reliefs of Germany's top brass of the day and the old 'warrior returns' theme, while here and there are figures of angels and the like - to say nothing of Old Father Rhine ogling a big-breasted Miss Moselle circa 1880. Completed in 1883, it was erected to celebrate Germany's unification after the Franco-Prussian wars of 1870/71. For all the help it gave me in the search for the Tasker woman, I might as well have stayed in bed.

Unable to deduce the significance of my quarry's interest in the monument, I wondered whether it might be no more than a rendezvous of some kind.

To avoid having to use the funicular on the way back down to Rudesheim, I decided to take a walk in the opposite direction - just in case there was something ahead that would help me to pick up her trail. I had plenty of time before meeting Klaus at the Krone Hotel.

It is a very lovely walk up there, through beautiful hardwood forest with the Rhine tracing the valley below and the steep slopes striped with vineyards and speckled with castles. If I had been on vacation, if I had had a girl with me ... but no such luck. I was stuck with a search for a woman who clearly would not have in mind what I would like to be doing in these woods! Even if I could find her!

After a while I met a man coming the other way, and in my halting German asked him whether the path through the woods led anywhere. It appeared that I could go on ahead and get to a place called Assmanshausen, and from there return to Rudesheim.

Sure enough, at the end of the path through the woods there was a way down to Assmanshausen - by way of a chair lift! I shall not dwell upon that mid-air descent, but be sure I made for the nearest brandy when I reached good old terra firma!

Nor was my journey any more useful than it was relaxing. There seemed to be no trace of Elizabeth Tasker in Assmanshausen. All I learned was that the quickest and pleasantest route back to

Rudesheim was by water taxi.

My taxi driver, or whatever you call him, turned out to be a guy with only one real peeper, and I had the crazy thought that he might only be able to see one half of the river at a time. But in fact he steered the tiny craft very well, and I suppose he had been at it for long enough. On the off-chance I took out the photo I had shown around so often and held it towards what I took to be his good eye. Apparently I was wrong, for he transferred it to the other side of his face and concentrated.

Yes, he had seen her. Only the day before he had taken her on the same route from Assmanshausen to Rudesheim. It proved no more than that she had been on the same journey, but I felt a satisfaction out of all proportion to this simple fact. I felt less as if I were chasing shadows.

While I was on my way up the mountain, Klaus was on the phone to his office, to be told that there was a telex message and photos for him at Wiesbaden, about thirty kilometres along the Frankfurt road. He drove there and picked up the following:

ATT. HOLTZ/LOCKHART
REF. ELIZABETH TASKER
NOW KNOWN LANSING LEFT NY
FOR LONDON QUERY EN ROUTE
FRANKFURT RUDESHEIM. IMPERATIVE YOU INTERCEPT PREVENT TWO
SUBJECTS COMING TOGETHER. IF

POSSIBLE DETAIN TASKER WATCH LANSING. NOW EVIDENCE THE BEAR IS INVOLVED WHAT NEWS YOUR END.

FOX.

ATTN. HOLTZ/LOCKHART SUBJECT: HUGO LANSING (LANZIG) BORN RUDESHEIM FED. GER. REP. 1929. ENTERED U.S 1946 UNDER PROTECTION COL. JOHN LANSING USAF. EDUC. MIT MASTER DEGREE BUS. ADMIN. 1954. UN SINCE. DIRECTOR UNPA 1969 MARRIED GRETA STANHOPE 1967.

A photograph was attached.

Needless to say, Klaus immediately noted the fact of Lansing's birthplace and that it gave us the link between an absconding UN secretary and a small German town. Within an hour he was back in Rudesheim, speaking to a clerk in the Rathaus (Town Hall).

He showed them his ID card briefly and gave out a spiel about being from the Registrar General's office, and wanting to do a spot check on some of their old files. It took them a while to dig out the pre-war ones, but eventually he was ensconced in a corner with two large and dusty tomes full of entries of births and deaths.

He was simply going through the policeman's routine: take nothing for granted; check every fact when and where you can. He was in for a surprise when he got to the birth certificates of 1929 ...

Intent as he was with the task in hand, he could hardly be expected to notice the rather insignificant looking little man who did not seem to have much to do except watch him as he made his inquiries.

CHAPTER 11

Willi Hauptner was an efficient bastard. His mother was one of the most active ladies in Bremen and his father - who knows?

Brought up in various institutions, Willi took to a life of petty crime as a leech takes to blood. Wartime Germany presented many opportunities, and he seized them with both greedy paws. By the time 1945 came with the end of the war in sight he was, although only twelve, a daring sneak thief with a vicious streak to his character that would have won him instant promotion in the SS had he been old enough to enlist.

He would certainly have liked to join, for the arrogant black-uniformed men who seemed to command respect wherever they went were his special heroes. He would run errands for them at every opportunity and revelled in the thought that he was part of their organisation, albeit unofficially. Then came the bombing of Bremen - which Willi thought was most unfair - and he was offered a lift out of the city by one of the SS officers. There was no room in the Captain's Mercedes, but Willi found a seat in the following truck.

Three kilometres outside the city a bomb fell between the two vehicles, throwing the car sideways off the road and overturning the truck. Willi was saved by the bodies of the two large soldiers between whom he sat. Dazed but uninjured, he extricated himself from the corpses and crawled out. Ahead of him, on the far side of the crater, lay the smashed wreck of the Mercedes. Before he reached it he knew that the Captain was dead.

Looking down at the twisted and still body, Willi felt a twinge of some emotion or other, but was so unused to such feelings that it went unrecognised. Instead he busied himself with the task in hand and, glancing quickly around, removed from the Captain's uniform a few things which he reckoned would prove more than useful - a pistol, a sizeable quantity of money and, most precious of all, a black metal cross. Willi turned it over in his hand and read the name on the back. He decided that it sounded much better than the Schmidt that had been given to him in the orphanage, and duly named himself Hauptner, deciding at the same time that having for a father a Captain in the SS, albeit a dead one, was a vast improvement on having no father at all.

Willi soon enlisted the sympathy of those in a following truck and was on his way south. A few days later he found himself in Frankfurt and remained there until the German High Command surrendered.

Like many others, he felt a sense of betrayal - for himself, his country, and in particular his SS heroes. When he heard the news on the radio he murmured an apology to Captain Hauptner - his 'father'.

At the time he was, however, more concerned with the day-to-day business of survival than with thoughts of the disgrace brought upon his country. He was good at surviving. He had the knack of being in the right place at the right time, and it was not long before he became involved in the black market.

The spanner of defeat had thrown the machinery of the German state into chaotic paralysis. Shortages were in abundance, supplies non-existent. Except, that is, for the allied armies who brought with them everything that post-war Germany could not provide. Willi soon tacked himself on to those who took advantage of the situation, and in no time he was running errands for them, quickly learning how to make a profit out of every deal in which he assisted. The US Army, being the most prolific source of supply, did not escape Willi's attention for long.

Hank Carlile was a soft-hearted guy. Having seen what the Allied bombs had done to Germany he had some sympathy for the civilian population, and especially for their children. He first encountered Willi one night on the way back to his depot. The boy was a pathetic looking scarecrow of a figure, cowering in a doorway. Hank paused and gestured towards the lad in a friendly manner, only to be met by a whimper of fear. It was an act that Willi had perfected, and it disguised effectively the fact that he was standing guard over his recently acquired stock of tinned fish nestling at the foot of the door. Hank decided not to press his acquaintance on the boy, but simply threw him a pack of chewing gum before going on his way.

He recognised the boy a couple of days later

when he saw him hanging around the depot gates and was pleased with himself for having made the friendly gesture as the boy seemed more amenable than he had on the first night.

'Hi there, come on in,' Hank called, waving the boy towards him. Willi hesitated, judging to a nicety the degree of reluctance expected of him. Hank waved again and Willi shuffled forward, putting his right hand to his temple in a passable imitation of a military salute.

This gesture of calculated cuteness had the desired effect, and Hank embraced Willi both physically and metaphorically. During the next few weeks the thin little German boy - he was not really very thin but his stolen army tunics made him appear quite undernourished and Hank's imagination did the rest - became a regular visitor to the supply depot at the perimeter of the airfield.

So many items were finding their way off the base that the comparatively minor contribution Willi made to this traffic was never noticed, and indeed he would never have been found out were it not for Helga. She was a healthy fifteen-year old who knew her way around. That she was so healthy was a testimony to the quality of American food supplied to their troops. The precise nature of the payment in kind that Helga and others like her gave in return for all this nourishment did not figure in Willi's thoughts, until one night when he was making his way out of the base after his latest sortie.

Stealing his way among the shadows and between the guards, he perceived up ahead a young woman engaging the Corporal on duty in conversation outside the small wooden hut at the main depot entrance. As Willi stood still in the shadow of a pile of empty oil drums, the two entered the guard's hut. He gave them two or three minutes to complete their business but when they did not emerge he decided it would be a good moment to creep out undetected. Swinging his sackload of spare parts over his shoulder, he tip-toed past the hut. As he passed the window, bending low to avoid being seen, the giggling-gurgling-gulping noises that came from within stirred his curiosity. He set his load down in the shadows and peeped inside the hut.

He knew immediately that what he was witnessing was the sort of activity alluded to in so many of the jokes that he had heard, but not understood. He watched, fascinated, as the performance came to an end, then, realising that it was never intended to be played out before an audience, he ducked out of sight, picked up his loot and scuttled off home.

That night he dreamed as he had never dreamed before, and the next morning determined to find the young woman who had figured so prominently in those dreams. He was not at all clear in his mind what he intended doing if he did find her, but that did not stop him making the necessary resolution.

For the next few nights he lurked in the shadows near the guard's hut at the base hoping to see her again and, though he did not consciously realise it, hoping also for the opportunity of witnessing the erotic show again. He was not to know that the Corporal who had cavorted with her that night had gone on furlough the very next day.

On the fourth night Willi set out to keep his vigil, but it was colder than ever and his steps grew less determined as the depot drew nearer. He turned back when its lights were in sight, deciding that whatever she had to offer it was not worth another night in the cold. As he did so the headlights of a jeep returning to the base swathed him in visibility and he dashed up the nearest alley, instinctively avoiding an encounter with authority. Nor had his instincts let him down for the jeep contained four M.P.s returning from town.

Disappointed at making no arrests that evening, they saw in Willi - a local lad returning from the direction of the base so late at night - an opportunity for spoiling somebody's day. In any case there had been talk about slack security at the base, and the amount of stores going missing had been the subject of acid comment from one of the HQ staff.

Sergeant Marty Madison leapt from the jeep while it was still moving and pelted after Willi with the speed of a greyhound. Willi, the hare, darted about disconcertingly and would have made his escape were it not for the fact that he had the bad luck to choose a blind alley in which to attempt it.

The struggle was outrageously unequal and Willi was soon sat in the back of the jeep between two large soldiers. It reminded him of the time he had escaped from Bremen in the truck between the two German soldiers, and he recalled how warm he had felt then, in bleak contrast to his present chilly situation.

When they reached the base he thought, too, about Captain Hauptner, telling himself that these Americans would not get away with interrogating him if his erstwhile protector had still been alive. However, the M.P.'s idea of questioning hardly matched up to Willi's imaginings, and when they realised he was little more than a grade five candidate they abandoned any idea of making a sensational breakthrough in the case of the missing supplies. Willi's silence they took to be a sign of innocence tinged with fear rather than the guilt sodden with contempt that it was, and the bed they gave him for the night was designed more for comfort than torment. The next morning he was given a big breakfast and sent on his way. As he reached the corner of the road he looked back and, to his surprise, saw Helga emerging through the gates. He turned the corner and stopped, pretending to tie his bootlace. Sure enough after a couple of minutes she came round - almost colliding with him.

'Sorry,' he said, grasping her arm to save her from falling.

'That's all right,' she replied. Willi saw for the first time how young she was and whatever strategy had formed in his mind was abandoned. All he could think of to do was to put on the look he knew Sergeant Carlile found most endearing, and to offer her a stick of the chewing gum one of the M.P.s had given him. For her part Helga thought Willi looked quite like a young brother she seemed to remember having years before when they were still a family, safe back in Stuttgart.

'Would you like a cup of coffee - real American coffee?' she asked.

Willi nodded his head and fell in step beside her. In silence they made their way through the streets, sometimes picking their way through rubble, sometimes walking along elegant avenues whose facades bore little witness to the destruction of war. They stepped off the sidewalk to avoid a queue of sullen women waiting at a bread shop and Helga led the way up a narrow lane and over a pile of debris, the pieces of a jigsaw that had once been a church. Down the far side the lane resumed its twisty course through a small clump of stunted ash trees, then petered out in a half-acre grass field. At the far side, seemingly guarded by an abandoned anti-aircraft gun, stood a stone building that bore the look of a stable.

Helga led the way up to it and, with a knowing look at Willi, put her arm through the broken pane of a window at the side of the stable door. After fumbling for a moment she contrived to release the upper half of the door which she then pulled open. Placing her foot on a convenient stone, she stepped up and over the lower half of the door. Willi had seen American underwear before, but only in a box.

Inside, the stable's dimensions were more generous than the outer appearance suggested. It was divided into four stalls and above was a hay loft which had clearly been turned into sleeping quarters by the men who had previously occupied the place. At the far end were piled the appurtenances of the anti-aircraft gunners' trade. Against the wall near the door was an iron stove whose chimney poked out through a makeshift hole in the roof. The gap left round it was plugged by sacking which, sooty and frayed, hung down like garlands round the chimney stack. Nearby hung a small paraffin lamp. Helga opened the door of the stove and pointed inside.

'You light a fire - you'll find some wood lying around. I'll get the coffee,' she said, and climbed the ladder to the loft. Willi looked around for some wood and found one or two bits which he stuffed inside the stove. He added some paper and put a match to it. His mind was not altogether on what he was doing, however. He was thinking about the coffee and what else she might have hidden up there. He stole across the stable and mounted the ladder as quietly as possible. Pushing his head up through the hatch, he looked around. It was quite dark, but he could make out, to his right, piles of straw against the wall, and in front of these an army-type canvas bed stretched on a steel frame. Next to that was a rough wooden crate which looked as though it had contained shells at one time, but which now served as a bedside table, and held a drip-encrusted candle nestling in a broken saucer beside an army mug. Against the far wall was what appeared to be the remains of a tent - a large stretch of khaki canvas suspended from the beams supporting the roof. That was all. No Helga.

Willi blinked in the semi-darkness and looked around again, but still could not see her. He climbed further up the ladder, pulled himself onto the floor of the loft and crossed to the piles of straw, sure that she must be hiding there. Lifting aside a few bales he discovered - not Helga but her cache of loot, the result of several months' work in and around the Allied camps and depots.

'I thought you were lighting a fire.'

Helga's voice made Willi jump. He turned quickly, tripping over a bale in the process. He fell sideways over it and lay there looking up at her. She stood near the bed, a bayonet held menacingly in her hand. For a moment he thought she was about to attack him, but dark as it was he could see that murder was not her intent. He tried to laugh and asked, 'Where the hell did you come from?'

Helga visibly relaxed.

'Back there,' she replied, nodding her head towards the canvas sheet. Willi frowned and rose from his awkard position.

'Look, over here,' Helga said and went over to the wall and drew back the canvas. Behind it Willi could see that there was an opening. In fact, this was the upper entrance to a small clock tower which an ambitious builder had tacked onto one end of the stable. From the outside it was obscured by a large branch which had partially broken away from the enormous beech tree which had afforded camouflage to the anti-aircraft gun. The lower part of the tower was filled up to the level of the loft with boxes and crates of spare parts and equipment for the gun. Above, Willi could see some light filtering in through wooden slats, and a ladder fixed to one wall led up to a tiny ledge beneath the clock. All around the walls of the little tower were hanging numerous items of female clothing, rather like some theatrical wardrobe.

'My dressing room,' Helga laughed self-consciously.

'Go and make the coffee now,' she said, waving the bayonet in the direction of the stove, 'But don't ever come up here again without I let you,' she added.

Willi descended the ladder and caught the tin of coffee she threw down to him.

As he made the drink Willi thought to himself that Helga had a very good place, better than the small room in the ruined tenement that he inhabited, and he began to think of ways of gaining occupancy. He came to the conclusion that the best way would be to get rid of Helga and simply take over. He knew that the stuff behind the straw must have been gained illegally, and wondered about informing on her. Then he remembered the activity he had witnessed several nights before, and realised that it was possible she had some protector at the base. He began to think about that night again. The sound of Helga descending broke into his thoughts, and he looked round. She stood at the foot of the ladder in a shiny red dress from her collection. It was a shade too small for her, and Willi's pulse increased as he looked at her. She laughed and said, 'Like it? It's my favourite.'

Willi simply nodded and gestured towards the coffee he had made. She came forward and sat down opposite Willi on a crate, with a canvas ammunition pouch for a cushion. The red dress was quite short, and as she sat it worked its way up her thighs. Willi tried to avoid looking at them, but did not succeed.

Helga observsd his furtive glances and began to realise that he was a little older than she had at first thought. His small stature compared to her well-built fifteen-year old body had given her the impression that he was only about ten. She began to regret her impulsive decision to invite him back. She had up until then managed to keep her hide-out a secret, leading a make-believe life there, quite separate from the commercial existence outside forced upon her by economic necessity. She drank the coffee in silence, trying to figure out what to do next. For his part, Willi was wondering how best to approach the subject uppermost in his mind. He felt sure, judging by the episode in the guard's hut, that Helga enjoyed that sort of thing but at the same time he felt that there had to be more to it than simply standing up and saying, 'let's do it.'

Helga's mind was working furiously, trying to think of a way of diverting Willi from the subject. She knew that if it came to the crunch she could probably overpower him, but she much preferred not to have to put that belief to the test.

Willi could stand the inactivity no longer and, sensing her nervousness, he leaned forward and put a hand on her leg above the knee. She stood up quickly and said, 'Stop it. You're not old enough for that sort of thing!'

'I am too,' he retorted and stepped towards her menacingly. The ugly glint in his eyes was something Helga had never seen in a child before, and her throat tightened up with fear. She knew she had no choice but to give in, or pretend to.

'All right, all right, but up there, not here.' She tried to smile, but with little success.

Willi was quite pleased with himself for finding the right formula for getting his way and he smiled back, with more success. Helga skirted round him and went to the ladder. Willi watched her, and she had almost reached the loft when he remembered the bayonet. He ran after her as fast as he could.

As Helga pulled herself up into the loft she too remembered it. She scrambled across the floor towards it, and her hand reached it as Willi gained the top of the ladder. Unfortunately for her, it lay with its point towards her and she was unable to grasp it before he caught hold of her ankle and pulled her back. Using her weight for leverage, Willi pulled himself up and rolled onto the floor beside her. He was now nearer the weapon, and she knew it. She smiled at him as best she could and said, 'You can't blame me for trying.'

Willi knelt up and slapped her hard across the face. He had never before experienced power over another person like this, and he found it exhilarating. His pulse was now racing and he had no doubts about his ability to complete what had to be done. He grabbed her by the hair and growled, 'Take your dress off!'

Helga looked at him through her tears, and knew that there was nothing she could do. She sat up and indicated the back of the dress. Willi undid the buttons and she stood up and peeled off the dress. Then she lifted the slip she wore up over her head and dropped it behind her.

Willi had never seen anything like it. Her ample young figure was the most beautiful thing he had ever beheld, and he almost gasped. Helga realised the initiative had passed to her. She stepped towards him, knelt down and began to untie the rope which served him for a belt.

Willi's hand stretched out and touched her thrusting young breast. He felt a tingle run all through him and he leaned towards her. She lay back on the floor and pulled him down.

This time her left hand was quite near the handle of the bayonet and she had little difficulty in grasping it like a dagger.

Willi closed his eyes to kiss her, his lips tightly pursed. He leaned forward, wriggled out of his trousers, and to take some of his weight, he stretched out his right arm placing his hand on her elbow just as she swung the bayonet at him.

Thus pinioned, Helga was unable to deliver the blow she had intended. Instead the blade only just entered his flesh behind the shoulder. With a howl of pained surprise Willi rolled sideways away from the waving bayonet, and Helga's next stab sunk the steel into the wooden floor through Willi's shirt tail. He tugged hard to free himself, and as he did so rolled further away and over the edge of the loft.

He fell through the hatch to the stone floor of the barn, landing on his back among some half-empty crates. He struggled painfully to his feet, pulled up his trousers, and made for the door.

Helga, meanwhile, had prised the bayonet from the floor boards and threw it after him. It clattered against the wall as Willi reached the stable door. He turned back and looked up at the naked figure with rank malice in his eyes. Helga saw the look, grasped hold of the top of the ladder and threw it down.

Willi was in too much pain to rejoin battle however, and made to leave when a torrent of abuse hit him. He looked up at Helga, marooned in the loft, and a nasty thought came to his delinquent mind. He lifted the paraffin lamp down from the wall, lit it with a stick from the fire, then tossed it through the hatch against the far wall of the stable. It smashed on the stonework and set the straw ablaze. With an evil smirk on his face Willi clambered over the lower half of the stable door and out. He looked around to be sure he was unobserved, then limped away. Helga's screams he ignored and without slackening his pace, he was soon out of earshot.

Inside the stable Helga tried in vain to put out the flames, flailing at them ineffectually with her dress. When it was obvious she would not succeed she tried to escape by climbing the ladder in the little tower. However, the canvas at the entrance caught fire, and by the time she reached the top of the tower it was filled with smoke. Suffocating and panic-stricken, she beat against the slats with her fists, missed her footing and fell, banging her head against the stonework on the way down. She lay unconscious among the smouldering straw while her life ebbed away in the smoke. As it happened, neither the straw nor the stable were as dry as they might be and the fire petered out shortly afterwards.

Willi went to ground and stayed there licking his wounds for a few days.

When he emerged, he decided that it would be as well to stear clear of the depot for a while lest anyone had observed him going off with Helga that morning. Hank Carlile missed the little urchin he had befriended and assumed that the reason was because the boy had been run in by the MPs. He upbraided Sergeant Madison for scaring the 'poor little cuss' away, pointing out that 'now that the war is over we'll have to help these poor Germans to rehabilitate themselves.'

As fate would have it, it was the same Sergeant Mike Madison who discovered Helga's remains. About five weeks after the fire his patrol was chasing a black marketeer who led them to within sight of the old stable, and, in the belief that he was hiding inside, they stormed it. Their disappointment at not finding him was as nothing compared with their surprise at what they did find.

Working on the assumption that their quarry (who did not look at all like Willi) had been the occupant of the stable, it was his description that was circulated in connection with Helga's death.

All Willi ever heard, however was that the authorities were at last after somebody for the crime, and that was enough to make him get out of Frankfurt as quickly as he was able.

CHAPTER 12

From the town hall Klaus made his way to the Krone Hotel where he phoned his office, to be told that an H. Lansing was listed as a passenger on the flight from London arriving at Frankfurt at three-fifty. He settled down with a drink to await my arrival, and, unable to make sense of what he had found in the town records, looked again at the telex messages he had picked up earlier in Wiesbaden.

The hotel receptionist approached him.

'Are you Herr Schmidt, please?' she asked.

'No,' Klaus shook his head.

A minute later she was at his side again.

'Excuse me, but the man on the telephone insists it is you he wishes to speak to. He described you, er, quite accurately.'

Puzzled, Klaus rose:

'Which phone?' he asked.

'You may take the call in that booth,' she said.

Inside, Klaus picked up the phone, but before he could speak a voice said:

'I may have the wrong name, but it is you I want.'

'And who are you, may I ask?'

'My name is of no importance. The name you are interested in is Lanzig, am I not right?'

'Yes, that is so.'

'Very well, I have some information which might

interest you.'

'What is that?'

'Not on the phone, Herr...' the voice paused.

'As you say, the only name of interest is the one you just mentioned. What is it you know?' countered Klaus.

'We must meet. After all I can give you details over the phone, but you cannot pay me for them over the phone!' The voice laughed.

'I see. Well, as you are apparently aware, I am in the Krone Hotel. Where are you?'

'I can meet you at Muller Bros. wine vaults in half an hour. I cannot wait longer as I must leave on business this afternoon and may not return for some time.'

Klaus looked at his watch. It was five past twelve.

'Very well, in half an hour.' The phone went dead.

Fifteen minutes later Klaus was in his BMW on the opposite corner from the entrance to the winery. He watched a few people come and go, but saw no-one who seemed to be looking for a rendezvous. After ten minutes a group of about twenty came round a corner led by a young woman with a large yellow and black lapel badge. A man came out of the main entrance and escorted them inside.

Klaus got out of the car quickly, crossed the road and tagged himself onto the end of the party.

As the tour proceeded he looked round to see if any of the others could be the voice on the telephone.

Willi Hauptner, in scruffy overalls, watched the group pass by him on its way down into the depths of the winery. He glanced into the tiny plant room to make sure the engineer he had sandbagged was still unconscious and securely gagged, and followed at a discreet distance behind the tourists.

As the tour proceeded through the dank and musty cellars, Klaus began to think he had made a mistake and should perhaps have been more open and gone straight to the winery office to see if anyone had left a message for him. Suddenly, he felt a light blow on the back of his neck. It was caused by a rolled-up greasy rag. He plucked it from where it stuck to his jacket and spun round. About twenty feet away a man in overalls beckoned to him to follow, and immediately turned a corner out of sight. Klaus glanced back at the tour party, but they were already disappearing from view.

He wrapped his fingers round the Luger in his coat pocket and walked slowly towards the junction of dim passages where he had seen the man. Cautiously he turned the corner and looked along the passage down which the man seemed to have gone, but could see nobody. There was, discernible in the distance, light coming from a half-open door. He moved warily towards it.

Willi had chosen his spot well and counted on Klaus' caution to give him time to climb up into some rafters shoring up the ancient cellar. As Klaus walked slowly towards the light Willi was directly above him.

At the last moment Willi's weight caused a rafter to creak, and Klaus spun round. Before his gun was out of his pocket the spanner Willi swung caught him behind the ear and he fell dazed to the ground.

Willi was on him like a weasel at a petrified rabbit. A length of wire round the neck, a knee in the upper spine and it was all over in seconds. Willi glanced round, although he was sure the silent killing had gone unnoticed. He found the big man's body very heavy but managed to lift it and carry it up a wooden ladder set against the side of a large wine vat. He had earlier opened the inspection cover near the top, and now lay Klaus' body across it, going through the pockets, removing the Luger, the telex and Klaus' wallet and ID card.

Pushing the arms through first, he launched Klaus' body into the dark red liquid murmuring 'have a drink on me' as it sank under the surface.

Willi had not, however, reckoned on Archimedes, and some wine displaced by the body spilled over the edge of the inspection hole and drenched his legs, at the same time wiping away his self-satisfied grin. He cursed roundly and quickly removed his borrowed overalls, but not before the wine had soaked his trouser legs. Before replacing the hatch he tossed the overalls into the vat, and with the spanner in the pocket they sank quickly.

Five minutes later he emerged into the sunlight at the front entrance of the winery and walked away without a backward glance.

Ten minutes after that he was in his hired VW on the way back to Frankfurt to report the success of his mission. He smoked a cigarette while mulling over the killing and the pleasure it had given. He was sure Klutov would be pleased too.

He pulled out of his pocket the telex he had taken from Klaus, and read it through. Very interesting. As usual, Klutov had not given him the why's and the wherefore's so he had had no idea why he had been on the lookout for anyone inquiring about Lanzigs.

'This Lansing fellow must be big-time to judge by his c.v. Handsome bastard too,' Willi mused, glancing at the photo. 'Another German working for Moscow. I suppose I'll have to nursemaid him when he gets here. One thing, I've eliminated the opposition so they will not be there to pick him up at the airport ... I could do that <u>then</u> report to Klutov. He will be very pleased, the slant-eyed bastard.'

It reminded Willi of when he had first met the Russian and of how the meeting had come about, all those years ago after he had fled from Frankfurt.

CHAPTER 13

Following his escape from the stable that was Helga's tomb, Willi drifted around Germany making a living out of the black market and petty crime in general, graduating from being a youthful petty criminal to being an adult petty criminal. By virtue of his innate cunning and the fact that he never spent very long in one place, he kept out of the hands of the law most of the time. He remained essentially a loner, never forming any personal attachments.

Some fifteeen years later in a Hamburg brothel - the only place where he was able to establish a satisfactory relationship with women - Willi found someone who measured up to his image of the perfect female. Dagmar was the very image of Helga. Tall and well-endowed, she had the same long rich brown hair and dark eyes. She even wore a tight red dress the first time he saw her.

He became an habitue of her establishment and went so far as to leave her more than the going rate sometimes - the only gesture of generosity he ever made to anyone. For her part she was quite prepared to give him his money's worth, especially as his demands were rather juvenile. It amused her to pretend she was only fifteen and that it was his first time.

After the initial novelty wore off, however, she became rather bored by this game and found Willi rather an unpleasant character. Somehow his insistence on playing the part of the callow youth seemed unhealthy, even by brothel standards.

One night, although she knew Willi was liable to call, she accepted a commission from Helmut, a sailor of her acquaintance. He was a big fellow whose long absences at sea left him with a straightforward appetite she was happy to satisfy.

Having done so, she was about to get dressed again when Willi arrived. Without ceremony he entered her little room, fully expecting her to be ready for him.

His 'Who the hell are you?' did not go down well with Helmut who, in spite of the indignity of being trouserless, drew himself up to his full height and without saying a word, swung an enormous ham of a fist at Willi's head.

Willi had not survived for so long without gaining some experience in self-defence and was a very dirty fighter indeed. Whereas the big sailor outweighed and outreached him by a long way, Willi was a quick mover and too wily to be caught easily.

Ducking under the initial blow, he aimed a pointed toe at the sailor's crotch and struck home. As the big man doubled over, Willi brought up a knee into his face. However, this had less effect than expected and the sailor, roaring like a mad bull picked up a cheap chair and smashed it over Willi's head. Willi was able only partially to parry this blow and went down under the onslaught.

Helmut was on top of him in a flash and his hands went for Willi's throat.

Willi struggled and squirmed, but could not stop the roaring tide of noise and blackness filling his head. His eyes went dim - all he could see was the white grimacing face pressed close to his. It seemed to him to be the face of Death. In a last desperate effort to survive, his hand groped around for a weapon. It found one in the shape of a splintered chair leg. With his last remaining strength he lifted it high and plunged it down at the menacing face. The improvised dagger missed the sailor's jaw and plunged into his neck above the clavicle.

With an awesome gurgling exclamation Helmut released his grip and put his hands to his neck. Blood welled up past the wooden weapon and he was unable to grasp it. Pallor swept over his face and he pitched sideways, his body twitching for a moment or two as he died.

Willi gasped and coughed and gasped again as his lungs sucked in air. He sat up covered in blood and gulped noisily. He could see the fight was over and looked across at Dagmar.

She stood petrified against the wall, naked with her slip held against her breast. One glance at Willi's face as he rose and she knew what was in his mind. She opened her mouth to scream, but he was at her throat before the sound emerged. His wiry hands tightened round her neck and squeezed the life out of her. Finding his face close to hers he leant a little closer and kissed her as she died.

He dragged her body across the room and lay her near the sailor, making sure she was well smeared with blood, and placed one oustretched arm in such a position as to suggest she had been the one to stab him.

Willi reckoned that with luck no-one had paid heed to the noisy goings-on (the lusty customers were not exactly silent lovers) and so it proved.

Pulling the door shut behind him he descended the stair and went out into the night. After a couple of blocks he divested himself of his bloody raincoat and stuffed it into a trash can. As he had stolen it in the first place he thought it unlikely it could be traced to him. He washed himself in a public toilet and slunk off to his two-roomed apartment on Giessenstrasse.

It did not take the police long to deduce that the two victims in the brothel had not killed each other and they were soon looking for a third party. One of Dagmar's colleagues recalled hearing that 'Little Willie' (as he was laughingly referred to by the women of the house) had been expected by her that evening and it was for this otherwise unidentified customer that the police began to search.

Willi realised next morning that he had probably not confused the issue totally and would have to seek another way out - particularly as he could not be sure that he had not left the odd fingerprint at the scene of the crime.

Although he had managed for most of the time to steer clear of the law, Willi had on occasion been taken into custody and could not be certain that the police did not have his prints on file somewhere .

His first thought was to try to establish an alibi, but he knew he had no friends who would be willing to perjure themselves for him. The idea of escaping to sea he entertained for an equally short time. Not only did he have a stomach-churning fear of open water (brought about by an incident in which he had capsized a rowing boat on a lake and nearly drowned at the age of seven) but he did not relish the possibility of being at sea with any of Helmut's mates close at hand.

The more he thought about it, the more it seemed likely that the police would turn up some clue to lead to him. He concluded that he must get out of Hamburg - but whither? A murder hunt would be sure to stir enough memories to make life very difficult indeed, wherever he chose to hide.

He drew on the stub of his cigarette, almost burning his fingers in the process, and cursed his luck. Then he cursed Dagmar, the cause of his trouble. Then he remembered Helga, and cursed her even more vehemently for starting it all.

His mind lingered in the past and he remembered his 'father,' Captain Hauptner. He went to the tin box he kept under his bed and lifted it up and placed it on the eiderdown he had stolen from one of Hamburg's bombed-out hotels.

Kneeling in front of it he opened the box reverentially and removed the contents slowly, savouring the texture of each item. There were several bundles of dollars - about two and a half thousands' worth in all - a lewd picture he had stolen from the brothel - he tossed it aside contemptuously - the Luger he had taken from Captain Hauptner's corpse, and the iron cross.

This last he put to his lips, gently kissing it with his eyes shut. It seemed to have a transcendental effect on him and he knelt there swaying to and fro very slowly before letting out a long sigh. Before him was a vision of his 'father ' - handsome and tall, daring and strong.

Willi was sure that HE would provide the answer. After a few minutes it came to him - he knew how to escape!

Fierenstrasse was a mean little street peopled on the whole by mean little people. Number twenty-nine lay between a stale tobacconist and a boarded-up bakery. Willi entered the short passage and looked for the name he sought on the list attached to the wall at the bottom of the stairs. In the semi-darkness the names were obscure and looked as though they had not been renewed since the building had opened. He peered closer and gave a start as a sound came from the darkness at the end of the passage. A door opened and half a face appeared at the crack. Willi pulled his felt hat further down almost to his eyebrows and half turned towards the face.

'Herr Grossman,' he mumbled with a feeble attempt at disguising his voice.

'Second floor, left,' grunted the face as the door shut.

Willi climbed the dishevelled stair tilting his head away from the single gas bracket that hissed and spluttered on the landing of the first floor. However, he need not have bothered for there was no-one about, the whole building having the air of an abandoned ship.

He knocked at the door marked W.E. G OS N, Wh les e Mer ant, and a bellow issued forth from inside. Startled by the sudden loud sound he stepped back and almost fell down the stairs, but managed to grab the bannister. He cursed himself for being so jumpy, and opened the door. Inside he found a small outer office with a counter on which were perched a calendar displaying the date of three months ago, a tube of glue and a brass bell - its bright shine seeming quite out of place - of the kind one pushes on top to attract attention. Behind the counter a wood and glass partition with a door in it separated off what seemed to be the office proper.

Willi struck the bell. Before its vibrato had died the partition door opened and an enormous figure confronted him. It waddled towards him, blocking out most of the light from the single grubby window.

'Well?'

The voice squeaked out of the inflated body like the sound from a child's rubber duck, and for the first time in days Willi felt like smiling. But the situation was not funny and he knew he must be careful not to antagonise the only person he believed might help him.

'You deal in import and export?' he asked, and

was surprised that his own voice sounded almost as squeaky as the other's.

'Yes.' came the monosyllabic reply.

'And personal problems?' he went on, emphasising the second word. The large figure nodded. Willi drew breath, cleared his throat and plunged on.

'I have a personal export problem ...' his voice trailed off as he thought he may have said too much all at once.

The voice paused for a long time before replying, 'Someone has sent you?'

'Siggi Lieberling,' Willi replied, giving the name of one of the more senior members of the black market ring he often ran errands for. Again there was a long silence before the figure turned away from him and went through the door behind the counter, squeaking, 'Come in!' over its shoulder.

By the time he entered the inner office the squeaker was sat behind a gargantuan desk strewn about with an abundance of papers, desk furniture and bric-a-brac. The room itself seemed surprisingly comfortable, with carpets which although old and dirty, seemed of good quality, as did the furniture.

For the first time Willi was able to see the other's face, in the light of a desk lamp. It was a flabby, pale face with a delicacy which contrasted strangely with the hugeness of its body. The hair was thick, black and wavy, and Willi was sure it was a wig, while the thin lips looked too red to be real.

A puffy pale hand gestured him into a velvet

chair in front of the desk. He sat down, not sure whether it was up to him to open this phase of the conversation.

'You have a passport?' he was asked.

He shook his head.

'Huh, then it is much more difficult, and expensive.'

The eyes bore into him asking an unspoken question. He delved into an inner pocket and pulled out a bundle of dollar bills.

The eyes dilated noticeably. He threw the money onto the desk with an air of bravado, pleased that he had made an impression. A podgy fist darted out and grabbed the bundle like a lizard catching an insect with its tongue.

'Take your hat off, have a drink.' The dollar-heavy hand gestured towards a bottle of Schnapps on the mantlepiece. While Willi helped himself the fat man set about counting the notes with the speed of a bank teller.

In spite of the more congenial atmosphere the display of dollars seemed to have induced, Willi still felt very much at a disadvantage and he surreptitiously felt the Luger nestling in his other inside pocket.

'For this I can get you a passport and give you a contact on a ship sailing for ...' a hand rifled through a sheaf of papers on the desk, '... Rotterdam.'

'I can't sail,' Willi piped up.

'Why not?' asked the other, then waved away his reply before Willi had made it.

'What about a long distance truck to Belgium

then?'

'I need to go to ...' Willi drew in his breath,'... the East.'

The eyes dilated again, this time even more. There was a long pause during which they contracted again and the too-red lips twitched towards a smile.

'That, my dear fellow, will cost a great deal more, if it's possible at all.'

The podgy fist tossed Willi's bundle of notes to the floor, and the huge body stood up as though the matter was over.

Willi's hand gripped the glass so tightly it almost shattered and his instinct was to throw the contents at the face behind the desk. But he knew that this was his only escape route, and he fought back the desire to strike out. Instead he took from another inner pocket a second bundle of notes and flung them to the floor, rather pleased when they came to rest on top of the first.

The pale face actually did crack into a smile this time, although the eyes remained cold. A fat finger stabbed at a button which Willi had not seen before, and he heard a buzz from the other side of the wall behind the desk.

What had previously looked like a crack in the dilapidated panelling now opened wide, and a burly young man with an ugly scar down one cheek emerged. He was wearing a fashionable suit.

'Hans, show our frightened little friend out. Little Friend!' the voice squeaked on before Willi could say anything, 'Come back tomorrow at ten. Meanwhile I shall make inquiries and if what you ask is possible then I, Grossmann, will see to it. Take your money and bring twice as much tomorrow.'

The huge figure sat down and busied itself with a pile of bank statements. Willi hesitated, looked at Scar-face, and knew he could only obey.

Back in his little room, Willi wondered whether he had done the right thing, but concluded there was no other source of help to which he could turn. He was convinced that East Germany would be the ideal sanctuary. The police would never dream of looking for him there - and even if they did, could do nothing.

He did not care about poiitics, and had heard that there was a black market there too. Once or twice he had met escapees from the East, and they had told him so. It was from them he had heard stories of the legendary Grossmann who could always be relied on to furnish good papers for escaping.

His only worry was whether the fat man could come up with papers for escaping, *to,* the East, rather than out of it. He turned over in his mind again and again other possible escape routes, but came up with nothing. No, the only place, the ideal place, was East Germany, Liepzig if possible - where his 'father' had come from. He reckoned he might even be able to make use of the connection, somehow.

He decided not to stay any longer where he was, just in case the police were already looking for him. Packing together a few essentials in a rucksack, he shut the door on his apartment without a second glance, and set off for a hideout under a railway bridge he had used once or twice in the past. His landlord was not at all pleased when he discovered the little man had skipped off owing a month's rent, but the police were the last people he would inform. Instead he told some 'friends' who specialised in debt collecting. Willi never realised he was being sought by some of his underworld peers as well as by the authorities.

The Fat Man provided documents - an East German identity card ('Who has a passport over there?' he had asked) and a pass to get through the Berlin Wall. The whole package cost two thousand dollars, leaving Willi with five hundred, plus some Deutsch Marks.

Once aboard the train for Berlin, Willi sat in the corner of the carriage trying his best not to look furtive. However, apart from a few frights when various uniforms entered the carriage - ticket inspectors, a guard, two soldiers and a brass bandsman - Willi passed an uneventful journey, and even managed to sleep part of the way.

In Berlin he felt quite safe somehow and began to have qualms about the rest of the escape plan. These were quickly dispelled when he turned a corner and almost walked into two patroiling policemen who looked at him very suspiciously - or so Willi thought.

His resolve strengthened, he renewed his search

for a certain street which led to a fairly busy crossing point. He had been well briefed by the Fat Man, who in turn had learned from a client who had escaped in the opposite direction.

At the appointed hour he observed a number of people from various directions entering the street and making their way towards the check point. He found it easy to join them as though he had made the journey many times, and it was not long before he was in the queue to pass through to the East.

As his turn came he felt a churning in his stomach and more than a hint of gelatine in his knees. He hardly dared look up at the tall figure who seemed to scrutinise each person for an age before letting them through. Just as he presented his identity card, a whiff of smoke from the guard's cigarette drifted up his left nostril and he was unable to suppress a sneeze. The droplet spray engulfed the guard's hand as well as Willi's document. The guard ostentatiously withdrew a handkerchief from his uniform and proceeded to wipe his bespattered fist. The pass he disdained to touch again and Willi was able to pick it up and be on his way with the minimum of scrutiny.

Unfamiliar as it was, East Berlin did not overwhelm him. He rightly assumed that the underworld is very much the same in any society, and he soon found his own level and forged links with the locals engaged in the same illegal practices with which he was familiar.

He thought it wise to maintain his role as an easterner, telling those who had to be told, that he came from Liepzig, relying on the underworld's usual code of ethics to prevent too many awkward questions being asked. In any case, he was usually able to divert their attention from that subject to that of the West with which (truthfully enough) he was able to claim a fair degree of familiarity. Indeed this gained him a certain status for few if any of his new acquaintances had ever been there.

He had never before been the centre of attention (apart from that of the police) and the experience warmed him. It also gained him quite a few free drinks - which also warmed him. Willi could hold his liquor, although he had never been a very heavy drinker, and it was not the level of his blood alcohol that led to his undoing, but the intoxication of having an audience listen with rapt attention to his garbled tales of life on the other side of the Wall.

In fact, Willi could spin a yarn with some skill, and by substituting himself for some of the bigger fish in the murky pools of post-war German criminality, he was able to tell quite a tale. Unfortunately for him he was also able to gain the ear of one of that species that always feeds on the criminal classes - the informer.

In this instance the insignificant looking labourer at the end of the bar did not go to the police with the story of Willi's accurate account of the West, but to a section of the State Security Service.

The following day, when he was unceremoniously bundled into an unmarked car and squashed between two large unsmiling men, proved to be the longest day of Willi's life.

CHAPTER 14

On leaving the car he was marched into what had at one time been a small hotel, past the reception desk where the man on duty paid him no attention, and down a back stair into what had been the modest establishment's modest wine cellar. Its various bays, now made into effective cells by supplying them with crude bars across their entrances, were all empty and at the far end of the cellar a single deal table stood on the rough floor, a copy of Pravda folded under one leg to keep it steady.

Behind the table sat a middle-aged man in a woollen cardigan and a bow tie. He did not look up from the single sheet of paper on the table until Willi stood before him, flanked by the two men who had brought him in. They said nothing, but each took a step backward, and although he was glad they were no longer pressing against him, Willi felt terribly alone.

'Name?' Bow-tie asked, without looking up.

Willi swallowed, although his mouth was totally devoid of saliva, and tried to speak. At first no words would come, but the evil look on Bow-tie's face as he raised his eyes to Willi's face proved very stimulating.

'Hauptner,' was all he could manage.

'Papers?'

Willi withdrew his forged identity card and stretched out his hand across the table. The eyes bore into him, but their owner made no move to take the document from his hand. Willi stretched further and leaned over the table, his hand approaching the other's face.

The eyelids dipped and Bow-tie looked down at the card, but found it difficult to focus due to the coarse tremor of Willi's outstretched hand. Suddenly Bow-tie's left arm shot out from behind the table and the piece of grubby card was snatched from Willi's unsure fingers, to be held quite still in the double hook of a mechanical hand. His scrutiny complete, Willi's tormentor ceremoniously opened a drawer in the table and dropped his identity card into it, then shut the drawer.

'And now, your real name, IF YOU PLEASE!' the words were screamed at him and the left hook landed on his temple at the same time. Willi staggered sideways and tripped on the uneven floor, landing in a heap at the feet of one of his captors. He looked along the floor under the table and saw that the man seated behind it had a large ugly boot on his left foot. All he could think of was what a perfect specimen his father - Captain Hauptner - had been.

'Hauptner, Hauptner, Hauptner!' he repeated, his voice breaking as the blood from his temple mingled with his tears. The two thugs who had brought him in hoisted Willi to his feet and stood him again in front of the desk. At an almost imperceptible nod from Bow-tie, the one on the left drew back his fist and punched Willi very hard over the kidney. Willi almost fainted and almost vomited at the same time, crumpling against the man on his right. He in turn jerked Willi upright by his collar, cutting off the air Willi was trying to gasp into his lungs. As Willi choked, one of the men bunching his fist in preparation, looked at his boss and asked, 'Again?'

'No,' replied Bow-tie, 'Number five.' He indicated one of the cells with his hook.

They marched Willi to the middle cell on one side and pushed him in through a metre high gap at floor level, closed after his entrance by a grille slid down from above. On all fours Willi looked around through misty eyes at the bare cell whose floor sloped away to the wall, with a drain in one corner. He half straightened painfully, and turned round just as one of the thugs came towards him carrying a bucket. Willi grasped two bars to help pull himself up, and was almost erect when a gallon and a half of icy water hit him full in the face and drenched him. Willi gasped, choked, and gasped again.

Unsmilingly, the man turned away and, placing the empty bucket on the floor, left the cellar. Willi wiped the water from his eyes with his wet hands and looked towards the desk, but it was unattended, and just then the only remaining light bulb went out. In the total darkness Willi felt very, very cold and very, very afraid. There was nowhere to sit except the cold wet floor, so he stood half crouched against the bars, shivering fitfully. An overwhelming desire to relieve himself beset him. He was afraid to let go of the bars lest he fall to the ground, so he simply let it come, the warm urine trickling down his leg. It was the only part of him that was warm - for a few miserable seconds.

Two hours later the light went on again, and another man appeared. Willi blinked his eyes and looked up from the floor where he had lain for most of the time. He was just in time to see another bucketful of icy water cascade towards him. The light went out. Left in the same sorry state for the second time, Willi was sure he was going to die, and came to the conclusion that he was not altogether sorry. Death did not come however - only awful, numbing coldness and nausea rising up from the depths of his belly. He turned towards the drain, but could not remember in which corner it lay. Half-way there he retched, but nothing came. He retched again and slumped down on his side his knees tucked up to quell the spasms of his abdomen.

He lay there for some time, his teeth chattering and his head occasionally bumping against the floor as his whole body shook. The light came on again and he was aware of footsteps coming towards him. He did not look up and waited for the arctic onslaught to be repeated, consoling himself in the knowledge that he could not feel any colder.

It did not come. Instead the grille was lifted and he was dragged out by one foot and hoisted to his feet, a man again on each arm. He was scraped rather than marched to the desk - his lower limbs were totally numb - to find Bow-tie in place again. On the desk in front of him were a pile of what looked like clothes on top of a thick blanket and a bowl of hot soup.

Willi looked, fascinated, at the steam rising from the bowl and involuntarily licked his lips.

'The whole truth - and they are yours. Anything less - you know what to expect.' Bow-tie sounded almost benevolent. In front of him on the table were the few things they had found on Willi - including his precious iron cross.

Willi could only nod. The men let go of his arms and he collapsed to the floor. On Bow-tie's instructions one of them brought a chair and helped Willi into it.

'Your story first,' said Bow-tie, his hook waving aside the Promised Land of food and clothes as though of no importance.

Willi croaked out an outline of his past activities and told of his latest and greatest crime. For a brief moment he thought of distorting the facts somewhat to make his part seem rather more heroic than it had in reality been, but his mind was too tired to do anything other than give out the plain truth of the matter.

When he had finished Bow-tie looked at him for a long few seconds before nodding curtly and standing up. The hook waved vaguely towards the things on the table before his inquisitor limped away.

Willi was warm and dry again, and the soup had damped down his stomach's partiality for trampolining. In an upstairs room he was seated in a comfortable armchair, and were it not for the ache in the region of his left loin, would have been asleep. He felt quite pleased with himself and the performance he had put up, under the circumstances. He knew that the authorities would not turn him over to the West German police ... at least, he thought not.

His thoughts were interrupted by the entry of a man he had not seen before. The newcomer wore a pigskin coat over his stocky frame, and had a faintly mongolian face. Without saying a word, he strode towards Willi and looked down at him. For some reason Willi felt compelled to stand up. The proximity to the other man made him feel very uneasy, and he retreated against the chair, falling back into it again. The narrow eyes bore into him and Willi got the impression that this man could be even more nasty than Bow-tie. He was unsure what to do. The silence unnerved him, but he found himself unable to speak.

The pain in Willi's back grew worse, and he badly wanted to visit the toilet again. He cringed visibly, sinking deeper into the leatherette upholstery.

A smile spread across the oriental features of his latest tormentor, but it did not reassure Willi. As the upper lip unfurled from the teeth, he could see that the upper canines on either side were duplicated by teeth protruding from the gum above them. It made Willi think of the wolf in Little Red Riding Hood. At last the man spoke. His voice was strangely high-pitched and did not seem to match his physique.

'Willi Hauptner, or whatever your name is, you are going to tell me all about the man who gave you this.' At this point he produced from his pocket Willi's false identity card and flicked it at Willi in the manner of propelling a frisby. It caught Willi on the nose, then slithered down into his lap.

Willi looked down at it. He knew that even if his inclination had been towards protecting the man who had given him his false papers, he would have been unable to withhold the information.

Alexi Klutov owed his features to his origins in Soviet Central Asia, and his peculiar voice to an old wound in the neck - inflicted by a woman prisoner with a broken perfume bottle. He was a very experienced and successful interrogator and a Colonel in the KGB to prove it.

Here he was, in possession of a lead to the man who had been forging papers for those escaping to the West. Never had he supposed that he would find someone coming FROM the West with similar false documents. When Mildegruber had first phoned him to tell of Willi's capture, he had thought it mildly interesting but simply a routine matter. Now he realised he had a considerable prize within his grasp.

For his part, Willi had been wondering how he could turn the knowledge he possessed to good advantage, but did not have the will to try any bargaining. He badly needed to relieve himself, an urgency increased by the memory that on the previous occasion in the cell there had been more than a trace of blood present.

Klutov bent towards Willi and permitted himself another smile as Willi cringed away from him. He put a hand under Willi's left shoulder and yanked him to his feet.

'Over there,' he said, propelling his captive towards a large desk. Willi, however, indicated his urgent need for relief without words, and Klutov added, 'In there first,' pointing to a door in one wall.

Willi's urine was even more blood-stained than before and the sight of it removed the last possible trace of resistance from him. Klutov saw it too, and it reminded him of the time he had watched his own blood flow down his chest from the wound in his neck. He knew that Willi would not give any trouble.

In a few minutes Klutov was in possession of all that Willi knew about the forger of Fierenstrasse. Having made the best possible use of him, Klutov's first thought was to cast Willi aside as one would an old pair of shoes. On reflection, however, he wondered whether his captive might not prove useful. He had more than once thought that it would be handy to have someone in the West who was familiar with the criminal world - someone who could pick up information and do odd jobs that more conventional agents were unable to undertake.

Under the threat of delivery to the Hamburg police, Willi readily agreed to work for Klutov. His first job was to return in the company of one of Klutov's men to assist in the downfall of the man in Fierenstrasse.

Willi led the way to the grubby office of W.E. G OS N, Wh les e Mer ant, but the cupboard was bare. A few inquiries revealed that the fat man who had run the business had died the week before - of a kidney complaint.

This news came as a disappointment to Willi, who had hoped to gain credit for helping Klutov to deal with the problem. However, his eagerness to be of assistance seemed enough to convince the Russian that he was worth keeping on.

Willi rather enjoyed his new role. He had never before received any sort of official recognition or privilege. Things were pretty hard for the masses in East Germany, but he was able to share some of the luxuries reserved for the New Masters and, if anything, his standard of living was better than it had been in the West.

He was only a tiny cog in the Kremlin's vast network of espionage machinery, but as time went by he proved a useful addition to Klutov's section. His upbringing in the shady underworld of petty crime in the West made him suitable for certain jobs that conventionally-trained agents simply could not do. Klutov sent him into West Germany from time to time, and on these trips he used the name Grossmann. His fear that he might some day be picked up and identified by way of a fingerprint as the Hamburg brothel killer made him extra careful. In fact he need not have worried. The only prints he had left behind at the scene of the murders were so smudged with his victims' blood that they were unidentifiable. The file on the case remained open, technicaily, but the overworked police department soon consigned it to a dust-gathering shelf.

His innate cunning rendered him a ready pupil and he added quite a few new tricks to his repertoire. Later he graduated to more important assignments, and eventually got the chance he had subconsciously been waiting for - the chance to kill. He enjoyed a repetition of that orgasmic thrill he had felt when killing Dagmar. The feeling of power was almost overwhelming as he watched his victim - a minor double agent who had outlived his usefulness - slump down to his death in the back seat of the taxi Willi had 'borrowed' for the purpose.

It was some years and many jobs later when Willi received a phone call from Klutov instructing him to make his way to Rudesheim to keep a lookout for anyone bearing the name, or showing an interest in the name, Lanzig.

'If you do find anyone showing too much interest in these records - birth certificates and the like - they must be got rid of,' Klutov said. For Willi that instruction could mean only one thing.

CHAPTER 15

Having returned to Rudesheim by river. I was waiting in the lounge of the Krone, wondering what was keeping Klaus late and what news he had from Fox. After fifteen minutes I went to the reception desk.

'Have you a message for a Herr Lockhart, please?'

'You are staying here, sir?' the girl asked.

'No, but I was to meet a friend here at one o'clock and he has not turned up.'

'Herr Schmidt? Ah, no, his name was not Schmidt.'

'Pardon?'

'There was here earlier a large gentleman who is also not staying here. There was a message for him on the phone, but his name is not Schmidt.'

It clearly sounded as silly to her as it did to me! At last I sorted out what she was trying to tell me. Klaus had gone off, God knows where, in response to a phone call from someone who clearly did not know him. I did not like the sound of it.

I put through a call to the Inn where we had a room, but Klaus had left no message there, nor had there been any sign of him since morning.

I had a couple of drinks at the bar, but after half an hour could sit around no longer. I left a message to the effect that I would return within the hour, asked them to look out for any messages from Klaus, and took off downtown. I had at least one concrete objective - to find out if Klaus had had the copy of Elizabeth Tasker's photo made. It had proved inconvenient having only one picture while two of us searched for her, and he had agreed to try and have a copy made in Rudesheim that morning.

I struck lucky in the second shop I tried. The man there confirmed that a large fellow had been in that morning to have a copy made of a certain photograph. At first he would do no more than admit this, pointing out that the commission should be handed over only to the holder of the ticket in question. After some persuasion and twenty marks he let me have both copy and original.

'Funny thing is, I know the lady,' he said quite casually. I stared at him, looked again at Elizabeth Tasker's picture to be sure he had not given me the wrong one, and exclaimed:

'You know her, this woman?'

'Well, I have met her. Here in the shop only yesterday.'

'Tell me about it. From the beginning.'

'We do not normally open on a Sunday, but at Oktoberfest I come in for two hours on a Sunday to sell films as there are so many visitors in town. Yesterday morning she came in and bought a camera. She had come on a visit and left hers behind, apparently.'

'What kind of camera?'

'A Polaroid instant.' He pointed to a shelf-full. 'Good for holiday pictures, nothing very special. Comes complete with film.'

'Is that all?'

'Yes, she left as soon as it was bought. She did not want it made into a packet.'

'Thank you very much.' I gave him another ten marks and left.

What, I wondered, did she want to photograph, or was it a question of whom?

I decided to make use of her pictures, and spent the best part of half an hour round the town asking if anyone had seen her. No luck. Back at the Krone there were no messages. It was two thirty-five by then, and I was worried.

I went into the bar for a drink and found it crowded. I elbowed my way forward and bought a brandy. As I turned away in search of a place to sit down I came face to face with Edith, of all people. I tried to pretend I had not seen her, but could not avoid her withering stare.

I retreated into the lobby and sat down. No sooner had I raised my drink to my lips than she was standing looking down at me.

'I heard you,' she said.

'Pardon?'

'A few minutes ago - you were asking for your friend the German, at the desk.'

'Yes I was, as a matter of fact.'

'You always seem to be looking for people, don't you?'

'I cannot see how it concerns ...'

'But I've seen him.'

'I know you've seen him,' I rejoined - then realised.

'You mean, today? Where?'

She smiled at me with the satisfaction of a cat contemplating a litre of double dairy cream.

'On the wine tour, a couple of hours ago.'

'Where?'

'At the winery we visited. He was going round with the tour party.'

'He was going round...?'

'Yes, I thought it rather odd. After all, you're not exactly tourists, are you?' she grinned knowingly, and for a moment I thought she really knew something. Dismissing the absurd notion, I went on, 'Are you sure?'

'Quite certain. He was at the back of the group as we toured the cellars. I'm sure he saw me but didn't say anything. I didn't see him again after that and, of course, he wasn't on the coach coming back.'

I was already on my feet.

'What's the name of the wine place?'

'I can't honestly remember,' she said, 'I expect they'll know at reception.'

'Thank you for telling me. It's been most helpful,' I said.

'What ARE you doing here in...' Her question tailed off as I gave her my most dismissive look, and made for reception.

The taxi drew up outside Muller's winery - next to a police car. As I paid off the driver my eyes caught something familiar over the top of his car. In the opposite corner of the little square I saw Klaus' BMW.

I barged in through the entrance of the winery and into an office from which came a babble of voices.

No Klaus! Instead there were two policemen, a manager and an engineer with a sore head and no overalls.

I had to be patient while the policemen asked me who I was etc. etc. At last it was my turn. I asked if any of them had seen Klaus. No. They showed little interest.

I gestured the senior of the two policemen to one side, took out my UN passport and Security ID and showed them to him.

'The man I am trying to find is a Security Officer of the Federal German Republic. What has been happening here? There may be some connection.' I paused to let it sink in. It did.

'This man, the engineer who looks after the plant, was knocked unconscious and tied and gagged. Nothing appears to be missing except his overall! He did not see his assailant. This happened about two hours ago. We were called twelve minutes ago when he was found. That is all I know.'

Just then an old fellow in a green apron came in, clearly upset. 'Herr Muller! The temperature in vat seventeen is very high ...' he broke off as he saw the policemen.

'Never mind, Karl,' said the manager-type, 'Get Joachim to look into it. I am very busy with the police.'

Karl waddled out. I felt myself go pale.

'What does it mean, the vat getting hot?' I asked.

The policeman looked at me and was clearly thinking the same thing.

'Show us the way, Herr Muller! Quickly!' he barked.

Even with the lights on, it was dim down there. We climbed the steps, wet with wine, and took off the inspection cover. Two feet away, floating on the frothy red surface of the wine, I saw the back of Klaus' head.

CHAPTER 16

'Dead!' Fox was clearly shaken. 'God Almighty, Lockhart, what the hell's going on over there?'

'You tell me! You're the clever one. I'm just a desk johnnie that's fished his mate out of a vat of wine to find he's been garrotted with a length of piano wire.'

'I'm sorry, Lockhart.'

It was the first time I ever remember him apologising to me for anything. There was a pause.

'I just got to the office here in Wiesbaden where I found your telex. Klaus didn't have his copy on him - nor anything else, come to that.'

'So you know about Lansing coming over. What time is it with you?' Fox asked.

'Three forty-five. Frankfurt's about twenty-five kilometres away so I doubt if I'll be able to get there in time. The flight could be late, of course, so I might make it.'

'Yeah, you better try. We know Hugo Lansing contacted a bear before leaving. It seems likely he was caught unawares by the Tasker woman's flight to Germany.' Fox paused. 'There's gotta be something fucking big behind all this, Lockhart, to bring them outta the woodwork and start killing.'

'I'm beginning to wonder if our Miss Tasker is still alive. There's just no goddam sign of her since she arrived here and went up to Germania.'

'Hell, I'd almost forgotten her. Where did you

say she is?' Fox asked.

'Has been. It's a monument to the unification of Germany built last century high above the Rhine near Rudesheim. She visited it almost as soon as she got here, and there's been no sign of her since.'

'What did she go there for?'

'I've no idea, but apart from buying a Polaroid camera, it's the only thing she did while she was here, as far as I've been able to determine. So, unless it's some kind of blind, it must mean something.'

'Some kind of dropping point?'

'Nothing seems very logical, quite honestly.'

'And you think she may have been rubbed out as well?'

'I just don't know what to think,' I said.

'Get after Lansing - if he has arrived already you'll probably be able to pick up his trail. But for Christ's sake stand off - they've killed once. Keep your distance until I get some help to you.'

'Who'll you send?'

'God knows. We're cut to the bone. How Congress expects us to do the job properly when they refuse us the money to. . . but that's not your problem, Lockhart. I'll find somebody.'

'That's what I'm afraid of.'

'Eh?'

'Nothing.'

'Never mind the wisecracks, remember the Kremlin's in on this - they're the big league boys. No farting around with them. Get in their way and they'll stamp on you.'

'I've seen what they do.'

'Yeah. Sorry about your pal.'

'Thanks. Well, I better be off to the airport. I'll keep in touch.'

'This number'll get me day or night. Good luck, Lockhart!'

The television monitor at the airport told me what I had feared - the flight had landed on time. I hung around in the hope that he had been held up through customs, but I was already twenty-five minutes too late and did not hold out much hope. Sure enough, there was no sign of him.

After a few more minutes, I made my way round to Passport Control, and found that he had indeed passed through - one of the first off the plane. He had probably only carried hand luggage anyway. It's what I would have done, I thought, and gave up.

I took myself off to the bar to think out my next move. I tried to put myself in his position and figure out what he would do after landing. Why had he come? In response to a plea from the woman? Or was he chasing her, and if so, why? She seemed to hold the key. If he was already in contact with the other side, could she be also?

I concluded that the most likely scenario was that she had met him off the plane and they were already on their way to some rendezvous with our Russian friends. With some top secret stuff? That seemed unlikely. And it did not tie in with what Fox had said about him being taken unawares by her departure for Germany.

All the same, it seemed worth following up. I finished my drink and set about trying to find anyone who had seen her around the airport. But no - she had not been noticed waiting to meet anyone off the London plane. It suddenly dawned on me that if I had been marking time in the bar, so might she. I went back there. The barman smiled his recognition as soon as I showed him her picture.

'Yes, she was in here earlier today.'

'Alone or with someone?'

'Almost everyone here is,' he laughed.

'But you did not see her meet anyone?'

He closed his eyes in an effort to remember.

'No, I cannot recall her even talking to anyone. All she did was have a drink, look at her ticket then dash off, presumably when she heard her flight announced.'

'She was leaving, then?' This was not what I had been expecting.

'Yes, catching a plane somewhere.'

'What time was this?'

'About midday.'

'Midday?'

'That's what I said.'

'You can't recall where she was going?'

'No, sorry.'

'Can you remember the colour of her ticket - you know, which airline?'

'Noooo... I think it was a red ticket, but I can't be certain.'

'No matter. Thank you for being so helpful.' I pushed a ten mark note across the bar, 'Have a couple on me!'

According to the barman, who seemed quite sure, Elizabeth Tasker was *leaving* again - had already left, in fact.

So it seemed much more likely that she was trying to avoid Lansing. She was certainly not there to meet him with open arms. Perhaps she was unaware of his arrival in Germany. He had, after all, left in a hurry to follow her, and may have had no opportunity to contact her. Maybe he did not want her to know he was following her.

There was so much I could speculate on and without any more solid facts that's all it would ever be - speculation. My only course was to get hold of one of the pair and find out what the hell it was all about. Lansing I was to follow but *not* intercept, as yet. No-one had ordered me *not* to question *her* - always assuming I could find her.

I knew she had left the airport on a flight somewhere that had been called about noon, and that her ticket was probably red. The inquiry desk narrowed it down to a Lufthansa flight to London, or an Iberia flight to Madrid.

Thank goodness it had not occurred to her to travel under an assumed name. The computer found her, on the passenger list to London. There was another flight there in an hour and a half, and I booked on it.

While waiting I considered phoning Fox, but decided that I would be more free to pursue this lead if I simply told him of my intention. I telexed him:

MISSED H.L. NOW FOLLOWING ORIG-

INL. INSTRUCTION IN PURSUIT OF E.T. TO LONDON. WILL KEEP IN TOUCH.

CHAPTER 17

Elizabeth Tasker looked at the pictures she had taken up at the monument. Were they good enough, she wondered, to prove the point? She was convinced - but would anyone else be? And then what? It seemed to indicate that he had ...

The air hostess interrupted her thoughts, handing her the gin and tonic she had ordered. Elizabeth thanked her and sipped her drink. She was glad the plane was half empty. It gave her a window seat all to herself. She would not have to worry about some stranger making unwanted conversation. She wanted all the time to think. To plan her next move. That would have to include a visit to the British Museum. Then what?

What indeed? What would she do with the knowledge? Damn him! Damn him for opening his mouth. Damn him for involving her. Damn him for everything - no, not everything. There had been good times - REALLY good times. She stared out into the clouds and let the memory wash over her like a comforting warm shower ...

They were lying together, relaxed and contented, her head on his chest She looked down his chest and over his abdomen to her favourite place.

'How old were you the first time?' she asked,

grinning.

'The first time what?'

'You know!' She extended her hand and stroked him. He began to respond and put his hand down her back and over the cool mound of her buttock.

'Tell me, how old were you the first time you used this on a girl?' she insisted.

'Twenty ...' he stopped abruptly and went quite limp in her hand.

'Oh!'she said, 'What's the matter?'

'Nothing, nothing at all!' He resumed stroking her hair. She frowned momentarily, but he could not see her face.

'Twenty eh? So what took you so long?' She was smiling again.

'I grew up in the thirties - well, forties, remember. There was none of this permissive stuff then. Girls actually stayed virgins until they were married - well, some of them!'

'And those that didn't - what happened to them?'

'Oh, they did all right. I remember the hottest lay in college ended up married to the music professor!'

'He must have wielded a pretty nifty baton!'

'Not all that nifty - he got the rythm wrong and her pregnant!' They both laughed then kissed, then ...

But it was spoiled for her by the fact that she remembered the first time she had thought she was pregnant. Not long after her parents had split up, it had been. Sixteen she was, and half drunk at the time. Jimmy somebody or other, in the back seat of a borrowed Ford. What a way to go. Then the worry three weeks later - and the relief a month after that.

There had not been another time for two whole years. Until that night 'Uncle Henry' had called round on the pretext of visiting her mother.

He had taught her a lot. No fumbling in the back seat for him. He liked to take his time. Almost too long sometimes. Like that night her mother had come home early from bridge. Had she suspected? If so, she never showed it. After that it had always been older men - except for Jules. That summer in Montreal had been idyllic. So natural, so innocent.

When he drowned she had been so near to a breakdown. How wonderful her mother had been <u>then</u> - just as a mother should be at a time like that. Such a pity she could not be as wise as she was sympathetic. Especially about Raymond Baron, the bigamous bastard! Mother should have seen through him, instead of encouraging her.

No use blaming someone else, it was her own fault. How could she have fallen for that line: 'My family come from Norfolk, near where you were born.' Had she been seeking security? Probably. Some security - married to a man with a wife and four kids!

If only her father had been around, instead of running off with the second flautist. Where were they now? Oh, yes - Sydney Opera House. If music be the food of love, play on indeed! She had been thinking about them that night at Carnegie Hall, the first time Hugo had taken her out. The Rite of Spring was playing and ...

The hostess leaned towards her with the lunch. Pulling down the folding table, she laid the tray on top. The plastic food looked up at her, limp and unappealing. She pushed it on to the tray of the vacant seat next to her and gestured to the stewardess as she came down the aisle.

'Bring me another gin and tonic, please.'

She took from her handbag a small tin of tiny black cigars, and lit one. When the drink came she sipped it slowly and watched the smoke from her cigar curl upwards, then disperse in the jet of the air conditioning. He had been surprised that night, when she lit one during the interval. His eyebrows rose and his smile, which always reminded her of Clarke Gable as Rhett Butler, broke out.

'Cigars, eh? Always smoke these?'

'Only when I'm drinking. Do you mind?'

'Why should I mind? Just haven't come across it before.'

'Some men have strange prejudices about women. You wouldn't be the first man to disapprove.' She thought about Raymond, who had not liked her smoking cigars.

'I won't claim to have NO prejudices when it comes to women, but I can't think of any right now.' He waved past her at someone in the crowded bar.

'Enjoying the music? Hope you like this sort of thing, classical music, I mean?' he asked her

'Oh yes, very much. Brought up on it, in fact.'

'You play yourself?' he asked.

'The piano, badly. My father was, IS, a violinist.'

Before he could ask her more a rather tall, latin

type wearing a cloak accosted him.

'Good evening Hugo, enjoying Stravinsky? Who is the lovely lady?' His words seemed to run away with him.

'Elizabeth Tasker, my secretary. This is Paolo Entes.'

Hugo stepped back as the other two shook hands. Paolo held hers a fraction too long, and for a moment she thought he was going to kiss it. The look he gave her said that he would have liked to kiss more than her hand.

On the way back to their seats after the interval she asked Hugo about him.

'Paolo?' He's with the Portuguese UN delegation. Quite a character, I believe. His family own a large chunk of Portugal. He rather plays at being a diplomat, I think.'

'He certainly fancies himself,' she said.

'You are not impressed?'

'No, I've met the type before.' Bloody well married one, didn't I?, she thought, but said, 'What's in the second half?'

That first night Hugo was scrupulously correct and bade her farewell outside her apartment. She fell asleep thinking that it was just as well. If she was going to work for him it would be better to avoid becoming too involved. On the other hand, that smile ...

Ten days later he called her into his office.

'I wonder if you would do me a favour?' he asked.

'Certainly Mister Lansing, what is it?' she asked in turn, not sure what to expect.

'Are you free tomorrow evening?'

'I think so,' she said, indecisively.

'I've just taken a call reminding me of a reception I said I'd attend. The invitation came a month ago, and I'd decided to go alone, but ...' he hesitated.

She said nothing. He continued, 'To be frank with you, I find it a little awkward attending these things without a partner. Oh, I'm sorry, that isn't very flattering to you, is it?'

'I'd rather you were honest, like the last time.'

He looked at her, not sure whether or not she was being serious.

'The last time? Well, it would have been a pity to waste a ticket for Carnegie Hall. And this time, it's more or less official business. A reception for the Leningrad Symphony Orchestra.'

'I'd sooner have gone to their concert.'

'But you will come tomorrow?' he pleaded.

'I'm not sure I have anything suitable to wear,' she said with a sly grin.

'I think you'd look great whatever you chose to wear.'

'I thought you were going to be honest?' she laughed.

'I am.' He sounded as though he meant it. She turned to leave.

'I'll need to leave early to be ready in time.' she said.

'No problem. Thank you for coming.'

'Thank you for asking me, Mister Lansing.'

The door shut behind her. He reached for the telephone.

CHAPTER 18

She wore a simple black dress of French design which she had brought with her from Montreal. It set off to perfection her tall shapely figure and long dark hair. She received quite a few admiring glances, among them that of Paolo Entes, who contrived to meet them as soon as they arrived.

'The beautiful Miss Tasker, is it not?'

This time he did kiss her hand. Hugo did not seem to notice. He was looking past the Portuguese at a group of the guests of honour. His eyes narrowed as he turned and walked away.

'I'll bring drinks,' he said over his shoulder.

'You enjoyed their concert?' Entes asked.

'I couldn't get a ticket,' Elizabeth replied, hoping it would put paid to the conversation.

'What a pity. I could have taken you, with the greatest of pleasure,' he beamed at her.

'I'll bet!' she thought. She looked round for an avenue of escape, but thought she had better stay where Hugo could find her. Entes followed her gaze.

'How can such great musicians be such dull people?' he asked.

'Pardon?'

'Russians - they are so dull.' He looked quite glum.

'Are they? I've never met any, as a matter of

fact.' She realised her mistake as soon as she had spoken.

'Allow me to introduce you!' Entes took her by the arm and walked her a few feet to where a stocky individual with close-cropped hair and steel spectacles was standing with a group of men and women to whom he seemed almost to be lecturing. The man turned towards them as they approached.

'Comrade Borsakov, allow me to introduce Miss Tasker,' Entes said, 'Miss Tasker, this is Ivan Borsakov, Cultural Attache to the Soviet Embassy.'

They were then introduced by Borsakov to the musicians, none of whom could speak English.

Elizabeth looked round for Hugo, but could not see him. The group were soon joined by others wishing to meet the artists, and she contrived to become separated from Entes and went off in search of her boss. She found him in the far corner of the room talking to a tall, lean, tanned individual who broke off and walked away as she approached.

'Who was that?' she asked.

'Senator Stanhope.' Hugo looked at her, keenly. 'I guess you know?'

'About your wife? Yes, I know.' Elizabeth had been filled in on as much of her boss's private life as the office knew about two hours after she had arrived from Montreal!

'I should have told you.'

'1 just told you - I know,' she said emphatically.

'Yes, but I should have told you myself. I'm sorry.'

'No need to be, I assure you. Forget it. Who's that over there?' Elizabeth referred to no-one in particular, wishing merely to change the subject, but just then Borsakov hove into view.

'Him? Some Russian guy, I think,' Hugo said without interest. Elizabeth refrained from enlightening him, meaning to surprise him with her knowledge some other time. Borsakov took off in another direction to greet a member of the orchestra with a bear hug and deep belly laugh.

Entes appeared just then, asking, 'Where's that drink, Hugo?'

'Oh, sorry, I'll get them,' Hugo said, and made off.

Elizabeth turned to follow but Entes stopped her.

'Much better wait here. Otherwise he'll never find us with these drinks. I'm parched.'

'Are you here alone?' Elizabeth asked

'Yes, unfortunately. The lady I invited is indisposed tonight.'

'I'm sorry,' Elizabeth said, with feeling.

'How kind of you to say so,' he replied, 'Ah, drinks,' he went on as a waiter passed. He deftly grabbed two glasses and handed her one. The champagne was cool and stimulating.

'How long have you been in New York, Senor Entes?'

'Please, call me Paolo,' he gave her his assymmetrical smile. Even that reminded her of Raymond. She wondered if Paolo had a wife in Portugal and one in New York. Probably not.

'... here in New York two and a half years now,' he was saying, 'And you? You are a newcomer, are you not?'

'Yes. From Canada.'

'Ah, what a lovely country!' he exclaimed.

'You've been there?' she asked.

'No, never.' He seemed unaware of the incongruity of his response, and bestowed his lop-sided smile on her again. She was unable to help herself responding in kind, and as Hugo re-appeared they were grinning at each other for no particular rsason. He carried with him three glasses of champagne. Elizabeth and Entes quickly drank those they already had and gratefully accepted those he had brought. Hugo looked from one to the other and strode off, murmuring, 'Excuse me, but someone's looking for me.'

Elizabeth, about to apologise, looked after him in dismay and Entes said, 'Ah, what it is to be a busy, important man.'

Elizabeth turned and looked at him, not sure whether he was serious.

Entes shrugged.

A few minutes later, when Entes had been distracted by the arrival of some fellow Portuguese, she took the opportunity to wander off through the crowded rooms, half looking for Hugo, half simply observing UN society at play. She eventually emerged into the foyer and saw him, apparently in conversation with a thick-set man whose back was towards her. As soon as she started to cross towards them the man walked past Hugo and into the gents.

He smiled as she reached him.

'Sorry I've been so long,' he said, 'Just a tiny bit

of business. Let's enjoy it from now on.'

They started back towards the reception and she asked 'Wasn't that the ... '

'Yes?' he interrupted.

'Nothing, doesn't matter,' she said. For some reason she thought it best not to pursue the subject.

They arrived back at her apartment at five to twelve. She asked him in for a coffee. While they drank they chatted about the evening, but she knew his mind was on lower things. She had seen that look in so many men's eyes before. She realised the time had come to make up her mind, for she knew it would not be the last time he would take her out. She stood up.

'Let me get you more coffe,' she said, and leaned across the low table, her long hair falling forward in front of his face. He brushed it away with the back of his hand, then pulled her head down to his. As they kissed she silently thanked him for making up her mind for her.

CHAPTER 19

He stayed that night, and many more.

Six weeks later he was away at a conference in Mexico City when her phone rang.

'This is Paolo Entes. Remember?'

'Yes, we met at Carnegie Hall a few weeks ago.'

'I have two tickets for a concert tomorrow evening. I wonder if.. '

'It's rather short notice. Have you been stood up?'

'No, no. I only now was given them. My dear Miss Tasker you would never be anyone's second choice.'

She could almost hear him smiling at the other end.

'I'mmm ....' she hesitated.

'It's Isaac Stern. I know you'll enjoy it and I shall be desolated if you do not come.' He sounded as though his tongue was firmly in his cheek.

'Very well, thank you. I will.'

'I shall bring a taxi at seven. Be ready then.'

She did enjoy the concert. She loved violin music and had once met Isaac Stern years before, when he played at a concert in Winnipeg. Entes sounded dutifully impressed when she told him, but she had the distinct impression that he was laughing at her. However, he seemed to be better on closer acquaintance, and she scolded herself for judging him prematurely.

'It's been a very pleasant evening, Paolo,' she said as they parted, 'Hugo's back tomorrow and I'd better turn in at a reasonable hour. Working girl, you know.'

He smiled, said nothing and leaned forward quickly, planting a kiss on her lips. Just as quickly he straightened up and, raising his wide-brimmed black velour hat, he strode away calling 'Adios' over his shoulder. She looked after him, not knowing what to make of him.

Hugo's return saw the start of a period of intense activity at the Agency as he sought to implement some re-organisation arising out of the conference. For the next few weeks they settled into a routine of working hard by day and spending two or three evenings and nights each week together. One afternoon Hugo phoned her from the main UN building.

'D'you remember the telex we got this morning?'

'The one about the Swede arriving this afternoon.'

'Yes. Can you recall the details?'

'No, I'm sorry, it went straight in to you,' she replied.

'That's right, you didn't see it. I'd forgotten. I thought I brought it with me, but I can't find it. Can you search around, see if it's on my desk. It must be there somewhere.'

'Hang on.' She went into his office and looked on the desk. She found no telex. She searched around the room, but could not see it. As she went to the phone, she noticed the waste-paper basket, and knelt down beside it. She pulled out various ends of memo pad, some torn bits of writing paper and a crumpled piece of the office heading with, printed in ink 'PATEL - 476 5493.' As she dropped it back in, she espied the typical edge of a telex message and, removing it, flattened it out on the desk.

'Got it. You'd dropped it in the waste-paper basket.'

She gave him its message.

Seven weeks later she arrived at the Agency office and Linda Schwartz at the front desk called to her.

'Elizabeth, do you remember that nice Indian guy, came here about a month ago to see the boss?'

'No. Why?'

'Wait a minute. You were away then, weren't you, visiting your mother in Winnipeg.'

'Yes I was away a month ago. What about this Indian fellow?'

'He's dead. Look.'

She handed Elizabeth the morning paper. On page three she read a brief report of the death of an Indian civil servant seconded to the UN. He had fallen from the 16th floor of the Chrysler building. She went into the office.

'Sorry I'm late, Hugo.'

He smiled briefly, but looked grim.

'Have you heard about this Indian, Patel?' she went on, 'I seem to recall his name - some connection with the office, I think.'

'Very likely. He's on file here. He didn't seem too promising. How right we were.' He grunted.

Elizabeth could not recall seeing the file in question. As she turned to go after taking some dictation, her eye lit upon the waste-paper basket. She remembered. When she reached the door she turned to speak, but the phone rang.

'That may be the Police now,' Hugo said, 'They phoned earlier to say they wanted a word about this guy Patel. Not that we can tell them much.'

He picked up the phone. She left the room.

That night, lying in the bath, Elizabeth thought about it. Patel. Common enough name. Odd though. I wonder if it was his phone number. She tried hard to remember it.

Then suddenly all thoughts of Indians, phone number and puzzling connections went out of her head. As her right hand spread soap suds over her left breast, she felt a lump. She felt it again. She lay still, a little sinking feeling in the pit of her stomach. Getting out quickly she dried, wrapped the towel round herself and went into her sitting room. She ran her finger along the bookshelf and selected a slim volume.

After a few minutes of study she plucked up courage and examined herself according to the book. There was no mistake. She mixed herself a stiff drink, and emitted a foul expression.

Next morning she went into Hugo's office and shut the door behind her.

'I shall have to go out this morning for a couple of hours, O.K?'

'Sure. Nothing urgent I can think of. Anything special?' He spoke the last two words slowly. She looked at him, wondering if ....?

'You know!' she blurted out, instinctively putting a hand up to her breast.

He nodded.

'Yeah. Felt it the other night when we were ....' he smiled.

'That's why you stopped in the middle!' she smiled for the first time since her discovery. Although she had intended not telling him, she was quite relieved that he knew.

He went towards her and hugged her gently, frightened to do any damage.

'It'll be OK, you'll see.' He cupped her face in his hands and kissed her tenderly. 'Anything I can do?' he asked in a whisper.

She went into hospital three days later. Coming out of the anaesthetic she dreamed she had lost both breasts and she stood naked in Victoria Park, Winnipeg. Her father looked at her, laughed and proceeded to play his violin.

That evening the Surgeon came to see her. As he approached the bedside she held her breath.

'It's OK,' he said, patting her hand, 'Good news. The frozen sections showed no malignancy.' His eyes seemed to be moist. He went on, 'The scar'll never show, unless you're an habitue of St. Tropez!'

'Thank you,' she said quietly, only just keeping the catch out of her voice.

She was sound asleep when the enormous bouquet from Hugo arrived.

Ten days later she was studying the small scar and silently congratulating the Surgeon on his skill when the doorbell rang. It was Hugo and he, too, was soon admiring the needlework.

'What a superb job. It's hardly noticeable. They're still the most beautiful tits I've ever seen.' His tone changed as he touched her and looked into her eyes.

'You carnal beast!' she said in mock horror.

'No, really, it's true. They are as beautiful as Miss Moselle's!'

'Miss Moselle! Who's she?'

'I'll tell you later.' He laughed and picked her up: 'Here or in the bedroom?' he asked.

'What makes you think ....'

'The look in your eyes,' he said confidently. In the bedroom she turned to him and asked, 'Who is Miss Moselle?'

'Jealous?' he asked in turn.

'No, just curious.' She tried to sound unconcerned. He laughed.

'She was a statue.'

'A statue?'

'Yes. Where I grew up.' His voice trailed off. She turned and looked at him.

'Well? Go on.'

'Nothing much to tell really,' he said.

'Please,' she insisted.

'There was, still is, I suppose, a statue on a hill above the town - Rudesheim. On it is depicted a Rhine maiden, Miss Moselle we used to call her. She's with Old Father Rhine.' He stopped.

'What about her boobs then, why the reference?'

'Well, she's naked and facing the old guy, you see. We used to go up there to play and sometimes climb up on the statue and mess around, you know.'

'Naughty boys and girls!' she grinned.

'No girls!' He sounded shocked, and laughed at himself.

'So that's where you learned to handle a woman. Dirty beast.'

She slapped his hand and sat up, propping herself up with her right hand on the floor and her left resting on her left knee, her right leg remaining stretched out.

'You look just like her,' he said, pretending astonishment.

'Well, show me how you used to mess around,' she said haughtily.

He put his hands on her breasts and pretended to be climbing up a statue

'Keep still!' he ordered. He knelt beside her saying, 'We used to stand on the ledge like this and ...' he sounded as if he was going to stop.

'Go on, don't stop now, Miss Moselle's getting interested.'

He ran his hand down her torso and onto her mons pubis, and beyond, guiding his finger gently between her love-lips.

'What was Old Father Rhine doing all this time?' she asked, and began to move in response to his probing.

'Keep still, you're a statue remember!' he ordered.

'Oh, you naughty boy, I would have to be a statue to keep still when you do that,' she whispered, 'But don't stop, will You?

Half an hour later, a gin and tonic in one hand and a cheroot in the other, she looked across at him and asked, 'Haven't you ever been back to Germany?'

'No, never,' he said curtly.

'Why not?' she asked in a puzzled tone.

'Oh, lots of reasons. I suppose I wanted to make a complete break. After all that Germany had done to the world I think I was, well, ashamed. I wanted to become American and stay American. Let's change the subject,' he added abruptly.

He stood up and crossed to her cocktail cabinet. As he poured himself another whisky he said, 'I shall have to go away for a few days, to Wyoming.'

'To visit your wife?' she said, without expression.

He turned round.

'Yes. Business. Got to.' He looked at her, unable to decide what she was thinking.

'I expect we can manage without you for a few days. That Security guy, Lockhart, is coming in next week, isn't he?'

'Yes, but there's no need for me to be there. Purely routine.'

'I suppose not,' she sounded doubtful. He looked across at her, but said nothing. He went over and picked up her glass.

'No more for me, thank you,' she said, stubbing out her cigar.

'What about dinner?' he asked.

'Well, what about it?'

'I came here with the intention of taking you out to dine.'

'You could have fooled me,' she said, with a hint of ice in her voice.

'What's the matter, Elizabeth?' He sounded puzzled.

'Nothing,' she said as she got up, 'I'll get dressed if you're taking me to dinner.' She went into the bedroom.

He shook his head and tossed back the last of his whisky:

'Women!' he muttered.

CHAPTER 20

'Will you require anything else?' Elizabeth asked as she reached the door. Lockhart looked up from the pile of files on the desk.

'No thank you, not at present. A coffee would not come amiss a little later. Possible?'

'But of course. Nothing simpler. In half an hour.'

She closed the door behind her. Straight ahead, through the glass panelling, she saw Paolo Entes in the outer office, leaning on his silver-topped cane. He raised his enormous hat.

'What are you doing here?' she asked as he came up.

'Do I need a reason to come to see you?' His eyes twinkled.

'Yes, you do!' she said in mock admonition.

'I cannot tell a lie, I came to see Hugo.'

'I'm afraid you're in for a disappointment. He's away for a few days. In Wyoming.'

'Ah. Wyoming. In that case, I've come to ask you to a concert.'

She laughed.

'You're incorrigible.'

He shrugged. One of the office staff passed just then and Elizabeth stopped her. 'Take a coffee in to Mister Lockhart in a few minutes, Jean.'

Entes raised his eyebrows.

'Visitor?' he asked, cocking his head towards Hugo's office.

'Only Lockhart, our security wallah. Going over some files.'

'Oh well, in that case I'll be off. Wouldn't want to get in the way of work. That would never do.' He turned as though to leave.

'Thanks for the invitation, pity I can't go,' she said, tongue in cheek.

'Ah!' he spread his arms, 'The concert.' He slapped his palm against his forehead in a dramatic gesture, 'How could I forget!' he exclaimed.

Elizabeth laughed, 'You are a fool!' she said.

'Yes, but a fool with two tickets to a concert! Friday at seven. Pick you up. Be there!' He swept out before she had a chance to say anything.

After the concert she consented to go with him for a meal at a small Portuguese restaurant he said he knew well.

'What do you think of our food, then?' he asked, half way through.

'You certainly know how to cook fish. The service is extremely good, too,' she said as the waiter topped up her glass.

'Well, it should be,' he said emphatically. She looked up.

'Did you enjoy the concert?' he asked, as though he wished to change the subject.

'Yes, thank you. It was very enjoyable. I was in the mood for something light.'

'Yes: "Peter and The Wolf." Charming. You know it, of course?'

'Funnily enough it was on the radio a few weeks ago. Hugo and I were listening to it,' she said, with slight emphasis on "Hugo" She paused and looked across at Paolo. He did not look up.

'Does he enjoy light classics?' he asked.

'He enjoyed "Peter and The Wolf." He remembers it when it came out.'

'Does he?' Entes sounded slightly surprised.

Elizabeth looked at him inquiringly, her mouth full of fish.

'He does not seem the type to have been brought up musically,' Entes said blandly, 'But let us change the subject. To you. I hear you have been unwell recently.'

'Who told you ...?'

'I called at your office two or three weeks ago and they said you were ill. 'Flu or something.' He looked at her as though expecting an explanation.

'Yes, that's right. 'Flu.'

'I called round at your apartment,' he said, not seeming to have heard her reply. He paused and looked keenly at her.

She blushed.

'I didn't answer the bell for three days.' She did not sound very convincing.

'Ah well you would not, would you?' He went back to his lobster. 'When is Hugo returning?' he suddenly asked.

'Next week, Monday or Tuesday,' she replied.

'Why do you ask?'

'I wondered whether you would be free this weekend?'

'I think perhaps ...'

'After your recent, eh, indisposition,' he went on, ignoring her, 'I thought perhaps some exercise would do you good. Have you ever done any horse riding?'

'Not for years. I used to when I was younger, in Canada.'

'Excellent. We will not be needing to go through the preliminaries then. I am sure they can find you a good mount.'

'They?' she asked.

'At my Athletic club. It is necessary to keep fit. I go there often at weekends.'

'Horse riding? Where, in Central Park?'

'Ah, no. It is out of town where I go. There is a city part for the busy man to go to in the week, but it is altogether too technical for me. All those rowing machines and weight-lifting devices. Very undignified.' He shook his head solemnly.

'Mmmmm, very,' Elizabeth shook her head in unison with his, but he did not notice.

'You will come, of course,' he said suddenly.

'Why not? I haven't ridden in years. It might be fun.'

They dismounted and passed the reins over to the stable boy.

'I did enjoy that. Thank you, Paolo.'

'You are a good horsewoman,' he said.

'Now, now. You know I almost came off.'

'What rider worth anything has not? Tell me that!'

'What else do you get up to here?' she asked, hoping to change the subject.

'There is archery, rowing, tennis, swimming, a gymnasium of course, shooting. Have you ever done any shooting?' he asked casually.

'You mean deer, duck and so on?'

'No, no. Pistol and rifle shooting, at targets,' he made a gesture as though holding a rifle to his eyes.

'I've never held a gun in my life,' she said.

'You must try sometime,' he said, as they entered the bar.

CHAPTER 21

'You're becoming quite a regular at the Athletic club,' Hugo said, after he had been back from Wyoming a few weeks.

'Yes, I rather enjoy ...' Elizabeth replied.

'The company of the flamboyant Mr. Entes,' Hugo interrupted her, 'Yes, I had noticed.'

Elizabeth opened her mouth to reply, but changed her mind. "If that's what he wants to think, let him!" she said inwardly. She decided not to tell him about her new-found interest. "If I get to the final I'll invite him along," she promised herself.

'Have you heard from your wife ...?'

'I'm sorry, Elizabeth, I didn't ....'

They both spoke at the same time. They looked at each other and smiled. They both opened their mouths to speak at precisely the same moment again, but neither said anything. Instead they burst out laughing, and fell into each others' arms.

Later he turned to her.

'Talking of your men friends ....'

Elizabeth began to protest, but saw the twinkle in his eye and bit her lip in time.

'That guy Lockhart is coming in again tomorrow. I should have mentioned it at the office, but it slipped my mind,' he went on.

'What does he want this time?' she asked, her smile fading.

'Why don't you like him?'

'I don't really know. I think he fancies himself rather.'

'Oh, does he?' Hugo sounded quite annoyed. 'He hasn't been making a pass at you, has he?'

'Not in so many words. It's just the way he looks at me.'

'Well, I suppose we can't stop him looking, can we? Anyway, I can't honestly say that I blame him. If I were only allowed to look ...' He took her in his arms, his hand through her long hair, pulled her head back and he kissed her. His other hand searched out her breast, and the pressure made her wince.

'I'm sorry,' he said and let her go, 'Is it still painful?'

'Only very little. And I don't mind,' she said softly. 'You needn't let it stop you,' she went on, pulling him close again, 'Show me again what you used to do to Miss Moselle,' she whispered.

He picked her up and strode towards the bedroom.

Two days later she sat in the office of Felix Jennings, MD, for what she hoped would be the last time. She picked up a copy of the National Geographic and rifled idly through the pages. Suddenly her eyes lit up and she opened the magazine out. There in front of her was an article on Rudesheim, with pictures of Germania, "Queen of the Rhine," as the caption ran. She looked closer and turned a page.

Suddenly a frown wrinkled her brow. She held the pages nearer and stared at one particular photograph. Slowly she lowered the magazine to the table, staring ahead of her.

'Miss Tasker,' the nurse said, 'Doctor Jennings will see you now.'

She started as though woken from a trance, the frown disappeared and she crossed to the consulting room, dropping the magazine on the table as she went.

Relieved and happy that she had been given a clean bill of health, Elizabeth was on her way home when she passed a bookstall and remembered what she had seen in the National Geographic. Retracing her steps, she scanned the ranks of magazines but realised, without asking, that the only naked women likely to appear there were those in Playboy or Penthouse. She hurried to a bookshop she knew and managed to buy a copy just as it was closing.

Back in her apartment she poured herself a stiff gin and tonic and sat down. Turning the pages she sought out the article she had seen in the surgeon's waiting room. It was not there. She looked again, this time more slowly. It was a different edition! She cursed all waiting rooms for keeping old magazines and tried to tell herself it was all a stupid mistake on her part. But, try as she might, she could not convince herself.

The following morning she thought of going back to the bookshop before work, but Hugo was preparing for a conference and she knew she could not turn up late without good reason. Half way through the morning she got out the telephone directory and looked up the bookshop number. Her hand had just reached the phone when it rang. It was Entes.

'You have not forgotten our date tomorrow evening, at the ballet?' He sounded quite light-hearted.

'No, I have not forgotten,' she replied, rather peremptorily.

'Anything wrong?' he asked, 'Hugo is going to be away in Washington until next week?' He sounded anxious now.

'Yes. No, nothing wrong, just a very busy day, that's all. I'll see you tomorrow evening, as arranged. I must go now, Paolo.'

'Goodbye.'

'Goodbye.'

As soon as the phone was down, the light flashed and she picked it up again. It was Hugo.

'Bring in the UN memo please, will you?' He was at his most business-like. She forgot about her own phone call and went in to him.

Elizabeth re-entered the stalls bar during the interval and looked around for Entes. Eventually she saw him at the far end of the crowded room, talking to a thick-set man with short, greying hair. The figure seemed familiar and she tried to recall where she had seen him, while threading her way through the crowd. She remembered. Then she remembered too, her attempts that day to obtain a back number of the National Geographic, and wished she had returned to Doctor Jennings' to look at it there.

She was glad, when she reached Paolo, that the other man had gone.

'Sorry I've been so long,' she said, picking up her drink and trying to open her handbag at the same time.

'Have one of these,' Entes said, proffering a packet of cheroots. 'They're Havana, but don't tell anyone,' he said, conspiratorially.

'Thank you very much,' she said as he lit it.

'I hope you are enjoying the evening,' he said.

'Yes, thank you, very much indeed.'

'You like classical ballet, obviously?' he went on.

'Oh yes I don't seem to go as often as I would like, I must confess.'

'Hugo does not take you? I thought ...' He left the question in the air.

'He doesn't care much for ballet, I'm afraid,' she said, remembering the times he had contrived not to take her.

'Is that so?' he asked, raising his eyebrows.

She looked at him, but he smiled blandly, and the interval bell sounded.

'Remember tomorrow,' he said, as they made their way back to their seats, 'It is an important day. I am glad Hugo is away at present. It will give you a better chance to concentrate on ...'

'Shhhh!' someone admonished, as the orchestra began to play.

That night as she lay in bed, Elizabeth thought about the ballet. How superb the music, how well it suited the dance and enhanced the story. Suddenly her thoughts turned to Hugo, and she wondered why - why did it make her think of him? Why should Coppelia make her think of Hugo?

She sat bolt upright, a chill feeling in her heart. She knew why! She knew what it all meant, all the little things that had made her wonder... They all added up to a conclusion she fought against accepting. But she knew it must be so. There was no other way to explain everything.

What could she do? Confront him and ask him to explain? But if ... what then? No, she had to be sure first, quite sure. There was only one way she could think of to do that: get evidence. And she knew where she had to go to get that - to the place where it must have started, whatever IT was. At the same time she could go to see the one person in the world she could trust. If she was right he would know what to do. She could rely on him, utterly.

How fortunate Hugo was away for a few days. She would have the chance to go there, and get back for that matter, without him knowing. Then she remembered what she had to do the next day. That was not important, except that Paolo would be there. The only way would be to see it through then catch a plane.

Yes, that should be possible. A fake telegram from her mother would give her reason enough. She would have to avoid having him see her off at the airport, but that should not be too difficult. And so it had proved.

She had caught the plane. She had been to Rudesheim.

'And now,' she thought, 'Uncle Simeon.'

CHAPTER 22

Not quite sure precisely where to go when she arrived at the British Museum, Elizabeth walked in through the massive pillars at the main entrance. Going up to the first attendant she saw, she said 'I am looking for Doctor Simeon Fletcher.'

'And who might 'e be, Miss?' asked the Attendant, eyeing her suitcase.

'He works here. He's an expert on porcelain.'

'Ah, well, that'll be the Academic Department. Not 'ere.'

'Could you show me please? Is it far?' she asked.

'Go back out, turn left and go to the end of the building. Turn left again and there's a door. Go in there and up to the first floor. You'll find a little office. Ask in there.' He smiled.

'Thank you. Thank you very much,' she said and picked up her suitcase. Round the corner she found the little office and tapped on the sliding glass panel that separated her from a tiny old-fashioned telephone exchange. A middle-aged woman sitting in front of it looked up from her daily paper.

'I am looking for Doctor Simeon Fletcher,' Elizabeth said when the window was slid open.

'Is he expecting you?' the woman asked, with some suspicion.

'No, but I think he'll see me. He's my uncle.'

'Oh,' The woman paused, 'I'll see if he's in.'

She plugged in a red rubber lead and dialled a

number on the dial fixed to the board in front of her.

'Is your professor in?' she asked, 'There's a young woman here to see him, says she's his niece.' She turned to Elizabeth: 'What's your name?'

'Elizabeth Tasker. I've come from Canada.'

She repeated the information into the phone, then waited, listening.

'All right. He says he'll see you.'

She unplugged the lead and took off the headset. Sliding down off her stool she stood on the floor, but was no higher than she had been whilst sitting.

'His secretary's coming down,' she said, and pulled out a book from a shelf below the window. 'You'll have to sign this,' she said, handing Elizabeth a government issue ballpoint. The secretary arrived and led Elizabeth along a corridor and up a winding staircase to an oak-panelled door. She knocked and opened it, ushering Elizabeth in.

Simeon Fletcher, a man in late middle age with thick white hair, half spectacles and a sagging bow tie, was already half way across the Turkish carpet to meet her. He held out both his hands. She dropped her suitcase and they embraced.

'Elizabeth, my dear, this is a surprise,' he said.

'Hello, Uncle Simeon,' was all she could say in reply.

'Kirsty,' he said to the secretary, 'Bring us some tea. And I'm not in, to anyone.'

He pulled up an old leather armchair and sat her down in it .

'You look very tired,' he said, 'Have you just flown in from Montreal?' He put her suitcase behind the door.

'No, from Frankfurt, as a matter of fact.'

'Really, how interesting. And how is your mother?'

'Very well, thanks. I saw her a few weeks ago.'

'Ah, yes, of course, you're in New York now aren't you?'

'Yes.'

'How is the new job? You're doing very well, judging by your mother's last letter.'

He removed his spectacles and folded them into his breast pocket. He looked keenly at her and was about to say something when the door opened.

'Ah, the tea. Just put it here,' he said, indicating a space he had cleared on top of his vast desk. 'Thank you, Kirsty, I'll manage now.' He proceeded to pour the tea and handed Elizabeth a cup. She smiled her thanks and drank thirstily.

'Now, my dear. What's worrying you, eh? What's brought you hot foot to see dull old Uncle Simeon?'

'I've come for your opinion. It's rather complicated and not easy to put into words,' she gulped more tea. 'I've no-one else to turn to.'

'Yes, such a pity about your father. Is he still with that randy cellist, by the way?'

'Yes, but she's a flautist. They're in Sydney - as far as I know.'

'Australia. Yes. Best place for him. Plays the flute? Mmmmm.'

Elizabeth handed back the empty cup. Simeon

refilled it and passed it back.

'Well now, what's the problem. You've not got yourself ... No. Wouldn't come to me with that sort of problem, would you?' He grinned.

'No. It's not that,' she said emphatically, 'It's something that's more in your line. It's about Germany. Well, it's really about a person. A man. He comes from Germany - at least I think he does.' She paused and drank more tea.

'My, but this does sound complicated - and interesting. I take it your trip to Frankfurt is involved. This German, does he ...'

'Actually, he's American.'

'I think you had better start at the beginning.' He sat back in his chair and clasped his hands on his paunch.

'For me it started a few months ago,' she said, 'But for him it seems to have started at the end of the war - World War two, that is.' She went on to tell him all she knew about Hugo Lansing, and what she suspected.

When she had finished he looked at her solemnly and said: 'I think you may be right, my dear. You may have stumbled onto something significant - and possibly dangerous.'

'I know. I realise that. What do you think I should do?' She sounded very weary.

'Of course, he doesn't have any idea where you are? By the way, does he know about me?'

'I think I once mentioned that you work here.'

'But he has no idea you have come here now?'

'No. He's in Washington at a conference. I took the opportunity to get away. I sent myself a telegram saying that mother was ill and left a message with someone in the office that I'd flown to see her. I thought I would phone her and get her to telephone the office to say I'm detained there, caught a bug, or something.'

'That ought to give you a few days' grace. But what then? What if we confirm your suspicions? You realise what you'll have to do then, don't you?'

Elizabeth nodded without speaking.

'Are you in love with him?' he asked quietly.

'I don't know. I don't think so - after this.' Her face crumpled.

'My God, girl, you're all in.' His voice almost broke with emotion. He stood up. 'You need two things. First, a good night's rest. Second, a quiet spot for a day or two. Recharge the batteries. Decide what's best. You get round to my flat now, have a bath and change, then we'll get off to East House.'

He picked up the phone and pressed a button on the front.

'Kirsty, get me a taxi, will you?' Turning to Elizabeth he said, 'It's just five minutes away as you know. You get round there and I'll just check on one or two points, dates and so forth. Then there's someone I know in the Foreign Office who might be able to help.'

'Please, nothing official, Uncle Simeon, at least not yet.'

He opened his mouth to argue, but thought better of it.

'All right, my dear, as you wish. Not tonight,

anyway. I can get away in an hour or so and I'll take you to the farm. We'll discuss it there when you've had more time to think.'

He opened a drawer in his desk and took out a key.

'The flat - spare key. Locked myself out so often I keep one here,' he grinned. She smiled back at him. 'That's better,' he said, giving her an affectionate hug, 'Always sorry your mother had to take you off to Canada. You're all the family I have now, with Rupert ...'

She returned his affectionate embrace. The door opened and Kirsty announced that the taxi had arrived. She took Elizabeth's case and led the way out.

When they had gone Simeon turned to his bookshelves and ran his eye along the regular ranks of books. He picked out two and for the next half hour or so consulted them closely, occasionally making notes.

By early evening they were on their way to Norfolk.

'I checked the dates and a few other points, my dear, and I think you are quite correct about this Lansing fellow.'

Elizabeth, who had been looking round the flat countryside that she had not seen for so long, turned to her uncle.

'Yes, but how significant is it? What does it all mean?'

'It seems unlikely that it is just a chance circumstance. Much more likely to be some hand behind it. The question is whose?'

'You mean - whose side is he on?' Elizabeth asked.

'That is precisely what I mean. We really have no idea, do we?'

'I suppose not. I had assumed that if he is not ...'

'Assumptions can be dangerous things. You know, my dear, I think you are too emotionally involved to make balanced judgments when it comes to Mr. Lansing. You may be jumping to totally the wrong conclusion. On the other hand ...' He broke off as the car rounded a bend and was confronted by a herd of cows. He slowed to a halt and turned to look at his companion.

'What should I do?' she asked, 'Go back and confront him? I don't think I could. But I can't just let it be, can I?'

'No, you can't do that. We come back to my suggestion of yesterday - we must consult someone who can advise you as to the best, and safest course.' He started the car up again as the cattle moved past. Elizabeth, distracted momentarily by a cow which seemed intent on joining them in the car, turned sharply to her uncle.

'You do think there could be some danger then?'

'There is no avoiding such a conclusion. Hopefully it will not materialise. When did you say he returns from Washington?'

'Wednesday. As I said, if we can phone mother she should be able to contact the office and tell them I'm not well and will not return until, say, next week.'

'Yes, that seems likely to give us time to sort this whole thing out, one way or the other.'

They rounded a bend in the road and East House Farm came into view. Elizabeth looked at the ancient house with its scattered outbuildings and memories of her childhood welled up inside her. She knew that for as long as she was there she would feel safe. With that thought came the realisation that she had been subconsciously afraid ever since discovering the truth about Hugo Lansing.

CHAPTER 23

At Heathrow the first thing I saw when I emerged from Customs was the line of car hire desks. She had not patronised any of them, I soon discovered. In any case it was more likely that she had taken a taxi.

At last my luck was in. About time! The policewoman controlling the queue thought she could remember her. Half an hour later I found a cabbie who recognised her picture.

'Piccadilly Circus,' he said in answer to my question

'Piccadilly Circus?'

'That's it, sir, I took her to Piccadilly Circus.'

'Did you see where she went after you dropped her there?'

'Sorry, no. But she may have been going to the British Museum.'

'What makes you say that?' I asked.

'I'm pretty sure she asked to go there first. I didn't hear very well and asked her to repeat her destination. When she did, it turned out to be - Piccadilly Circus!'

'This is definitely her?' I showed him the photograph again.

'Yes. That's her all right, sir.' He nodded.

'OK. Take me there - the museum, I mean.'

'I doubt we'll get there before closing,' he said,

switching on the meter. He was right. The museum was as dead as Tutenkhamen's tomb. I got the taxi to take me round as many nearby hotels as I could find, in the hope that she had registered at one of them, but to no avail. I booked myself in at the Russell on the way round and ended up there - in the bar.

I was forced to admit to myself that I was at a dead end. Chasing this woman seemed to have that effect, and I didn't like it! I was feeling very tired and had the distinct impression that I was not thinking very straight. I tried to put myself in her position, but gave that up as a bad job. I had no idea why she had flown the coop in the first place, far less what she was doing flying round Europe, visiting monuments and museums.

I decided the time had come to report in, so I put through a call to Fox.

'Where the hell've you been, Lockhart?' was his warm greeting.

I brought him up to date.

'British Museum, eh? Well, that figures,' came the cryptic reply.

'It does? Well, let me in on the secret. What is there at the British Museum? Which exhibit ...?'

'Not what, Lockhart, WHO!'

'Who? How the hell do you know she met someone at....'

'Shurrup and listen, Lockhart. The WHO in question happens to be Doctor Simeon Fletcher. Her uncle.' Fox could not keep the smirk out of his voice.

'How did you ...?'

'Elementary, my dear Lockhart, we asked her mother. He is the only relative she has in England. They've always kept in touch.'

'You don't happen to have his address and phone number, do you?'

'East House Farm, Wickham, King's Lynn, Norfolk. Wickham 2390,' Fox barked, ignoring my sarcasm. 'He has a flat in London, but the mother only ever writes to the farm. It's been in the family for generations, apparently. My guess is she's gone to earth there.' He sounded pleased with himself.

'Yes, but why? What's it all about?' I asked, 'What's she...'

'That's what you're paid to find out, Lockhart.'

'Not bloody enough, I'm not,' I muttered.

'What was that?'

'Nothing. Is there any news of Lansing?'

'How can there be? You left him in Germany somewhere, remember?'

'I thought the best thing was to stick to my original job and find her. I still think she holds the key to this ...'

'Yeah, okay, I think so too.' Fox sounded quite reasonable when he agreed with me, even if he did keep interrupting.

'Right. So, I'll keep after her. What about Lansing?'

'I don't think you need to look for him.'

'Why not?'

'Because I think he'll find you. He's crossed the Atlantic after her and when he doesn't find her in Rudesheim, the chances are he'll pick up the trail to London just as you did, and from there ...'

'To the farm.' It was my turn to interrupt, and I enjoyed it.

'Exactly, so watch your step. You may not be God's gift to the Security Services, but you're all we've got at the moment.'

'Thank you for the testimonial.'

'For Chrissake stop being such a smart-lip, Lockhart,' Fox snapped.

'Sorry, sir.' (I have to call him SIR every so often.) 'What do you want me to do then, sit tight until he turns up or what?'

'No, get her back here as quick as you can. We want him back in our territory.'

'Do you think he'll follow? Won't he just make for Moscow?'

'Why should he? He's not certain his cover's blown. Dammit, it isn't in a sense. We still don't know what the hell this is all about. Until we do, we've got to keep playing him. Moscow won't call him in yet if he can still be of value. They're much more likely to take a chance that he can still be of use. They can always offer an exchange if we do reel him in. The main thing is to try to find out precisely what he's been up to. The girl seems to hold the key to that. If she doesn't actually know, she has a damned good idea. That's why she's flown to Germany and London.'

'Okay, I'll do my country yokel thing and follow her down to the farm. Then I'll use all the charm at my disposal to get her to come back with me. God knows whether she'll fall for it.'

'It's your job to see that she does. I'd send someone else, but you'll have to do. In any case, she knows you, doesn't she? That should help - unless you've been trying to ball her at some time, Lockhart!'

'Not guilty. Not my type. I go for ...'

'Good. Well, see that it stays that way. Just get her back here and find out what she knows in the process, if possible.'

'I'm on my way.'

'One last thing. If you do need to call in the marines, use this number. O1 - that's London - 935 7216. The name's Murchison.'

'Okay, got it, thanks. I'll try not to disturb him.'

'Oh, and Lockhart, be careful. Are you carrying a weapon?'

'What, the agent's friend? Never without it. Take it to bed with me. I ...'

'Goodbye Lockhart. Keep in touch this time.'

I put the phone down, and went back to the hotel. I found fifty-seven entries in the telephone directory marked 'Fletcher, S.' Guessing that a guy who worked at the British Museum would have a flat in the Bloomsbury area, I picked out one of them. The address was in Kenilworth Mansions, a likely name for what would probably be an old block. I was there in fifteen minutes.

Sure enough, it was one of those Edwardian blocks, all red brick and fancy sandstone, taking up a short street to itself. As I walked along, a beautiful old Lagonda passed by. Unfortunately, the flats had been modernised to the extent of having an entryphone installed and the main door was locked. I could hardly see them opening the door if I announced myself, so I stood back in the shadows and waited. It was ball-freezing cold, and I had only a light rainproof over my suit. After five minutes I saw the lift arrive in the hall, and a woman got out. As she crossed the short distance to the outside door I walked towards it, holding a bunch of keys in my hand. When she unlatched the door I pushed it in and held it for her to emerge.

'Good evening, Mrs. Clarke, cold for the time of year, isn't it?' I said, and was in. I reckon she is still trying to figure out who I am!

Number fifty-four was on the fourth floor. I put my eye to the spy-hole, but could see no light. I placed my thumb over it and rang the doorbell. There was no response. I looked again, but there was still no light. I rang once more, but knew there would be nothing. I walked along to the next flat and rang the bell there. After a couple of minutes, a light came on and I could sense an eye giving me the once-over. The door opened two inches, held by a massive brass chain.

'I'm sorry to bother you,' I said, 'But my wife's not well - we just moved into number thirty-nine, and I'm trying to raise Doctor Fletcher.'

'That won't do you any good, young man, he's not that kind of doctor.' The voice came from an apparition in beads and black. 'He's not medical at all. He's a professor. Works at the British Museum.' There was a throaty cackle as the door shut: 'No use to you unless she's going to be a mummy!'

With a sense of humour like that, I thought, you should be an exhibit yourself.

An hour later I was on my way north-east out of London in a hired car. I drove for an hour and a half and began to feel very tired. I pulled into a lay-by, put the seat back and went to sleep. I was awakened by the drumming of rain on the car roof. To the east the dawn was doing its best to see through the rain. I had been asleep for hours! I was still tired and very cold.

For the life of me I could not get the bloody car to start!

After half an hour a truck came along and I jumped out of the car and waved him down. By the time he stopped he was two hundred yards along the road and I was drenched when I climbed up into the cab. He dropped me off at a transport cafe on the outskirts of King's Lynn. I felt marginally better after two cups of tea and a clean-up in the toilet. I asked the way to Wickham and if anyone was going that way, but none of the few drivers present seemed to be. Instead, I was directed to a garage half a mile along the road where there was a chance of picking up another car. It was not due to open for some time, however, so I had some breakfast and was surprised at how good their coffee was.

It had stopped raining when I set off to the garage.

'You're not from round these parts, are you?' was the garage man's brilliant opening line, when I asked him if he had a car I could hire. Pity his efforts at help were less than brilliant by comparison. No, there was no car for hire. Not even for a hundred dollars. Did I not know that we were in Britain and not America - and so on. He did offer to go back and try to fix the car I could not start - but not until Charlie arrived to relieve him at the pumps. When would that be? When he finished his milk round!

I walked another mile or so into the center of the town and found the sign of the car hire company whose customer I already was. I had to wait half an hour until they opened. I went through the formalities of hiring a car in the usual way, trying hard to hurry them up as we went along. At last I was driving out the yard and I wound down the window and handed the clerk a bundle.

'That's the hire agreement and keys of one of your company's cars. I got it in London, but it broke down about twenty miles back along the London road. You'll find it parked in a lay-by. Sorry I didn't have time to explain earlier. Must be on my way.' I took off while his mouth was still open.

I had brought with me a map bought at the Russell Hotel's bookstall, but it did not show the numerous country roads around that part of the world, and although I knew I was going in the right general direction, after about half an hour I was lost. However, at the next crossroads there was a signpost - Wickham three miles. Once there I found the post office and discovered there were only two more miles to my destination.

The country round there is very flat, but I was quite near to East House Farm before I saw it. The centerpiece was a beautiful old three-storey brick house, with a portico at the front door and tiny dormer windows in the roof, making it look, from the end of the drive, rather like a Victorian dolls' house. Beyond the house I could see the scattered farm buildings. Among them, next to a tractor, stood an old-fashioned sports car which looked very much like a Lagonda! I must have just missed them at Kenilworth Mansions. I crunched to a halt on the gravel and got out. There was an ancient iron bell-pull at the side of the front door. I pulled on it. The door opened and a thick-set beetle-browed guy frowned at me. He was not entirely clean, and certainly not my impression of the butler such a house seemed to rate.

'Is Doctor Fletcher at home, please?'

'I don't fink so,' was his rather odd reply.

'Could you please find out, I ...'

'Wait 'ere,' he said, and shut the door in my face.

I decided to look for myself and set off along the front of the house. As I passed the second window I thought I saw a movement inside, but the reflection of the sun which had now broken through made it difficult for me to be sure. The front door opened again.

'Ey, come back 'ere.' It was the same man beckoning to me. 'In this way, sir,' he said, almost politely.

He led the way into a typical small sitting room of an English country house, with chintz-covered chairs and a Sheraton escritoire against the wall. The French windows led out onto a small terrace at the back, giving a long view of the surrounding countryside. In the distance I could see someone riding up a long slope and disappearing among some oak trees. I heard a sound behind me and turned.

''E's not in,' he said, back to his neanderthal best.

'Go and tell Doctor Fletcher that I know he is here. I have seen his car - the Lagonda, right? Tell him I am a friend of his niece. Is she here by the way - Miss Elizabeth?'

He opened his mouth to speak, but changed his mind, paused, then said, ''Alf a mo,' and left again. As soon as he had gone I followed quietly into the hall and stood still, listening. I could hear nothing and tip-toed towards the stairs. My hand was on the bannister when a sound came from behind me. I turned - and looked straight into both barrels of a twelve-bore shotgun. Beetle-brows was at the other end of it. It was an old weapon with hammers and they were both cocked. He waved it sideways, without a word, indicating where I should go. I did not argue. I went along a corridor at the side of the stairs, off which were the kitchen and pantry, etc., and at the end I could see a door to the outside. He marched me through and out into the farm yard. I looked around for an avenue of escape, but decided that it would be unwise as long as he remained so close. I saw the tractor again, but no Lagonda.

He grunted at me to keep going and we crossed to a long barn. By now the sun was shining with as much brightness as it could muster. As we entered the barn I anticipated the darkness by shutting my eyes for a moment then, just as I judged he would be finding it very black, I dropped to one side, twisted round and went for his legs. I brought him down and the gun wavered in his grasp, both barrels blasting a hole in the door as he fell. I was onto him like a mongoose at a cobra, and put a hammer lock on him - or so I thought. He grunted louder than ever and seemed to shrug me off with ease. Before I could get hold of him again he kneed me in the chest, and the last thing I remembered of the encounter was seeing, out of the corner of my eye, the stock of the shotgun homing in on the side of my head.

When I came round I was lying in the loft of the barn, my hands and feet tied with the string from some bales of straw. My head throbbed as though the gun was still trying to knock it off my shoulders. I struggled to my knees and looked around. It was very dark, but a crack of light was showing through what proved to be a small door at one end of the loft. It was one of these doors for loading the loft, and a stout beam projected from above it, both inside and out, with a block and tackle on the outer portion. However, a means of lowering myself was of little use as long as I remained bound. I hopped about looking for a tool of some kind, but without success.

Suddenly I heard the creaking of a ladder and I fell down among the straw and lay still. A hatch in the floor swung upwards and rested against a bale of straw. After a moment Beetle-brows' head appeared, his face no more than six feet away. I watched him through one half-open eye. He seemed satisfied that I was still unconscious and sighed. I could smell his breath. He stretched up, grasped hold of the hatch and began to descend, lowering it after him. I rolled sideways until the hatch was at my feet and at just the right distance.

I pulled up my knees and gave an almighty kick with both feet in the middle of the square of wood. Poor guy. I think as he heard me he stopped his descent, and the hatch crashed down on the top of his head. He must have dropped like a stone after that. I managed to lever up the hatch again, and looked down at his inert figure. He sure was not playing games. I hopped down the ladder from rung to rung and in a matter of moments I had found a knife on him and was cutting myself free. I returned the compliment on him, taking the precaution of tying his hands and feet together - round one of the pillars of the barn.

I went back to the house and sluiced my head in cold water before helping myself to some of Doctor Fletcher's brandy which I found in what seemed to be his study. That helped a little but my head still felt as though a flock of woodpeckers had been using it for practice.

I sat in the deep, comfortable leather armchair, and in spite of my head, felt an overwhelming desire to go to sleep. I looked at the brandy, and for a moment had the crazy idea that it had been doctored. I stood up and felt dizzy, and then was sick all over his nice carpet.

Another dowsing under the cold tap improved my equilibrium, but not my temper, and I stalked out to the barn. He was still out cold. I decided it was time to get some help, and put my hand in my pocket for my wallet. It was not there. Nor was it on him, and I had no idea what he had done with it. I could remember the name Fox had given me - Murchison - but the phone number I could not recall. Back in the study, I considered calling Scotland Yard, but if they sent the local police .... I was staring at the phone when I saw next to it on the desk, a small phone directory. On the open page was a name - Jeremy - and a number, 2757. I picked up the phone and dialled it. After three rings the line opened. I could hear music at the other end.

'Hello,' I said, 'Is that Wickham 2756?'

'No, 2757.' Very superior voice.

'Oh, are you sure?'

'Of course I'm sure. This is Wickham 2-7-5-7. Knowsley Hall.'

'Ah, Knowsley Hall. Sorry to disturb you.' I put the phone down. It was worth a try, and with Beetle-brows still out for the count, the only lead I had. I went out to the car and was glad to see my flight bag was still there. My car keys I still had, thanks to the fact that my jacket pocket had a hole in it. I fished them out of the lining and got the car going. Knowsley Hall was marked on the map. With a bit of luck, I thought, I can catch up with her at last. Has she got some explaining to do. And how!

It took me only twenty-five minutes to get there. It would have been fifteen if I had known the roads. If East House Farm was an example of a fine country house, Knowsley Hall was more of a stately home. As soon as I could see it, I stopped the car and scanned the view. It was one of those houses with a staircase sweeping down from the front door. I groped about in my bag and got out my Magnum Special. No farting around this time, I muttered to myself, and clipped the holster to my belt. I had had enough of Miss Tasker and her uncle. I drove on up.

CHAPTER 24

Drummy Nugent shuffled into the study without knocking.

'There's a car coming,' he announced in his dull monotone.

'Did you recognise it?' Simeon asked.

'I fink it's a Vauxhall,' Drummy replied, pleased with his powers of observation.

'No, no, I mean, is it one that belongs to anyone we know?' Simeon's tone was that of a man who was used to Drummy's simplicity.

Drummy just shook his head. Simeon turned to Elizabeth.

'You must get away. Whoever it is, we're not ready for any questions yet. Take Bruno - you can still ride, can't you?' He lead the way towards the back of the house.

'Go over to Jeremy's. Wait there. I'll follow in the car. Drummy'll do his best to keep him here to let me get away. Quickly now.'

As Elizabeth trotted out of the stable yard Simeon and Drummy were already back in the house.

'He'll be here any minute. Whatever you say, Drummy, you must keep him here long enough to let me follow Elizabeth. Pretend to be looking for me, take him into the morning room, anything. But keep him here. Understand?'

Drummy nodded vigorously.

Simeon went back into the study and collected the notes that he and Elizabeth had been discussing when interrupted. The telephone rang. He picked it up after the first ring.

'Hello. Wickham 2390.'

'Is that you, Simeon? Peter Thorburn here. I phoned earlier but you weren't at home.'

'Ah, it was you. Drummy said there was a call but he couldn't remember who it was.' As he spoke he heard the sound of a car drawing up in front of the house.

'I'd like to consult you about rather a nice piece of Meissen that's just come my way I was wondering if perhaps you ...'

'It's rather awkward at this very minute, Peter, I'm just walking out of the door. Could you Phone me tomorr ...?'

'Flying to Brussels tonight and ...'

'Well, look. I must dash right now. I'll give you the number I'm going to. Ring me there in, say, half an hour. Come to think of it, there's something you could help me with. Rather a sticky problem. He stretched across the desk and opened a small book. 'Here's the new number. Wickham 2757. Got it?'

'Yes, indeed, 2757. Ring you in half an hour. Toodle-oo.'

Simeon put the phone down gently and hurried as quietly as he could across the study. He opened the door a crack and saw Drummy close the front door and turn towards him. He opened the door fully and put a finger to his lips. Stuffing his notes in his pocket, he whispered to the other, 'Remember, keep him here at all costs,' and went out along a passage by the side of the staircase.

Twenty minutes later he was in the drawing room of Knowsley Hall.

'Infernal cheek this fellow has, forcing his attentions on Beth like that.' The speaker was Jeremy, Lord Knowsley.

'I've told Jeremy all about it, Uncle,' Elizabeth said. Then, as their host bent over the drinks tray, she shook her head vigorously at Simeon. He nodded briefly to indicate that he understood, then said:

'Very good of you to receive us unannounced. Jeremy, I'm afraid we just ran for cover when we saw him coming. I ...'

'Don't mention it. You know you're always welcome here. Pity you can't come more often, Beth. You cut a fine figure riding in on Bruno.'

The door opened.

'Telephone for Doctor Fletcher, m'Lord,' announced Berry, Knowsley Hall's butler, general factotum and one remaining servant.

'I hope you don't mind, Jeremy, but just as I was leaving, Peter Thorburn phoned - wants some advice about a purchase he's made. I took the liberty of giving him this number.'

'Not at all, old boy. Welcome. Take it in the study, eh?'

Simeon picked up the telephone in the study and waited for Berry to close the door.

'Hello, that you, Peter?'

'The very same. So you're at Knowsley. How's Jeremy these days?'

'Oh, in good form. Didn't know that you and he were ...'

'Yes, indeed. Married a second cousin of mine. Of course, poor Marjory ... tragic business that. He should have remarried.'

'Yes, I suppose he should.'

'Well, to business, Simeon. You were saying earlier that you thought I might be able to help you with something. A sticky problem, I think you said.'

'Yes, it is. It's to do with my niece, Elizabeth.'

'Your niece?'

'Yes, she's come over from Canada. My sister and her husband went over there quite a few years ago.' Simeon paused. 'Look here, it's not really something one can discuss over the telephone.'

'Ah, well now. Why not come over. Cambridge isn't far, and you can look at that piece I mentioned.'

'Good idea, Peter. Only too glad to be of some help in return.'

'Why not bring young Elizabeth with you, especially if this problem of yours concerns her.'

'Thank you, yes, I will.'

'That's settled then. I'll see you here in my rooms in about ...'

'An hour and a half?'

'Excellent. See you. Toodle-oo.'

'It's simply exquisite,' Elizabeth said, gingerly handing the Meissen figurine to her uncle. He took it from her and crossed the room to the window overlooking the Cam.

'The light's better over here,' he said, and turned it up to look at the base.

'Sherry, my dear?' asked Sir Peter Thorburn, his hand hovering above the decanter.

'Yes, thank you,' replied Elizabeth, sinking into the velvet of the chesterfield drawn up by the side of the fire.

'It's very nice to meet you. Your uncle has mentioned you on more than one occasion.' Sir Peter smiled across at her.

'It's nice to be in Cambridge again, such a beautiful city.'

'How long do you think your visit will last?'

'I'm not sure ...' She looked at her uncle as he left the window and took the piece of porcelain to a table in the center of the room, where he set it down, a faraway look in his eyes.

'Well, what do you think of it?' Sir Peter asked eagerly.

'A very fine piece, without a flaw.' Simeon picked up the sherry his host had poured for him and sipped it thoughtfully.

'Of course I know it's nothing to the collection you have, so to speak, but I'm quite proud of my acquisitions.'

'You have every right to be, Peter. You're one of the country's connoisseurs.' Simeon laughed lightly. 'If ever you're in need of a job, come to me at the museum!'

Sir Peter returned the laugh, then his face straightened as he asked, 'What about the problem you mentioned? You said I might be able to help?'

He looked keenly at Simeon.

'It's rather a delicate matter and it may be rather presumptuous of me, but I thought that with your connections with the Foreign Office you might be in a position to ...' Simeon tailed off.

'Only too pleased. Spell it out and I'll do what I can.'

'It's my problem really, Sir Peter,' Elizabeth said, then stopped, unsure how to continue. She fumbled in her bag and pulled out a box of cheroots. Her hand shook a little as she lit it. She smiled nervously towards her uncle. Simeon took his cue.

'I'm afraid it concerns a man. He and Elizabeth ...'

'Yes, of course, I guessed as much. When a young lady has a problem ...' Sir Peter chuckled. 'But how can I help? Sounds like an affair of the heart, and an old duffer like me isn't likely to be of much use.'

'Well you see, it's also a professional matter. The man in question happens to be a very senior official - as well as being married.'

'Oh?' Sir Peter looked over at Elizabeth with a frown.

'Elizabeth works for the UN in New York, and a few months ago became involved with a man called Hugo Lansing. He asked her out a few times and one thing led to another, and ...'

'We've been having an affair, Sir Peter,' Elizabeth broke in decisively.

'And he's a married man,' added Sir Peter, nodding as if to indicate he understood the difficulty.

'But there's more to it than that, I'm afraid, ' Elizabeth said, and again turned to her uncle. Sir Peter took their glasses and went to his sideboard. As he refilled them he said over his shoulder, 'I guessed there must be. You wouldn't be here asking my advice just because you had been having an affair with your boss. Not my line, advice about that sort of thing.' He smiled at Elizabeth as he handed her and her uncle two more glasses of sherry. 'What's the problem, eh? What have you been worrying over these last few days. Something to do with the FO did you say Simeon?'

'Well, it's the United Nations connection, you see. With Elizabeth working there, anything to do with her job is their concern, and we wondered whether you could help her get a job here in England. You see,' said Simeon after a pause, 'She's decided not to go back.'

Elizabeth coughed.

Simeon took her cigar and stubbed it out.

'But surely,' said Sir Peter, 'Whatever you think about this man, there's no need to abandon your career. Even with all the help I could get you, you're unlikely to find such a position again. Why take such drastic action?' He looked intently at Elizabeth.

'I've not told you everything, Sir Peter,' said Elizabeth.

'It's my sister, you see,' said Simeon, interrupting, 'I never mentioned it before, but Elizabeth's father ran out on them a few years ago. The only reason for going to Canada was his job in an orchestra. He played the flute, you see, and ran off with a woman from the second violins. Carrie, my sister, is very unhappy in Canada now - she's only stayed there because she wanted to be near Elizabeth. Now that this unhappy affair has occurred - there's no hope, apparently, of getting a divorce - Elizabeth wants to come back to England, but she's blotted her copybook at the UN by running off like this ...'

'Running off? I don't quite understand,' said Sir Peter.

'I left without warning and they're terribly security conscious over there,' said Elizabeth.

'But surely if you go back to explain...'

'That's just it,' said Elizabeth, 'I'm afraid that if I go back ...'

'Well?'

'That I won't be able to finish with him. I ...' Elizabeth shrugged and turned her head towards the fire.

'Mmmm. So you want me to use what influence I have at the FO to straighten things out for you, and perhaps find you a job into the bargain?' Sir Peter asked, not without a hint of condescension.

'That's it in a nutshell, Peter. I know it's a lot to ask but ...' Simeon spread his hands in a gesture of appeal.

'Only too glad to be of help. Give me a few days and I'll be in touch,' said Sir Peter with some enthusiasm, at the same time giving the impression that he might have other, more pressing business.

'Thank you, you've been most kind,' Elizabeth said, shaking his hand.

'Yes indeed, we're most grateful,' added Simeon.

'Not at all. Thank you for giving me your opinion of the Meissen. I'll ring you at the club, Simeon.' He ushered them out. 'Goodbye.'

As they descended the stairs Elizabeth turned to her uncle:

'What was all that about? I thought we were going to ask him ...'

'Wait 'til we're in the car,' he ordered in a harsh whisper.

CHAPTER 25

The front door of Knowsley Hall was open, and as I entered I wondered whether the front door of a stately home is ever locked. The entrance hall was of fairly modest proportions with oak everywhere. There seemed to be no-one about and I could hear nothing. Straight ahead of me was a half-open door, but for some reason I decided it might be wiser to take the one on my right. I tiptoed over to it and opened it quietly. I looked in at a very old-fashioned toilet with floral porcelain and a mahogany cistern.

There came a cough of the discreet variety from behind me and I spun round, my right hand hovering near my gun.

He was a tall, lean, long-faced guy wearing a black apron and holding a potted plant.

'Can I help you?' he asked in a moderately supercilious tone.

'I'd like to speak to Doctor Fletcher - and his niece.'

'They're not here.'

'I have reason to believe otherwise,' I said, investing my voice with what seemed to me a good deal of authority.

'Who are you?' he asked, apparently unimpressed.

'I think I ought to speak to ...'

'Lord Knowsley?'

'Exactly.' At last I was getting through.

'Follow me,' he said. He lead me to a small morning room, then made as if to leave.

'Don't be long,' I ordered, 'I get nervous if I'm kept waiting - and leave the door open.'

He slid out of the room without saying anything. I took up a position by the fireplace so that when Lord Knowsley appeared he would have to come right into the room before seeing me. Thirty seconds later I heard footsteps and felt myself go tense.

'I believe you wish to see me?' he said with a flicker of a smile. It was the same guy, only without apron and flower pot.

'This is not the time for silly games. Now where are they - Fletcher and his niece?' My head was beginning to hurt again.

'You are the fellow who has followed Elizabeth from the United States, aren't you?' He was not smiling anymore.

'Yes, and ...'

'She doesn't want to see you.'

'She has no choice in the matter.'

'Now look here, my man, this is ...'

'No, Lord Knowsley, if that's who you are, YOU LOOK HERE! I've come a very long way to interview Elizabeth Tasker. I've bloody well nearly been killed in the process, and I'm in no mood for being fobbed off by you. Now, where is she?'

'They left some time ago. You may search the house if you wish.' He was obviously telling the truth.

'Where are they now?' I asked.

'Before I answer that I think I ought to know who you are.'

'Lockhart's my name. I'm a United Nations security officer.'

'I see. You're here officially, are you?'

'I am and I suggest you ...'

'May I see your identification?'

'I don't have it with me.'

'How very careless of you.' He was getting to be supercilious again - but not without reason I had to admit.

'If you must know it's somewhere at Doctor Fletcher's farm. It was taken from me at gunpoint.'

'By a small, rather hirsute individual?'

'Yes.'

'I see ... and how did you ...?'

'I left him with a very sore head.'

'Funnily enough, I'm inclined to believe you. However, I still think it's up to you to prove your bona fide before I tell you.'

'Lord Knowsley, I think it's time you faced up to the gravity of the situation. Miss Tasker may be involved in a murder. It was certainly done in connection with her flight from the US. Since then her uncle and yourself have been aiding and abetting her - to say nothing of the character who committed an assault on me with a deadly weapon. As if that were not enough, there is the possibility that the aforesaid Miss Tasker is herself in danger. She mentioned to you that someone has followed her. I do not think she meant me. I am sure she does not know I am in Britain. If I can get hold of her ...'

'What precisely is she accused of?'

'At the moment, nothing. But her flight from the US may involve a breach of security, and over here, as I've said, there is the question of the attack on myself. I could put that in the hands of the police here. However, there are other considerations - my prime task is to interview her and persuade her to return with me to clear up this whole matter, if possible.'

'Would you like a drink? You look as if you need one.'

'I need to know where Elizabeth Tasker is - but a brandy wouldn't come amiss, thank you.'

I followed him over to a tantalus on a table by the window and watched him pour some brandy into a glass.

'Cheers,' I said, raising my glass without drinking. 'Now, where is she?'

He poured himself a drink from the same decanter and looked at me keenly as he sipped it slowly. I drank some of mine and relaxed a little as I felt the delicious warmth of it on my palate.

'They've gone to Cambridge to see a mutual friend who may be able to help. They promised to let me know the outcome. Then, I think, they intended going back to the farm.'

'Thank you,' I said, and drank more of the brandy. 'Who did they visit in Cambridge?'

He hesitated.

'I would rather not say, just at the moment. You still have not proved to me who you are, Mr. Lockhart, if that's your name.' I was forced to admit to myself that the guy had something. In his place I would have been unwilling to reveal what I knew to a complete stranger, even if he sounded highly convincing - and I could not be sure that I did. Apart from waving my gun at him (in any case I doubted the efficacy of such a ploy) I could think of only one way out of the impasse.

'Are you willing to come back to the farm with me?' I asked. 'If the guy I laid out has come round I can get my ID and maybe convince you of who I am and, if Fletcher and his niece are there, or turn up, they might be willing to listen to me sensibly if you are present.' He looked at me long and cool. I willed him to agree.

'I was about to suggest the same thing myself,' he said.

He showed me a short cut back to East House Farm and we were there in twenty minutes. On the way he asked, 'What exactly did you do to Drummy Nugent?'

'To who?'

'The man at the farm - you said you left him with a sore head.'

I told him.

'What did you say his name is?' I asked.

'Drummy Nugent. He came from London as an evacuee during the war. He was rather a simple child, but contrived to bring with him his favourite toy - a drum, which he played incessantly. Poor thing, his parents were both killed in the blitz a few weeks after he came and as no-one else seemed to want him, he stayed. He's been with Simeon - Doctor Fletcher - ever since.'

'Simple he may be, but he's no pushover,' I said

with conviction.

'Indeed not. He has the intense loyalty one finds in those of low intellect. I am afraid he rather overstepped the mark with you, but he thought he was doing the right thing, I'm sure. I do hope you have not done him any serious injury.'

In spite of the fact that the guy had nearly knocked my head off, I found myself hoping the same thing. When we arrived at the farm we went straight to the barn and found him still tied around the pillar. He was conscious, but it was obvious his head was playing the steam hammer game, and the look he gave me would have shrivelled a rattle snake. Fortunately Lord Knowsley was clearly top of the hit parade in Drummy's eyes, and he accepted our attentions as we untied him and led him inside.

There was obviously no-one else about, and I left the two of them in the kitchen while I went in search of a drink. My head was still throbbing. I found some booze in the sitting room I had been in previously and was pouring myself a stiff one when Lord Knowsley appeared.

'Care for one?' I asked.

'Yes thank you,' he replied, and tossed my wallet onto the table beside me.

'Where was it?' I asked.

'In his tobacco jar.'

I rifled through the contents. Everything was there. I looked across at him, and it was clear he had seen my ID card.

'Yes, I believe you,' he said in answer to my silent question.

'Well, can you tell me now where they went in Cambridge?'

'To see Sir Peter Thorburn.' He looked as if the name ought to mean something, but it did not. He went on without waiting for me to ask.

'Peter is a Cambridge don and has connections with the Foreign Office. They seemed to think he could help.'

'What exactly did Elizabeth Tasker tell you?' I asked.

'To be perfectly candid, very little. It appears she took off from New York on impulse to get away from a man with whom she seems to have had a .... relationship. The circumstances are such that she may choose not to return. That's all.' He obviously did not believe that it was.

'And you thought I was that man?' I added.

'It seemed a reasonable assumption at first.'

'Well, now you know better.'

He said nothing.

'Lord Knowsley, are you willing to help me?' I asked suddenly.

'To what end?' he responded.

'To get Elizabeth Tasker to tell me exactly why she fled across the Atlantic.'

'What precisely have you in mind?'

'You said they were likely to return here. They will clearly be on their guard when they find I am waiting for them. If so, I have a feeling she will be ready with some story - no doubt laced with enough truth to make it difficult to deny - that will land her in more trouble than she is in now. Believe me, she badly needs to come clean over this business. More evasion and she could be in real trouble. I MUST know why she went to Germany.' I tried hard to sound convincing.

'You place me in a difficult position. Whilst I am more than willing to help the forces of law and order, I cannot connive at any attempt to make Elizabeth incriminate herself if such is the case.'

'I am only interested in the truth. There is something behind this business, and, as I already pointed out, someone has died trying to find out what that something is. All that I want you to do is be here when she returns. If she sees you ... well, she will feel less threatened. She may feel able to tell the truth.'

'I think you have more than that in mind, Mister Lockhart.' He looked right through me. He was nobody's fool.

'OK. I thought perhaps if I stayed in the background when they first arrive ...'

'You would catch her with her guard down and get her to spill the beans.'

I could not avoid smiling. I nodded.

'Yes It's a tactic I've used myself before now,' he said.

Before I could ask him to explain he went on - 'Very well, but on one condition. That I am to remain while you ... hear what she has to say for herself.'

'Agreed.'

'Then let's have a drink on it,' he said. Half an hour later we heard the Lagonda drive up. Lord Knowsley went out and told Drummy Nugent to stay in the kitchen, and went himself to the front door. I sank into a wing backed armchair and waited. Between me and the door of the room stood an ornate carved wooden standard lamp with an enormous shade. I kept very still.

The door opened and they came in. Lord Knowsley was speaking.

'... I thought perhaps a drink might be indicated.'

'What a good idea. I certainly need one,' Elizabeth Tasker said in a voice whose timbre almost served to mask the tremor I could just detect. She turned towards the sideboard and I saw how strained she was. Her uncle came round the other side of the lampshade and drew in his breath as he saw me. Lord Knowsley said:

'Oh yes, you have a visitor.' He sounded almost as though he were enjoying it. She wheeled round and I stood up. Her finely chiselled jaw sagged.

'Lockhart!' she gasped as though I had come from Mars.

I thought for an instant she was going to pass out. Instead she took a large swig of whisky.

'Jeremy what the...' Uncle Simeon said.

'I'm sorry, Simeon, Elizabeth, but Mister Lockhart ....'

'Needs to know exactly what's been going on,' I continued.

I took out my wallet and made sure Uncle Simeon caught sight of my Magnum as I did so. I showed him my ID.

'Where's Drummy?' he barked.

'He's all right, Simeon,' said Lord Knowsley, 'Only a sore head.'

'You know this man?' Simeon asked Elizabeth

Tasker.

'Yes, he works for the UN in New York.' There was no mistaking the catch in her voice now. I felt sorry for her, but it was no time for sympathy.

'Well, Miss Tasker?' I did my best to sound menacing.

'Say nothing, Elizabeth.' Uncle Simeon again.

I glared at him but he did not flinch. I felt myself running out of menace. Lord Knowsley came to the rescue.

'Simeon, please listen to Lockhart.'

'Jeremy, we have been betrayed ...'

'That's putting it rather strongly, I think,' protested Lord Knowsley.

'I was not referring to this ... performance.' Simeon sat down beside Elizabeth Tasker as he spoke. 'I mean this afternoon - in Cambridge.'

Elizabeth Tasker fumbled a cheroot out of her handbag and Knowsley lit it for her. She gave a tiny smile. I had another attack of sympathy.

'What about Cambridge?' Lord Knowsley asked.

I thought he was getting away from the point.

'Miss Tasker,' I began.

'Mister Lockwood,' Simeon said, 'I do not think this is the time ...'

'On the contrary,' I said, with some venom - nothing makes me madder than to have my name deliberately mistaken - 'It's high time I was told just what's been going on - and why. Why, for instance, did you, Miss Tasker, take off for Germany without warning and try to cover your tracks on the way to Rudesheim?'

It clearly came as something of a blow to her

that I knew so much of her movements. She gulped at her whisky.

'... Why, for instance, did you, Doctor Fletcher, give orders to your man Nugent to assault me with a deadly weapon, viz. one shotgun?' He went rather pale. I waited.

'I think,' said Lord Knowsley, 'That you should tell Mister Lockhart everything, from the beginning.' He handed Simeon a drink and sat down facing them. Almost imperceptibly he gestured to me to do likewise. Elizabeth Tasker looked at her uncle. His shoulders sagged and he gave a little nod. She turned her pale grey eyes to me, and I tried to smile reassuringly, but felt it came out more as a leer. However, she sank back in her chair and, after sipping her whisky, began:

'It all started some time ago. As you know, I am secretary to Hugo Lansing, Director of the Agency. You will be aware that he was ...' she paused '... born in Germany - Rudesheim in fact and brought over to the USA and adopted by a General Lansing, a distant relative. In the course of, eh, conversation, he said something about his childhood and Rudesheim.

Later I came across an article about the place in the National Geographic, with pictures. Something in the pictures did not quite fit with what he had said, but I let it pass. After all, he had been away a long time. Later the subject came up again and I was still left with a niggling doubt. After that, I found myself thinking about it when I shouldn't have been, and I thought his attitude to Germany - he had never been back since the war - not quite right. Something else he said later about his childhood did not quite fit with his age - I honestly can't remember what exactly, but it fed my doubts.

If there had been nothing more I don't suppose I would have done anything, but one night at a reception he denied knowing someone who was there, and later during the evening I could have sworn he was talking to the same man. Not in a casual sort of way, but in a conspiratorial sort of way. When I came on the scene they broke off rather suddenly.'

She paused for a drink and sucked at her cheroot.

'The man was the Russian Cultural Attache ...

One other thing ... There was an Indian diplomat who committed suicide. He had visited the office some weeks before, but at the time of his death I found a piece of paper with the same name and a phone number on it crumpled up in Hugo's waste-paper basket. You came round then, Mister Lockhart, but Hugo denied any recent contact with the dead man. Again, it was nothing conclusive - just something else which kept me wondering.

Finally, on the night before I flew to Germany, I went to the ballet. It was Coppelia - you know, the story of the doll that plays other parts. It came to me right there that that was the only possible explanation - he was playing a part, impersonating the real Hugo Lansing.

I was ... shocked, frightened, confused. I didn't know what to do. I decided the only thing was to prove, or disprove, the idea. And I thought I must go to Rudesheim to do so. The opportunity arose right then because he was away for a few days in Washington, and I simply took off. I left word that I had gone to visit my mother in Winnipeg because she was ill. With Hugo away, no-one would question it. It's still only Tuesday,' she went on, 'He's not due back in New York until tomorrow. I could fly back ...' her voice tailed off. She obviously did not relish the prospect.

'Why did you not go to the authorities with your suspicions?' asked Lord Knowsley.

'It all seemed so vague, just a few silly incidents. Besides, who would I have gone to?'

'What about Mister Lockhart here?' Lord Knowsley asked.

She looked at me and said very slowly, 'He works for Hugo, doesn't he?'

'Not quite accurate. Miss Tasker,' I said, 'I work for the UN. If you didn't trust me then why tell me all this now?'

'Perhaps I can answer that,' interposed her uncle. 'This afternoon we had rather a nasty experience. On top of everything else it has left Elizabeth rather badly shaken. Oh yes it has my dear. I think she now needs someone official to confide in. Someone, hopefully, she can trust.'

All three of them looked at me as though willing me to shrivel up and die if I could not be trusted. I did not reply to the unspoken challenge, but instead asked:

'What happened this afternoon?'

'We went to see Sir Peter Thorburn,' Simeon replied. 'He had offered to help. I know he has connections with the Foreign Office. It's been rumoured that he has some sort of role in Security. I suppose I thought he could sort this whole mess out whilst protecting Elizabeth.' He took a large mouthful of whisky.

'Well, what happened?' asked Lord Knowsley.

Simeon looked from one to the other of us and said, 'He's a ... I don't know exactly what, but he's not what he purports to be. If the Russians are involved in this - he's one of them!'

'What!' exclaimed his Lordship.

'Can you please explain?' I sounded very sceptical, 'How is it that the one person in England to whom you turn for help just happens to be a communist agent?'

'But you see,' continued Simeon, warming to the subject, 'It's not as wild a coincidence as it might at first appear. HE called me.' He nodded vigorously. 'While we were evading you when you came here this morning, my phone rang. It was Sir Peter. He told me he had acquired a piece of Meissen - he's known as a fine amateur collector - and wanted my opinion. Knowing his reputation in the field of, well, security and so forth, I in turn asked him to help with Elizabeth's problem.' He gulped his drink again, and Elizabeth took up the story.

'When we got there he showed uncle the Meissen then asked what he could do for us. I could hardly get a word in and uncle told him it was simply an affair of the heart, I didn't want to go back to the US and could he help me get a job over here. Then Uncle Simeon started talking a lot of rot. He got mother's name wrong and gave father the wrong instrument and ...'

'You've lost me, I'm afraid,' I had to say.

'And me,' agreed Lord Knowley.

'I was trying to warn Elizabeth not to say too much. You see, Sir Peter Thorburn had given himself away.' Simeon held up his hand to stop further protests.

'I'll explain, ' he said. 'You may not know, Mister Lockhart, but I am an expert on European porcelain. That's my niche at the British Museum. He showed me a piece that he had said on the phone he had JUST acquired. BUT, I knew of that item and he must have bought it AT LEAST SIX MONTHS AGO. His sudden request for an opinion therefore seemed rather odd. THEN, he made a slip when we were discussing Elizabeth's dilemma. She said she was having an affair with a man, <u>but</u> later he mentioned her <u>boss.</u> I am certain she had not described him so.' He paused for another drink, but his glass was empty.

'You mean ...?' Lord Knowsley left the question unfinished.

'YES. He already knew. He <u>knew</u> what we were going to ask. The request for my opinion was just a ruse to enable him to get in touch with me. Don't you see? - he must have known Elizabeth was here - he KNEW what the problem was.'

'What he really wanted,' Elizabeth said, 'Was to find out precisely how much I really knew - or how much I suspected!'

'But that's absurd,' interjected Lord Knowsley, 'How could he know Elizabeth was here, far less that she is your niece. She just said that her departure went unnoticed.'

'Not so,' I said. They all looked at me.

'What you don't know is that Hugo Lansing himself reported you missing on Saturday night, Miss Tasker.' Her jaw did its sagging trick again.

'Reported me missing!'

'Yes, it sounds incredible, but apparently he came back from Washington on Saturday evening, went to your apartment and found it empty. He returned later and was stopped by two cops who were keeping an eye open for a prowler in the neighbourhood.'

She nodded.

'He had to explain his hanging about, and reported that you weren't in when you should have been. Once they got onto your security rated status, they had to follow it up.'

'You mean they ...'

'Yes, they discovered you had flown to Frankfurt!' She swallowed the last of her whisky. I wished she had kept some for what was to follow.

'That's not all.' I paused to give her a chance to prepare herself. 'Hugo Lansing followed you. He flew to Frankfurt on Sunday night!'

This time she kept her teeth firmly clenched, but her face went very pale.

'And if he knew she had gone to Frankfurt,' said Simeon, 'He must have guessed ...' He took Elizabeth's hand and squeezed it. Her eyes were closed, and a single tear coursed down her cheek.

'Doctor Fletcher,' I asked,'Do you think this Thorburn guy was convinced by your story - that your niece simply wanted to get away from an affair?'

'I, I... think so,' he replied.

'Did you mention Elizabeth's visit to Germany?'

'No,' he replied.

Elizabeth Tasker got up and went over to the window. Lord Knowsley poured us all more drinks.

'Just as well, isn't it?' he asked.

'Not really,' I said, 'If THEY are behind this, then they know about her going there and it will seem strange that she never mentioned it to Thorburn.'

'I never thought of that,' said Simeon with a grimace.

'You did extremely well. It was most astute of you to sus. him out and put together a plausible tale on the spur of the moment. If you had told him the whole truth you might not be talking to us here and now.'

Elizabeth turned from the window.

'That's rather melodramatic isn't it? Surely you're not suggesting ...' She put her glass to her lips.

'A colleague of mine was murdered in Rudesheim yesterday while assisting me to find you.'

My head began to throb again.

'Oh, no,' she said, and made for the safety of the nearest seat.

'Yes, I'm afraid you've got yourself into a nasty game.'

'What do you think we should do now?' asked Simeon.

'My orders are to take your niece back to New York. I'm not sure that that isn't the best thing.

Thorburn has probably reported back to whoever controls him by now, and if they are not satisfied with your story - if they suspect that you know the truth about Hugo Lansing - there's no knowing what they might do.'

'Do you really think there's danger, even here?' Lord Knowsley asked.

'Probably not right here. If they know she is here, as though giving herself a few days to think things over, the most they'll do is keep an eye on her. There would be no sense in making a move as long as it seemed possible that what she told Thorburn could be true. But I suspect that if she were to do anything that could be construed as going to the authorities - well ...'

There was no doubting now that they were all perfectly aware of the seriousness of the situation. I needed to know what to do next.

'I shall have to make a phone call,' I said, and took out my wallet to get Murchison's number.

It was time to call in the marines.

CHAPTER 26

'Is Mr. Murchison there?' I asked from the phone in the hall.

'Hang on,' came the reply.

'Murchison.' The one word was enough to indicate Scottish ancestry.

'This is Lockhart, UN. Fox gave me your name.'

'Is he the one who wears spotty bow ties?' For a moment I forgot the response, and cursed the school-boyish penchant the Department had for passwords.

'Only when he's wearing a velvet smoking jacket.'

'Oh, aye, that'll be him. What can I do for you?'

'Do you know Sir Peter Thorburn?'

'Affirmative.'

'I have reason to believe he may be .. on the other side.'

'What evidence have you for such a .. fanciful idea?'

'I'm over here to find a missing secretary, one Elizabeth Tasker.'

'What's the connection?'

I told him the story that they had told me, and had to admit to myself that it sounded rather feeble. Could they, after all, be imagining Sir Peter Thorburn's sinister role in the affair?

'Verrry interestin'.' There was a long pause. 'There's not much to it, is there?' the voice burred on, 'This Doctor-fellow, he's at the British Museum, you say?'

'Yes. He seems a pretty sharp guy, but I agree the evidence is weak. Maybe he was mistaken, maybe ...'

'Oh, I don't think he was mistaken.'

'No?' I could not conceal my disdain at his enthusiasm for jumping to conclusions.

'We've had our eyes on yon Thorburn for some time now.'

'Oh?'

'When did this take place, the conversation with the Taskers?'

'This afternoon.'

'What's your number? I'll ring you back in half an hour.'

I gave him the number and rejoined the others. Lord Knowsley spoke as I re-entered the sitting room.

'Elizabeth's all-in. I think she ought to have a rest. What do you think, Lockhart?'

'Yes, I agree. My contact's calling back in half an hour. Why don't you go to bed and lie down, Miss Tasker?'

The other two had apparently been exhorting her to do just that while I had been phoning. She agreed, and Simeon saw her out. As soon as we were alone Lord Knowsley turned to me:

'What's the score, Lockhart? Is there real danger for her here?'

'I doubt it, at the moment. If Thorburn believed her that it is simply a question of a confused woman in love, then there's no reason for him to make any move against her. On the other hand, he will surely report to his masters, and if they know - as they must - that she has been to Rudesheim, they may conclude that she DOES know the truth. Then it will depend on whether they decide Lansing is worth keeping.'

'You mean, they might decide to cut their losses and let things take their course.'

'They never let anything take its natural course! No, they'll either get him out or else force him to go back to New York and bluff it out.'

'Surely that's dangerous - for them, I mean?'

'At worst, they'll lose an agent, and we're not sure we can prove anything against him. There's no question of any real espionage. Nothing he knows is top secret. I doubt if there's any sort of charge we could bring against him. Of course he'll be watched by them very carefully in future, but that can be turned to advantage sometimes.'

'In what way?'

'Resources are always limited. If you have someone like him being watched by them, then that can take the heat off someone who really IS up to something on our behalf. Then again, you can use such a person to plant a false trail sometimes, thus diverting attention from what you are really up to.'

'So he could return to the States and take up where he left off?'

'Not quite. He'll be subjected to a rigorous interrogation to establish just what's been going on. Depending on the outcome, he'll be left alone or asked to resign, or maybe charged - if they think they've got something that'll stick.'

'You've been very candid, Mister Lockhart.'

'Why shouldn't I be? I've told you nothing you couldn't work out for yourself, apart from which, you've already been helping Miss Tasker, and I think you're entitled to some sort of explanation of what it's all about.' I could imagine Fox's face if he heard me discussing the Department's business with an outsider!

The phone rang. To my surprise it was Fox, not Murchison. 'Lockhart! Fox here.' I could tell he was in a neanderthal mood.

'Yes, boss, I ...'

'Shurrup and listen, Lockhart. Are you alone?'

'Yes.'

'Is there an extension?'

'I don't know.'

'Well, go and find out and if there is - pull it out!'

'Come on, boss ...'

'DO IT Lockhart! For once just do as you're bloody well told!' I put the phone down and made for the stairs. Simeon was coming down. 'Have you an extension to this phone?' I asked.

'There's one in the kitchen with a bell in the yard. Why?'

'Sorry, but you'll have to manage without it for a while,' I said, on my way to the kitchen. When I got there Drummy Nugent was sitting at the long kitchen table with a steaming mug of something in front of him. The extension was a wall model and I went up to it and traced the cable down to the skirting board where it entered a connection box. I took hold of the wire and tugged - with little result. Drummy got up and came over. I squared up to him, but he smiled and tore the box from the wall and bit through the cable.

'Well?' I said, back on the phone in the hall.

'You're sure we can't be overheard?' asked Fox.

'Not unless we're bugged, Boss,' I replied.

'We're not. I checked while you were away,' said Fox.

'What the hell's all this about?'

'Listen, Lockhart, this thing's blown up in our face. It's no longer a question of finding this dame and what she knows about Lansing. That's now irrelevant. You've gotta get Lansing himself and bring him back, one way or another. We're pretty sure he's got hold of something big. It's possible he hasn't passed it on. We think we would have heard if he had. He must be stopped from doing that. But we've gotta play it cool. Our shock troops might put the frighteners on him and if they don't snatch him clean, first time, there's no knowing what he might do, apart from the fact that he'll realise there's something very big in it if they *do* turn up. He knows you, Lockhart, and if you can persuade him that the dame's just been bloody stupid about him he MIGHT come back with you. Then, back in New York, we'll have him. At all costs you must get him back there.'

'I'll do what I can, Boss.'

'You've got twenty-four hours, Lockhart.'

'How long?' I gasped.

'That's it, twenty-four hours. If he's not on a plane for the States in that time, he's not going anywhere.'

'You mean ...?'

'Yes. One of the elimination boys will take over. They're on their way to pick up his trail already. It was touch and go whether we used the subtle approach via you, or the other. That's why you've only got twenty-four hours. For god's sake don't fail.'

'Can I know what this is all about? If I might be in the firing line ...'

'You can only know one word, Lockhart, and that's only so's you'll know if Lansing mentions it. If he does, it means he doesn't know the value of it and hasn't passed it on. The word is 'ACME' - the 'ACME' project. You're one of only about a couple of dozen people who know such a thing exists.'

'What the hell is it, how do ...?'

'I told you Lockhart, you only know one word.'

'Okay, okay. But there are one or two questions.'

'Such as?'

'What about the girl?'

'Leave her there with her uncle. We'll get someone to put her on a plane to New York tomorrow. You concentrate on Lansing.'

'But what you don't know is that they went to a certain Sir ...'

'Yes, I know. It's taken care of. I'm with Murchison now.'

'What, here in London!'

'Yes, Lockhart, here in London.' He was back to his most sarcastic.

'Well, it must be big to bring you over here. So I leave the girl. But what about Klaus?'

'What about him?'

'Have you forgotten he was murdered on Sunday, on this job. How can I persuade Lansing that this is all some silly dame's escapade when someone's been killed. If we don't pursue it he's bound to smell a rat.'

'Not necessarily. For one thing we know by the time factor that *he* didn't do it. It's possible that whoever did will not tell him. You know the rule - never discuss more than you have to, etc. Besides there's another point. The German police have a theory that it was a revenge killing by some nut-case who had threatened Klaus - some guy he put away years ago who's just got outta jug. It's been in today's paper over there. So he'll not be worried about that. We think there's a chance he'll take the opportunity to come back with you, if only to find out more about ...'

'Acme vacuum cleaners!' I broke in.

'Don't joke about it, Lockhart, this thing's ...'

'Yeah, I know, bigger than both of us.' I could hear him sucking in his breath at the other end. Before he snorted fire at me, I went on, 'Twenty-four hours isn't long. I'm here in the depths of Norfolk, don't forget.'

'There's a flight to Brussels from Birmingham airport tonight at 20.00. You can connect with a flight to Frankfurt at ten thirty-five and be in Rudesheim tonight. That gives you most of tomorrow. The last plane leaves there tomorrow night at eleven thirty for Paris - then New York. BE ON IT - WITH HIM!'

'I'll do my best.'

'It's gotta be better than that, Lockhart. Otherwise it's bury-time for him and a pension - a very small pension - for you.'

'Thanks a lot!'

'Yeah, well you better get on with it. And Lockhart ...'

'Yeah?'

'The Department's relying on you. I'm relying on you. In fact I told them I thought you could do it. We need him back Stateside - BADLY.'

'I'll see you there, sir.' The phone went dead.

I apologised to Simeon for the damage to his phone and promised him it would be repaired, then explained that Elizabeth Tasker would be O.K at the farm. They were both anxious about the Thorburn angle, but accepted my assurance that all was taken care of, and she would be safe. I ate a hurried sandwich washed down by some good English beer, the like of which I hadn't had in a long time. By the time I drove off I reckoned I would just have enough time to make it to Birmingham and the plane to Brussels.

About three miles along the road the car developed a bad cough and began to lose power. Try as I might, I could not keep it going. I cursed it to hell and back, and still had some bad language left for the hire company who could give a man two lemons in two days. Up ahead about a mile away I could see a farm and I reckoned it would be quicker to walk there and phone back to East House for Simon's Lagonda than to fiddle under the hood. I set off along the road. There was almost no traffic, and the only car I saw was a large black Mercedes going in the wrong direction, looking singularly out of place in that rural setting.

I knocked on the farmhouse door. It was opened by a middle-aged woman.

'May I please use your phone?' I asked.

'Don't 'ave un 'ere,' came the brusque reply.

'Damn!' I said. 'Sorry, but I must get to Birmingham airport tonight, and my car's broken down.' I waved down the road. 'I hoped to phone back to Doctor Fletcher to ask him for help, but ...'

'You a friend o' 'is?'

'Yes, I just left there a few minutes ago and ...'

'Abr'am!' she shouted, back into the house. A tall bony guy appeared by her side. 'Is 'nother friend o' Simeon Fletcher!' she said, and gave a short laugh.

'Well now, ain't he pop'lar this day!' he responded.

I looked, puzzled, from one to the other.

'Them fellows in that 'ere black job wanted the way to the farm,' he said in explanation.

'To East House Farm?' I asked in amazement.

'Just so.'

I closed my eyes to recall the faces in the Merc. There had been three of them, stoney-faced, atavistic types. I realised why I had thought the car so out of place. It was the passengers, not the vehicle, that had seemed so incongruous.

I knew what they were! And who they were after! Curse Fox for his assurances: "Thorburn's been taken care of" - like hell!

They were the Moscow Heavy Brigade - after Elizabeth!

'Have you a car I could borrow? PLEASE!'

'Dunno 'bout that,' he drawled.

'I've no time to explain, but I must get back to the Fletcher's and quickly. They may be in danger. Miss Elizabeth Tas ...'

'Miss Elizabeth there is she?' asked the woman, and I could detect real concern in her tone.

'Yes,' I replied, 'She's the one they're after. For God's sake, can you help?' I sounded desperate, even to myself.

'You 'er young man?' the woman asked as the man went inside. 'Yes,' I lied, hoping it might help.

Her husband reappeared in rubber boots and an old duffle coat tied round the middle with string. He carried a double-barrelled shotgun under his arm. Without a word he walked round the end of the house, and nodded me to follow.

Round the corner I found him cranking a tractor into life.

'Is this all you've got?' I asked.

'Yum,' he replied, 'Over the fields it'll be quick enough. Me car's conked.' He nodded towards a shed where an ancient Ford V-eight stood guard over its engine. I climbed aboard as the tractor stuttered off.

In five minutes we were crossing a field of stubble behind East House and he turned the wheels towards the far corner where we would be hidden from the house by the outbuildings. I took out my Magnum and checked it. I found myself shaking.

He looked at me, but said nothing. Ahead there seemed to be no activity. I began to wonder if I had been imagining things. The tractor drew to a halt and we climbed down. He grabbed his shotgun and ran, crouching,to the back of a barn. It was the one I had been put in by Drummy Nugent. I ran after him and stopped in his shadow. He peered cautiously round the end, holding me back with his free hand. A thought came to me, and I asked, 'Where have you done this sort of thing before?'

'Deepie,' he said and, 'Shhh!'

Before I could stop him he stepped out from the shelter of the barn and with a whispered 'You stay 'ere!' he walked towards the house. I stayed put, but surveyed the house as he advanced towards it. A flutter of curtain caught my eye. It was at an open dormer window. I saw Elizabeth. She was lying on the roof against some boarding that had been erected to prevent snow falling on a greenhouse built against the back wall of the house.

Just then the side door opened and a big guy in a trench coat came out. He saw Abraham and stopped.

'Good evenin',' said Abraham, and the man plunged his hand inside his coat. But Abraham was quicker.

The noise of the twelve-bore shattered the still evening air and the trench coat disintegrated around its owner. His pasty face never had a chance to change expression.

I saw a movement behind the dormer window above and fired a tentative shot at it, shattering a pane. Abraham ran forward and flattened himself against the house. He broke open his gun and inserted another shell. I fired again at the window and ran forward to join him.

'There were three of them in the car,' I whispered to him. He nodded. 'Miss Elizabeth's on the roof,' I added.

'I seen 'er,' he said.

'I'll go in the back door, you stay here,' I said, feeling it was time I took control.

'There's another way in, through there,' he whispered, indicating the greenhouse. 'I'll go that way,' he added and took off. To get there he had to pass a large window. He put up the hood of his duffle coat and ducked past the window, but not quite low enough. A shot rang out, but was just too high, and he made it, followed by the shattered glass from the window.

With one dead outside, one upstairs and the third shooting at Abraham, I reckoned the back door a good bet and pelted round the side of the house and straight in.

I was in the passage I remembered being led along by Drummy Nugent that morning. It was gloomy and I blinked to get my eyes used to the light. As I emerged into the hall I saw Drummy. He was sitting at the foot of the stairs. Dead.

Above my head I heard a creak. Someone was coming down the stairs, but not quietly enough. I drew back into the shadows and waited. My hand was very sweaty round the Magnum. Firing practice was never like this. My head began to ache again. I made a conscious effort to ignore it. But it would not stop, and I realised that something was pressing down on top of my head.

'Drop!' a guttural voice ordered, and as I

dropped the Magnum he descended the stairs, sliding his gun from the top of my head down to my neck.

I was very sorry that Abraham had been so trigger happy. With one of his buddies blasted away, Guttural-voice was quite likely to waste me in the next few seconds. I tried to figure out why he had not already. Then he told me.

'Where is Miss Taxer?' he asked, jabbing me in the ear with the barrel of his gun. He was still descending the stairs, and as he reached the bottom Drummy Nugent chose that moment to sink slowly sideways.

The movement caught him by surprise, and for an instant his gun wandered off me. I grabbed at his wrist with both hands and forced his gun hand in the air. He gave a roar and put his other hand through the banister and round my throat. I pushed against the side of the stair with both feet to get free, but he held on and I dared not let go his gun hand.

My head began to burst and I heard a drumming sound. There was an echoing crash and everything went black for an instant. I blinked and realised I was free. I still held his wrist, but it was limp now and he lay crumpled on the stairs.

Elizabeth was there, taking the gun from his hand. She had come down the stairs and dealt him a dreadful blow across the forehead with a large pottery water jug that now lay in pieces on the stairs. He was bleeding profusely from a gash above the eyes.

I shook my head vigorously to rid myself of the

waves of nausea that insisted on lapping over me.

'Where's the other one?' I whispered.

'In there,' she answered, pointing to the sitting room, 'Drummy shot him in the legs, but he's still got a gun, I think.' Just then a voice came from where she was pointing.

'Mikhail!' it called feebly.

I gestured to her to keep an eye on her victim, although it seemed unnecessary, and tiptoed across the hall. As I reached the sitting room door which was half open I saw him. He was a pathetic sight. He sat in an armchair with some material tied round both legs above the knees. His trousers, shoes and a large portion of carpet were soaked in blood. I did not think much of their first aid lessons.

I pushed my outstretched hand with the Magnum through the door first. He looked up. His gun was in his lap and he just swept it to the floor with a weary hand. He was very pale.

Elizabeth pushed past me into the room. Simeon was lying on the couch, barely conscious and stripped to the waist. She knelt beside him, cradling his head in her hands. Beyond them, on the floor, lay Lord Knowsley, his crumpled posture indicating he had been unconscious when he hit the floor. I went over to him. His pulse was fairly strong and his breathing even. There was a cruel weal across his forehead with blood oozing from one end. I laid him on his side and turned to Simeon. His eyes were open and he said, 'Who's come, Eiizabeth?'

'Mister Lockhart,' she replied as I came into

sight.

'I thought he'd deserted us?' he said, his voice regaining some of its vigour. He sat up, pushing her away gently.

'I'm not so bad,' he said, 'I was putting it on rather for their benefit.' He looked up to the window - and started. However, it was Abraham. He was retracing his steps from the greenhouse. I had forgotten him in the excitement. We waved him in.

'What did happen to you?' Elizabeth asked me, unable to keep an accusatorial tone out of her voice.

'I was assured that there was no danger to you in staying here. My orders were - still are - to go back to Germany to find your Mister Lansing. I was to catch a plane from Birmingham to Brussels. My car broke down up the road. I went to Abraham's,' I nodded towards him as he came into the room, 'To use the phone, but they don't have one. However, he does have rather a neat line in tractors, to say nothing of his tactics. Where did you say you learned how to fight like that, Abraham?'

'I told thee - Deepie.'

'He means Dieppe,' explained Simeon, 'He was in that show with Jeremy. How is HE?'

'He's unconscious, but alive all right. We'd better get an ambulance.' I turned to Abraham:

'Can you check on the guy on the stairs - Elizabeth laid him out just as he was strangling me to death - Thanks, by the way.' She shrugged and gave a wan smile.

'Thank you for coming back,' she said.

'Abraham here's the one to thank. Without his

cross-country assault I would probably have walked up to the front door and not been half so successful. How did these guys get in, in the first place?'

I found the drinks on the sideboard and poured everyone a stiff brandy. We could hear Abraham out in the hall talking on the phone. Simeon sipped his brandy and answered my question.

'Elizabeth was asleep upstairs and you had gone. Jerry and I were in here when I heard a car. I looked out at the front, and although the car looked out of place, my suspicions were allayed when one of them got out holding an open map. We get people round here, it being a dead end, looking for the way. I opened the door, he came up to me smiling, then I saw the gun. They forced their way in, leaving one at the front door. When we were all in this room and they were asking us where Elizabeth was, we heard a shotgun blast, followed by two pistol shots. I guessed it was Drummy. He had come along from the kitchen and let fly at the one at the front door. Him,' he said, indicating the one leaking blood. 'That's my shirt he's got tied round his legs.' He shivered.

Abraham came in. 'Amblance comin',' he said, 'That un out there was astirrin', but he's out again.' He waved a ham of a fist to indicate the weapon he had used. I handed him a drink and said, 'It's not enough, but thank you.' We shook hands and I had a sudden urge to hug him, but thought better of it.

Elizabeth came back with a tweed jacket which she put round Simeon's shoulders. She handed me a Mauser automatic held gingerly between finger and thumb.

'You left that out there,' she said, a twinkle in her eye. I noticed for the first time that she was still wearing night clothes. She looked very good in them.

'Now Mister Clever Dick,' she suddenly burst out, 'I think it's high time you told us what this is all about.'

She looked venomous! How dames can change!

'I can't tell you more than you already know. These guys were sent to snatch you, presumably to find out how much you do know about Hugo Lansing. For them it all went wrong. It should have been a quick in and out job, without doing any more than roughing you all up a little. They couldn't have reckoned with the opposition they met.'

'Who in God's name are they?' she asked.

'KGB goons, I should think. They'll have diplomatic passports for sure. Can't bring charges against them. They would have been transferred to some other Embassy in some other country to serve the same purpose. I expect they were nominally drivers or cooks, or the like. Useful to have around and when the need arises the local KGB guy winds them up and points them in the right direction.' I shrugged.

'Who winds you up?' she asked.

I had a headache again.

WOMEN!

CHAPTER 27

By the time the ambulance came Lord Knowsley was beginning to stir. The police arrived just afterwards. I had hoped to get away before their arrival to avoid lengthy explanations, but what with the reaction to the violent activity - not to mention two brandies - I had not had the energy to make the effort. Anyway, I had missed the flight from Birmingham and had been working out what to do next. Another talk to Fox was clearly indicated, but with so many ears around I could hardly do that there in the hall among the bodies.

Thankfully Lord Knowsley still regarded my credit rating as good, and when he had fully come round he sorted out the police. Which was not difficult as he turned out to be a local JP and chairman of the police committee! He also remembered what I had told them while Elizabeth was asleep and could see I was anxious to be off.

'You'll need to phone your man for new instructions and bring him up to date with this fracas, won't you?' he asked. I nodded.

'Go upstairs and use the extension,' he said, 'I'll see to it that no-one listens in.'

I turned to Simeon but my protestations melted when I saw how shaken he still was.

'You didn't give me a chance to tell you there is one in the bedroom as well as the kitchen,' he said with a wan smile.

I grinned. He was quite right, of course. They used to say that 'Thorough' was my middle name. I had to be slipping.

I dialled Murchison's number and asked for Fox. Murchison came on.

'Is someone looking for a Mister Fox?' he asked.

'Yes, the one that wears spotty bow-ties and lies through his teeth. This is Lockhart here.'

'Hold the line.'

'Fox here. Where are you now, Lockhart?'

'I'm still at East House Farm, and I ...'

'You should bloody well be on your way to Frankfurt, Lockhart. What the hell are you doing still there?'

'You listen to me, Fox, you bastard,' I countered, 'You told me everything was taken care of this end. I told you about Thorburn.'

'What's happened? Just tell it straight, Lockhart, with less hysterics, PLEASE.'

'Only that three KGB goons came here to snatch Elizabeth Tasker and damn near succeeded. They killed one man and damn near another - one Lord Jeremy Knowsley, JP.'

'Oh Christ!'

'You may well invoke deity, Fox. You lied to me. You told me it was OK, I could shove off for Germany after your precious Acme and leave her here. You ...'

'Tighten your big lip, Lockhart, and listen. I've no time to explain my assurances - even if I had to. You don't seem to have gotten it through your thick skull how important this Acme thing is. Whatever happened there can't be helped now. Do your best to get Lord Thingummy to keep it quiet and get the hell out of there for ...'

'Keep it quiet! With two dead bodies, diplomatic passports soaked in blood, aristocratic skulls split open and ...'

'You have been busy, haven't you? Are you still fit?'

'Just about.'

'Then leave everything at this end to me. I'll see to things. But we must get you to Germany to find Lansing. Hold on a second.'

I laid the phone on the bed and went over to a wash hand basin and sluiced my face in cold water. It stopped my head aching. For about thirty seconds.

Fox came back on the line.

'Do you know a place called Brize Norton?'

'Yes, I think so. It's an RAF base.'

'That's it. Well get yourself there as quickly as possible. They'll fly you to Frankfurt military air base. Then you're on your own until that plane to New York tomorrow night. You've GOT to do it, Lockhart. This attack on Elizabeth Tasker MAY mean that they <u>do</u> have an idea about you-know-what. If so, it's more important than ever that we get him back alive, so's we can get at the truth.'

'Yeah, okay Boss,' I said.

'Just a minute, Lockhart! This girl Tasker, is she all right?'

'She's a good-looker, Boss, but I'm not all that ...'

'Not that sort of all right! I mean is she okay after all that mayhem?'

'Fortunately, yes She managed to keep out of the way. As a matter of fact, she just about saved my life.'

'She did, eh? Then take her with you, Lockhart.'

'What? You mean ....'

'Yes. Take her over there. She could be very useful in getting Lansing back Stateside. He won't know about today's thing. If you and she turn up together he's all the more likely to believe that we know nothing except that she's a silly dame with a mixed-up heart who took off to think things over.'

I had to admit there was some logic in that. Getting her to agree was another thing.

'It may be a good idea, Boss, but I'm not sure I can persuade her.'

'Use your charm, Lockhart, use your gun if you have to, but get her to go with you and help. Tell her, if necessary, that there'll be no charges against her if she co-operates.'

'But what charges could we bring?'

'None. But does she know that?'

'You bastard, Fox.'

'I didn't hear that, Lockhart.'

'I'll do what I can.'

'Good. Remember, you're all we've got - for the next twenty-four hours. After that it's ....'

'Goodbye,' I said and put the phone down.

Downstairs I found the place crawling with cops and forensic guys - the whole shooting match. Elizabeth came up to me.

'Now that you've vacated the bedroom, Uncle Simeon and I are going to pack. We've decided to go with Jerry to his place for a day or so.' At the foot of the stairs, she paused.

'Is Hugo Lansing responsible for all this?' she asked, gesturing towards the activity in the hall.

'Yes, indirectly.' I looked at her, trying to figure out what she was thinking. Some hope!

'And you're now going over there to try and get him back to New York?' She sounded sceptical about my ability.

'Yeah. There's a chance he doesn't know about any of this. If he can be persuaded that you chased after him for purely personal motives, he might believe that we don't know he's not all that he pretends. Incidentally, we still don't know EXACTLY who or what he is.'

'I know exactly what he is,' she said with venom. I let that pass. I was trying desperately to figure out how best to persuade her to come along with me. She turned her pale grey peepers straight at me.

'I'm coming with you,' she said, as cool as a frigidaire.

'You're what?'

'Don't try to stop me, Mister Lockhart, my mind's made up. If you take him back now I may never see him again - I'm thinking seriously of staying in Britain now. Well, I do want to see him again. It's the only way I'll get him out of my system. Apart from the fact that I owe him something for Drummy.'

She looked down at where the poor guy had bled to death on the stair carpet. I followed her gaze. She could see I did not understand.

'You forget, Mister Lockhart, I grew up here. He

and I were childhood friends. For all his lack of intelligence, Drummy was a good friend to me.'

There were tears in her eyes - and nearly in mine too. I needed another drink.

'Well?' she asked, defiantly.

'I don't know what the hell you expect to do to Hugo Lansing if you did come with me, but don't forget my orders are to get him back to New York in one piece. I'll brook no intereference in that objective.' I tried hard to sound masterful.

'You sound as if you are agreeing to take her.' It was Lord Knowsley who had come up behind us.

'I think it's a crazy idea,' I said.

'I could help you,' she said quietly, 'And you owe me.'

I tried hard to give the impression of giving in reluctantly.

'What do you think?' I asked Knowsley.

'I'd like her to come back here for good, but with a clean sheet, so to speak,' he replied. I wondered if he had ideas in her direction. I wondered if he had any heirs. He guessed what I was thinking, but he did not elaborate.

'What does your uncle think?' I asked. Might as well have everyone's opinion.

'He doesn't know, yet,' she said.

'Are you willing to act under instructions, and no funny business about taking revenge?' It was my turn to sound sceptical.

'I think so,' she said.

'Now look here, Miss Tasker ... Oh, get packed. We leave in five minutes.' I grinned. I was rather pleased with myself. She did not grin, but was equally pleased with herself.

The Inspector who had arrived in the second wave of police wanted his statements and so on, and I could not help but see his point of view, but there was no time for formalities. Fortunately, a combination of my ID card plus a few Scotland Yard names I was able to drop, and Lord Knowsley's assurance, proved enough for him. When he agreed to let us go without further delay, I dropped it on him.

'How about some active help?' I asked.

'In what way?'

'I've got to get to Brize Norton in a hurry. Your boys could drive me.'

'It's over the county line,' he said. It reminded me of the regulations I had been pleased to jettison when I had left Scotland Yard. He looked from me to Lord Knowsley, and back, then shrugged.

'Sergeant!' he called out, 'You've some fast driving to do.'

CHAPTER 28

It was rather cramped in the plane the RAF provided and I would have liked to sleep, but could not. I turned to Elizabeth. She looked like I felt.

'I never got round to asking you more about Rudesheim. What, if anything, did you find out there?'

'I confirmed my suspicions about the monument. It didn't quite fit with what he had said about it.'

'In what way?'

She took a picture out of her shoulder bag.

'This is a picture of the monument thing,' she began.

'So that's what the camera was for!' I said.

'Pardon?'

'Never mind - go on,' I urged.

'You see this couple - Miss Moselle and Father Rhine. Well, Hugo told me he used to climb up on there when they were boys and eh .. fondle her .. ' she broke off, blushing.

'It's a bit high, isn't it?' I suggested.

'Exactly. And he seemed to be talking about a nude statue but she is covered.'

'Except for her well-endowed top half,' I added.

'So it just didn't seem ... well, authentic,' she concluded. 'Are we going back there, to the Germania thing?' she asked.

'We could do, yes.'

'Then you'll see for yourself when we get there.'

'OK.'

'I found out something else,' she said, 'Hugo Lansing wasn't born in Rudesheim.'

'No, you said he wasn't the real one.'

'No, I don't mean that. I mean that there was no Hugo Lansing born in Rudesheim in 1929. There's no such birth certificate.'

'How did you find that out?'

'They showed me at the Town Hall. I pretended I was with a genealogy club in the States and was looking for ancestors of my mother. They were quite co-operative.'

'Are you sure?' I asked.

'Certain. I checked both 1928 and 1930 into the bargain.'

'No Hugo Lansing? So whoever he is ...'

'He's not who he says he is,' she said.

I lapsed into silence, trying to figure out what it meant. With no success. Whoever he was, all that was important was that he had to be found, and quickly. Because of ACME - whatever the hell that was! Something he knew of but not, perhaps, its importance, Fox had said.

I wondered whether to tell her about ACME - if she was going to confront Hugo Lansing, it might be useful for her to know about it. I looked across at her, but her eyes were closed. My head began to ache again, and I stopped trying to think.

'You're not quite what you appear, either, are you?'

Her question broke into my attempt to fall asleep.

'Pardon?'

'Well, you're not an American are you? I've noticed it in your voice. When we were at the farm you sounded quite English.'

'Did I? You may be right. I'm originally from Bristol, then we moved to London when I was five.'

'How long have you been in the States then?'

'Nine years now.'

'Did you take out citizenship?'

'Yes. You don't have to - you retain British nationality as well - but I think it helps.'

'How long have you been with the UN?'

'My, we are in a curious mood today!'

She shrugged and turned away.

'I'm sorry, I was just trying to be funny - with my usual ineptness.'

She looked at me again with a tiny smile. I liked that.

'I went over to the States with the UN. I had joined the Met - that's the London police - when I was young, then a few years later was seconded to Interpol. I was quite good at languages in those days. From there I got a job in Geneva, then New York.'

'Were you never involved in checking on Hugo?' With the mention of his name her smile faded. I liked that too.

'No. The top man was vetted twice. Once at the beginning - he was one of those who started it, you know - and again when he was appointed its head. I wasn't there the first time, and when he got the top job he was vetted by some of the big league boys. They're supposed to be the best.'

'Huh!' she scoffed.

'I don't think you can blame them. Whatever the truth about Hugo Lansing, it's something that only somebody who's been very ...'

'Intimate is the word you're looking for,' she said.

'Yes. Sorry.'

'No need to be. There's no secret about it now. I suppose half the police forces in Europe know by now that Hugo and I were lovers.' She gave an empty laugh. 'Are you a married man, Mister Lockhart?'

'No, never have been.'

'Good for you. Of course you'll know that I was. You must have done your vetting thing on me when I joined Hugo.'

'As a matter of fact, no. You joined the Agency in Montreal, remember, and the RCMP checked you out. In any case I am more concerned with the UN personnel in the files than with the actual employees.'

'Oh, I see. Class distinction rears its ugly head again.'

For a moment I thought she was serious, then we both laughed. I had that feeling again - just a twinge - but it was there. "Oh hell," I thought, "Don't let this thing get complicated by ..." She was looking at me and I wondered if she knew what I was thinking. I turned away.

'How long now?' I asked the pilot.

'Ten minutes.'

He was a big guy, the one waiting for us at Frankfurt. We landed at the military part of the airport and were spared the usual formalities. He showed us to a car, an Audi coupe, and handed me the keys.

'How can we be sure Hugo Lansing is still around here somewhere?' I asked.

'He was seen earlier today in Rudesheim when we were called in. Since then he ain't left the area. We got it sewed up tighter than a Jew's purse!' he concluded emphatically.

'Mmmmm' I replied sceptically, recalling that the last Jew I had known had been so careless with his purse as to die a pauper.

'You're on your own until midnight tomorrow,' he said, 'Then ...'

'Yeah, I know, it's ...' I remembered who was beside me, and bit my lip.

'What did you mean?' she asked as we drove off.

'Well, it's like this,' I stopped talking to negotiate a road junction and give myself time to think. I had to decide whether or not to tell Elizabeth Tasker that if we did not get Hugo back to the States in twenty-four hours it would be the end of him. I decided to stall.

'We've been given until the midnight plane tomorrow to persuade Hugo Lansing to return with us to New York. If we don't succeed it will be taken out of our hands.'

'Which means?' she asked.

I just shrugged.

'You say WE have heen given twenty-four hours.

That sounds like you need my help.' I could tell she was looking at me with those grey eyes, but I stared straight ahead at the road.

'Yes. I'm hoping for your co-operation. I want you to tell Hugo Lansing when we meet him - if we catch up with him - that you flew over here simply to see where he was born and think about how you feel for him, etcetera. There's to be no mention of your suspicions, or of what happened at East House Farm. We've got to persuade him that ...'

'You BASTARD!' she exclaimed.

'Pardon?'

'You bastard. You let me come thinking I had forced you to, while all the time you wanted to use me. Use me against Hugo.'

'Yes. I let you think that. It was the easiest way to get you to come. But I'm not using you against Hugo Lansing. Believe me, it's in his best interests to come back with us.'

'Oh, sure,' she retorted, her voice deep with sarcasm.

'Anyway, the last time you mentioned him it was with revenge in mind, so why should it bother you to ...'

'MY revenge is one thing, helping you to trap him is quite another. That would be betraying him, nothing less.'

'And what has he been doing all these years?'

'He may have been impersonating someone else, but that doesn't necessarily mean that he's a ... traitor or whatever.'

'You're kidding yourself if you believe that.' I

turned to look at her. There was a little tear at the corner of her eye.

'Bit of dust,' she said, wiping it away with a tissue. We drove on in silence for a while.

'How do you propose getting in touch with Hugo? Advertise in the local paper? Wanted, one traitor by the name of ...'

'We'll just have to make systematic inquiries. Leg it round hotels and so on.'

'What about your ... colleague back there. Haven't they been watching for him?'

I had thought of that. Singularly unhelpful he'd been, in the matter of Hugo Lansing's exact whereabouts. I detected the hand of someone who maybe did not want me to find him. Someone who preferred the other option.

'I think they're keeping a low profile so as not to scare him into any rash move. No, it's up to us to find him,' I said.

'And persuade him to return to New York with us,' she added.

'Well?' I asked.

'Well what?' she responded.

'Are you going to help me to get him back? Without your co-operation ...'

'You mean my lies.'

'Okay, your lies. But without them I doubt if he'll go back with me. If he suspects that we're on to him - although I've no idea what his precise game is - he'll run for it. Probably to Moscow.'

'That's it!' she exclaimed.

'That's what?' I asked.

'Nothing, it's not important.' I could see that it

was but let it be. She would tell me in her own time, whatever it was she had thought. Meanwhile I had to get her to help me.

'What about it then?' I asked.

'I suppose I'll have to. But don't rely on me too much. I'm not used to this sort of thing. I'm not sure I can get him to believe me.'

'You'll have to. I'll do most of the talking when we get to him. I'll tell him I was sent over to fetch you back because he reported you missing. Then I'll say that I was about to leave from London for New York with you when they told me he had also flown to Frankfurt, and that I have come over to tell him you are with me and ...'

'We can all fly home like some happy family!'

'Something like that,' I said, but I could see what she meant. It sounded a bit flimsy.

'Do you think he'll fall for it?' she asked.

'Probably. For one thing, it's what he wants to believe and there's nothing like self-deception for ...'

'Yes, you used it on me!' she interrupted.

'... and for another, there's you. I'll do my best to keep you from having to lie too much - although I never met a dame yet who wasn't damn good at it - but you MUST convince him that there is no more to all this than a lovelorn girl trying to sort herself out.'

Just then I saw a familiar gateway, and turned the car into a driveway.

'Where are we going?' she asked.

'Yesterday when I left Rudesheim I checked out of this place. It's an old Inn. It was the only place we could find to stay on Sunday. Maybe the room's still free. It's very late now (it was almost eleven o'clock) and we'll need a bed for the night.'

'Would you mind rephrasing that?'

'What? .. oh yes, TWO beds.'

'TWO ROOMS, if you don't mind.'

We went in and I approached the tiny reception desk they had made under the stair. The place was busy inside, but there was no-one at the desk. Suddenly Elizabeth turned and walked out again. I chased after her and caught up with her in the car park.

'What the hell are you playing at?' I demanded.

'He's in there, in the bar.'

'Who's in there?' Then it dawned: 'Hugo Lansing?'

'Yes. He had his back to us, but I'm sure it was him. He was talking to a little dark man.'

'Well, let's get back in there and talk to him! That's what we came for.'

'I couldn't - not right now.'

'Why not, for God's sake?'

'I just couldn't go through with it. I'm too tired and ... I'm just not ready for him. If you force me to do it now I know I'll give myself away. Please!' Even in the darkness of the car park those grey eyes!

'Okay. Just let me think a minute. Maybe he's staying here. He could have got that room we had. In that case ...' I stopped.

Two men had come to the Inn's front door from inside. They were silhouetted against the light. I could not be sure but ... I dragged her down behind a Mercedes holding a hand over her mouth. I pointed through the car windows towards the door.

'Is that him?' I whispered. She nodded. They stood there lighting cigarettes, and as the lighters flared, I saw Hugo Lansing's face. I knew that if they left I had to follow. I could not be sure they WERE staying here and we might lose them for good if I waited to find out. She would have to come too. If only there had been enough time to get her off to bed somewhere and leave me a free hand.

The two men came towards us. I crouched lower, almost falling on my arse in the process. They were talking.

'They said she might return tonight, so we'll give it one more try. After that it'll have to be a talk with ...'

Hugo Lansing was speaking. His companion, a runt of a guy who barely came up to Lansing's jaw grunted something I could not make out and opened the door of a VW station wagon on the other side of the Mercedes. They got in and drove off, the little guy at the wheel.

I dragged Elizabeth to our car and followed the VW down the hill to the main road. I looked at her. There were tears in her eyes this time.

'You'll spoil your make-up,' I said.

Not surprisingly, she did not reply.

We had been very lucky indeed to catch up with Hugo Lansing so soon, but I was afraid that we would find it difficult to take advantage. I had not reckoned on him having someone with him. It should have been obvious, of course, that they would give him some help. I wondered if it was the little guy who had done for Klaus. If so I had ... but personal vengeance was not our game, as I had pointed out myself. It seemed that they were going to look for Elizabeth Tasker somewhere close by - probably in Rudesheim. I decided we would watch them for tonight, see where they bedded down, then proceed in the morning, separating the two if possible. I could alert the local police that the runt was Klaus' killer. That ought to keep him busy while we went to work on Hugo Lansing.

They drove to Rudesheim and up through the town to the Krone Hotel. No, they went on past and took the road up the hill - the road to Germania! After a few hundred yards I slowed down and watched their lights disappear round a bend. I pulled up and stopped.

'What's wrong?' Elizabeth asked.

'I smell a rat,' I said. 'There's nothing up this road but that monument, right? And nowhere that you are likely to be found at this time of night. It could be an ambush. Round the next bend, their car across the road ... no thank you!'

'But how could they know ...?'

'Are you sure he didn't see you, back there at the Inn?'

'No, I mean yes, I'm sure. He had his back to us as we went in ...'

'What about as we went out? It's just possible he did see us, isn't it?'

'Even if he did, Mister Lockhart, surely talk of an ambush is a bit, well, melodramatic?'

'Have you forgotten what happened back at the farm already?'

'No, but Hugo wasn't involved - well, not directly, and he's not ...'

'Shh, I think there's a car coming!'

Headlights came round the bend towards us from the direction of the monument. The car slowed down as it approached and drew to a halt opposite us. Hugo Lansing got out and crossed to our car.

I had my Magnum pointing through the door at him as he reached my window. I wound it down. He spoke as though meeting us at a vicar's tea party.

'Good evening. It IS Mister Lockhart! I thought I recognised you at the Inn.' He looked past me at Elizabeth. 'Good evening, my dear. I've been looking for you.'

'Good evening Mister Lansing,' I replied, before Elizabeth could speak, 'I think it's time we had a talk.'

'And this is not a very convenient place, I agree. Would you be willing to follow me back to the Krone Hotel? We should be able to find somewhere private there.'

'Lead the way,' I said, and wound up the window.

I swung the car round in a U and followed them.

'He's certainly a cool customer, your Hugo,' I said.

Elizabeth said nothing. Her mouth was set in a firm line.

At the hotel I let Hugo do the talking. He soon

arranged for us to have the use of a small private sitting room, recently vacated by some revelling wine buffs.

'May I introduce Willi Grossman, from Bonn,' Hugo said when we were inside. 'He kindly came down to assist me from the UN secretariat there.' Like hell. We shook hands and sat down.

'Willi, go and bring us some drinks, will you please?' he said. I wanted to keep Willi in my sight, but could hardly demur as I was about to try and convince Hugo that the whole business was of no great importance!

'Well, Mister Lockhart, the floor is yours!'

'On the contrary, Lansing, I think you owe us an explanation for tonight - to say nothing of what you are doing in Germany when you are supposed to be in Washington.'

He did not like that. I waited.

'I suppose it did seem a little strange, but there is a simple explanation for tonight's little - meeting,' he began.

I said nothing. I looked at Elizabeth to prevent her speaking.

'As you must be aware, my purpose in being here is, was, to find Elizabeth,' he went on, 'To-night as we left the Inn I thought I saw her - and you - in the mirror at the bar. Then you were walking out through the front door. I called on Willi and we followed but when we got outside you were nowhere to be seen. I thought I must have been mistaken, so we set off for this hotel where I had been told someone like Elizabeth had been seen. On the way Willi thought he saw a car following us, and I wondered again if it were you. I was afraid if we stopped you might drive on past and I'd lose contact again. Then I remembered the road up to the monument. We drove up there, knowing you would have to stop in the car park if you did follow. Well, of course, you did not, so I thought we had been mistaken. We were on our way back down here when I saw you in our headlights. Why did you stop, by the way?'

It was all very plausible. I might have been taken in by it, except for one thing. I recognised Willi for what he was.

'I'm sorry, Mister Lansing. I guess in my job you get suspicious of everybody. I was beginning to wonder what was going on, you leading us along a dead end road! You must have been quite surprised to see us parked at the side of the road. The fact is we were ... I'm afraid I've got to be rather ungallant and blame Miss Tasker. At the Inn and again up the road she was singularly ...'

'I just couldn't face you, Hugo,' she came in right on cue.

'Why ever not, my dear?' he asked.

'It wasn't the right time or place and ...' she turned to me, 'He was there!' She combined just the right amount of protest and scorn. Willi entered just then with our drinks. It gave me breathing space which I needed, and a brandy which I needed even more. It was the local one - rather a different flavour, but I liked it.

'Well, Mister Lockhart, Miss Tasker and I would like to talk - alone. Do you have any objection?' Hugo Lansing asked.

'No, why should I? But Miss Tasker may not feel up to it just yet. She has had a tiring day. You and she will have plenty of time to talk on the plane tomorrow.'

'On the plane?' He tried not to sound too surprised.

'Yes, I'm afraid my instructions were to escort Miss Tasker back to New York. I assume now that you have found her, you will be coming back with us?'

'Yes, of course, but is it really necessary to escort her back? You sound rather officious, if I may say so, Mister Lockhart.'

'These are my orders.' I tried to sound even more officious.

'I appreciate that, but surely there's no sort of, no question of a charge against her?'

'Not that I'm aware of.'

'Well, surely ... I can vouch for her. Is that not enough?'

'Not quite. You see - you, too, have been missed.'

'I see. I suppose I should have been in touch with the office, but my concern was for Elizabeth. I was rather worried about her.'

'I can understand that, Mister Lansing. I better tell you that Miss Tasker has told me everything.'

'You know ...'

'Yes, I know the extent of your relationship. I can appreciate the situation. Mine is a thankless task, but I do have my orders.'

'What about a private talk? There can't be any harm in that, surely?'

I turned to Elizabeth. She was smiling at him!

I stood up.

'I have no orders that say you can't speak to each other ' I grinned and my face felt lopsided or something. My head was pounding again - and circling, or something. I felt very sick. I looked at them. They were circling too. All three of them, round and round. Lansing and Elizabeth and Willi. I did not like the look on his face, but could not focus on it for long enough to determine what it meant. It reminded me of something. I took a step towards him, but could not feel my feet. He was grinning. I put my hand down towards my gun, but there was nothing from the waist down.

He caught me as I fell, and held me like a cotton wool vice. He lowered me to the ground. I heard voices:

'What's wrong? ... ill ... nasty blow ... car accident today ... doctor ... hospital ...' Then nothing. For a long time, nothing.

CHAPTER 29

When there was something, it was nasty. Still that pounding in the head, nausea in the stomach and not much anywhere else. I was blind. I could not see a finger in front of my nose. I tried not to panic. I vomited instead. That brought on flashing lights, but not the kind you can see by. I felt around. I was lying on a rough stone floor.

Then I began to remember how I came to be there - wherever that was. I remembered the look on Willi's face and knew what it meant. It was the same look that the guy had had just before he shot away my kidney. Evil personified.

'Elizabeth!' I croaked. No response. Was she there and unconscious - or worse? Or was I alone? I took several deep breaths and felt a little less hellish. I dragged myself to my knees and crawled round the floor.

Alone.

I sat up and rubbed my eyes. They did not FEEL blind. Slowly I stood up and felt my way round the walls until coming to a crack. The door. I put one eye to the gap at the floor, but in bending down my head began to swim again. I straightened up and there was light! Only a glimmer coming through a crack - but light!

I felt the rough wooden door and at eye level there was a grille about six inches square with three iron bars. Outside it was covered by a piece of wood - presumably a sliding panel. It was from the edge of this that I could see the tiny light.

With this evidence that I had not lost my vision, I felt less desperate. I began to think.

It must have been the brandy. How pathetic I had been to let Willi bring drinks like that. But there, in a hotel with so many people, and while we were still at the stage of trying each other out I had not been fully on guard.

Excuses! I had failed. I had failed Fox - and Elizabeth. I had failed her. Or had I? Was she even now laughing at my predicament, in the arms of Hugo Lansing? I tried to remember her face as I passed out. She had been saying something, something about a car accident. I must have been hearing things. No-one had had a car accident. I turned my thoughts to my present predicament. My cell appeared to be just that. Somewhere very old, by the feel of it.

One of the castles! Some were bound to be unoccupied. They must have gained access to this one with the express idea of using it for this purpose. More than likely it was not habitable. But all the better for a prison!

I felt in my pockets. Nothing. No chance of a light. I explored every inch. No furniture, no potential tools, not even a nail. My only hope of escape would be to surprise my jailer - presumably Willi. I felt round the door. It was a solid thing which would not move a millimetre. I poked my fingers through the bars at the hatch and it moved a little. I pushed against it and the tiny crack of light widened. There was just enough room to get a grip of two of the bars and I heaved on them with my feet against the door. All I got was more headache. I cursed and swore - and there was a little movement of the bar in my right fist. I drew breath and redoubled my efforts. I could feel the wood splintering as I wrenched until my head burst. Letting go the bar I felt for where the wood was giving way and picked at it with my fingers. Eventually a fairly large piece came away and underneath it the wood was no longer solid. Using the first splinter of wood as a chisel, I grafted away, gouging out the door where the bar was embedded. After about ten minutes I freed its lower end and, taking a fresh grip, pulled for all I was worth. Gradually, by pulling and pushing it in every direction, I loosened its upper anchorage also, and at last I was able to twist it loose altogether, and remove it.

Now at least I had an effective weapon - a piece of iron about ten inches long and sharpened at each end. Enough to kill a man. And I was in the mood for killing! I stabbed furiously at the base of the next bar along, but the wood there seemed hard. The blow made a noise which echoed round the cell. I raised my makeshift chisel again and a sound came before it descended. A footstep!

With my ear close to the little hatch, I listened. Someone was coming down a flight of stairs. More than one person. I pressed myself against the wall at the side of the door. A voice grunted and the hatch began to move. He would see the missing bar!

It opened only half an inch, then seemed to jam.

The voice cursed in German and a narrow shaft of light pierced the darkness. More muttering and the squeaking of a tight rusty bolt followed. I gripped the iron bar like a dagger and held my breath. The door swung open, and as more light flooded into the cell I saw someone step inside. I raised my weapon. It was Elizabeth!

She was suddenly propelled forward, stumbled into the far wall, the door shut and it was dark again. The hatch began to rattle and inched open.

I took three quick steps across the cell and lay down - very still. There was a knocking as the hatch was opened all the way with the help of a stone. A shaft of light landed on my face and I was hard put to it to keep my eyes closed. After about three seconds the hatch scraped back into place and the footsteps faded away.

'Elizabeth!' I whispered. There was a sharp in-take of breath.

'Who's that?' she asked in a croak.

'Lockhart. Are you all right?'

'If you can call it that. I thought you were dead.'

'It hasn't felt much different, but no, I'm still alive. What time is it by the way?'

'About six o'clock in the morning.'

I was sitting up by then and I stretched my hand out towards her. I touched her on the shoulder - and ran my hand down her arm. I gave her hand a squeeze. She began to sob.

'Come on, don't despair.' It was the only cliche I could think of.

She sniffed 'But you don't realise - I've told them everything. I thought you were dead.'

'I expect they knew most of it anyway. It's not your fault, it's mine, I should never have fallen for that old Mickey Finn thing - the brandy.'

'So it was drugged?'

'Of course it was. What else do you think made me pass out like that?'

'At first we, well, that is, I, thought you were ill. You had a big bruise on the side of your head and Hugo pointed to it and I said you must have had it in a car accident.'

'What car accident?'

'Well there wasn't one of course, but I couldn't let on about what happened at the farm. I was still trying to play Miss Innocent, remember.'

'What happened then?'

'We lay you on the couch and Willi went off to phone for an ambulance. I had a look at you and you certainly looked pretty ill. Then ...'

'Go on.'

'I fell asleep. I'm sorry.' She began sobbing again.

'Don't be. You probably had some too.'

'Some what?'

'The latest in knock-out drops. Methylthalassinate. I reckon I had about three times as much as you in my brandy. They gave you just enough to put you to sleep for a while. Right?'

'I suppose so. I woke after ... I don't know how long. You had gone and Hugo told me you'd been taken away in the ambulance.'

'And then?'

'I didn't feel too well. I went to the ladies and was sick. I thought it was the drinks on top of no food and ... everything else. When I came back Willi had returned. He said they had taken you to hospital. I wanted to go and see how you were, but Hugo persuaded me to wait and that he should try to find me a room so that I could get some sleep. I refused to go to bed - there wasn't a bed to go to in any case. He suggested taking me back to the Inn. You were right - he did have that room. Anyway we started talking and of course he asked me why I had flown to Germany.'

'Which, of course, was the whole point of getting me out of the way - to pump you on your own,' I said.

'I wondered that myself, but your illness seemed genuine enough. But I kept my end up. I told him I had been going to fly home to my mother to talk things over, but she hadn't been in when I phoned, and that on impulse I flew to Frankfurt and went to Rudesheim to sort of help me sort myself out with reference to him.'

'Sounds a bit weak.'

'It did to me, but there seemed some merit in that. It wasn't the sort of slick tale he found it impossible to believe.'

'And did he - believe it, I mean?'

'If he didn't completely fall for it he was certainly in some doubt. So I threw in what I thought would really convince him ...' She paused.

'Yes?'

'I told him I had missed a period.'

'You clever little minx. And you said you were no good at lying. You haven't, by the way, have you? Missed, I mean?'

'None of your business!'

'Sorry, go on. Wait a minute, what about Willi. How did he react to this bombshell?'

'Don't be stupid, I didn't say that in front of him. He had gone at the time.'

'Well Hugo then? What did he say?'

'Eh, let's just say he seemed to believe me.'

'So what went wrong?'

'Nothing, just then. He asked me where I had been, why he had been unable to find me in Rudesheim. I told him I had gone to see Uncle Simeon, about him being an expert at the British Museum. I thought the more true bits I could get in the more he would be likely to accept it. Then he asked me a strange question. He asked me if the Acme exhibition was still on.'

'The WHAT?' I gasped.

'The Acme exhibition. I'm sure that's what he said. Why? What does it mean?'

'Never mind, he was just testing you. What did you say?'

'What could I say? I've never heard of it, that's what I said.'

'OK, tell me the rest.'

'I said that you had caught up with me in London and that you were about to take me back to New York when you learned that he was here and that you had to come over and take him back too.'

'You did very well. I think I would have believed you!'

'He did. He told me that he had followed me from New York on impulse when he learned that I had come here. He said that he spent Monday and

Tuesday looking for me and had decided to give up and go home by today if he had not found me.'

'It all sounds very cosy. So how come you're here?'

She sighed 'Willi returned and whispered something to Hugo. I guessed something was up, but wasn't expecting it.'

'What?'

'He suddenly announced that you had died! I'm afraid that's when I gave myself away.'

'How?'

'I said, "No, not him too" or words to that effect. Hugo got hold of me and said, "What do you mean, who else had died?" I tried to bluff it out but he looked me straight in the eye and I could tell that he knew I was concealing something. Then Willi took over and was very nasty.'

'What did he do?'

'It wasn't so much what he did as what he threatened to do. Hugo told me I had better tell the truth or ...' she started sobbing again. I waited and said nothing. The sobbing subsided and I squeezed her hand.

'Hugo said that he would turn Willi loose on me if I didn't speak up.'

'The bastard!'

'And so say all of us,' she said very quietly.

'How much does he know?' I asked after a decent pause.

'I told him about you chasing me to the farm and about those men who tried to get me there. About Drummy Nugent - that he was the other man who had died.'

'What else?

'Only that after that you had said we had to find him to see whether or not he had been responsible.'

'Didn't you tell him that you suspected him all along and had flown to Rudesheim to prove he was an imposter?'

'No.'

'How did you get away with that? He must suspect that you know something of the kind.'

'He asked me - or rather ordered me to tell him, but I persisted with the story that I was just very mixed up and found him strange, that sort of thing. I avoided any specific suspicions. I emphasised that I had to decide about him because I was, well, pregnant.'

'Do you think he believed you?'

'He did after Willi ...'

I turned to look at her although I could not see a damned thing.

'After Willi what?' I asked very softly.

'It was back here. They brought me here first. Then Willi threatened to ... he said my condition was ... very vulnerable. He made me ... anyway, I broke down. I swore that I had told them everything.'

'But you hadn't.' I put my arm round her shoulders and held her close.

'No. I tried to hold back from telling what I know about Hugo. I reckoned that if I did it would leave them no alternative but to ... to kill me.'

'That's probably true. On the other hand, it may not make all that difference. They've shown their hand now and must be wondering whether it's worth keeping us alive. Maybe they reckon we could be used as hostages in some way. I don't want to wait to find out, that's for sure.'

I gave her an encouraging squeeze and crossed to the door. Using the iron bar I had already removed, I set to work on the one next to it.

'What are you doing?' she asked. I explained.

'Come and help. It's better than sitting and waiting for them, and we might be able to get out of here.'

After a few minutes I got the second bar out and gave it to her. I could get my fist through the gap now and went to work on the wooden panel. I could have smashed through it with the help of the iron tool, but had to keep the noise to a minimum. While trying to prise it open I asked her about where we were.

'It's an old castle. Up in the woods somewhere, about a mile from the monument. I couldn't see much in the dark. Upstairs it's a bit of a ruin, but there's one room that's habitable. It's got an old table and two or three chairs. No lights, just candles.'

'What about the door?'

'It's got a big iron bolt. That's all, I think.'

I was trying hard to prise open the little hatch, but it was not yielding more than an inch. I remembered that Willi had had to use a stone on it.

'Something must be preventing this bloody thing from opening.'

'Yes,' she said, 'He tried to look in before he opened the door, but couldn't get it to move more than a crack.'

'After he pushed you in he knocked it open with a stone, but it could only have been a short way or he would have noticed the missing bar. Now I can't open the bloody thing at all. Can you tell me the position of the room they're using, relative to this place?' I asked her.

'Up there I think,' she said, pointing up to the right of the door.

'Well, let's start here,' I said, feeling my way along the wall to what I took to be the opposite corner of the cell. 'This place is pretty old and half in ruins. Maybe we can dig our way out.'

'What? A tunnel?' she asked.

'No. We'll try to pick out the mortar and loosen some of the stonework.'

'That's a hell of a job, isn't it,?'

'We can't get that door open except perhaps by knocking out that panel at the hatch and that would make too much noise. Besides we'd still have to get the bolt open. If Willi's upstairs there's no way of getting out that way without attracting his attention. No, it'll have to be some digging. I'm not sitting waiting on him. We're only alive now because it suits their purpose. If that should change - we're finished.'

I was already at work with the bar, scraping out the crumbling mortar between the old stones. It offered little resistance and in minutes I had the first stone loose. As I prised it out a tiny shaft of light appeared. I handed the stone to Elizabeth. 'Lay that down quietly!' I ordered. Soon there was a sizeable pile of them on the floor and a hole in the wall at the level of my head. I stuck my hand through and felt another layer after a gap of about six inches. I scraped and gouged out one of them and handed it to her. Through this gap I could feel soft earth and, as it began to trickle down, some of the stones came loose and, before I could do anything about it, fell away into the gap between the two layers of wall. The noise echoed round the cell. I waited for some sort of response from above, but none came.

'There's no-one up there,' I whispered.

'Are you sure?'

'Don't you think they would have heard that?' I asked.

I turned to look at her. There was more light filtering through now and I could see her for the first time since Willi had pushed her into the cell.

She was a mess! Her blouse was torn and seemed to be missing some buttons. Her hair looked like a bird's nest gone wrong and, as she turned to face me I could see dried blood on her chin.

'You're no beauty yourself,' she said, and I was glad to see there was still some life in her lovely grey eyes.

I made for the door and started hacking at the hatch with my iron bar. It splintered and I soon had it out of the way. I thrust my arm through and stretched down the door on the other side. I could feel nothing. I used the piece of iron and felt it make contact with metal. I tapped away and discovered the lug of the bolt. I swung at it with the iron bar in my outstretched fingers and caught it a blow, but lost my grip in the process and dropped the bar.

'Damn the bloody thing, it's too tight. Give me your one.'

I swung with the other bar held firmly like a hammer, but could not free the bolt.

She began sobbing again. I was getting very angry. I marched back to the corner where we had been at work and stabbed wildly at the stones, loosening more and more, letting them tumble round my feet. I attacked the inner layer likewise and the stonework began to collapse inward. I jumped back and pushed Elizabeth to the other side of the cell.

The whole of the corner of the cell caved in and stones and dust filled the air, choking us.

When it subsided there was a hole clear to the sky. I clambered up the pile of stonework and looked up. I was looking up into the ruined part of the castle. Above me, embedded in the structure, was a smooth surface of some kind. I wiped it with my sweaty palm and it was solid, metallic - and menacing.

I had seen something like this before, in London years before. It was a bomb. An unexploded bomb!

Cautiously I stepped back down the rubble - and it gave way under my feet. I fell among it and looked up. The bomb stared down at me threateningly, but did not move. Slowly I backed away on all fours.

'Are you hurt?' Elizabeth asked and came towards me.

'Careful!' I rasped in a loud whisper, 'Keep still!'

'What's wrong?' she asked.

'There's a bomb up there! An unexploded bomb!'

'A what?'

'You heard me. A bomb, embedded in the outer wall. You said that part of the place is a ruin - now you know why! Christ knows where it came from.

'I think I know,' she said quietly.

'You do?'

'Yes. The RAF raided here during the war in an attempt to get the Germania thing. They missed it altogether. It was in the National Geographic.'

'Well, now we know what they did hit. If that bloody thing comes down now it could go off and we'll be two very late casualties of World War Two.'

I picked up a stone and once again thrust my arm through the hole I had made in the door. I stretched down as far as I could until I felt the blood supply almost cut off from my arm, and swung at the bolt. The second blow loosened it and the third and fourth freed it. I pulled the door inward very slowly in case it was holding the wall up, making a gap of only a foot or so. I pushed Elizabeth through and, pausing only to pick up my iron bar from the floor, I tip-toed out, drawing the door closed behind me. I pushed the bolt into place and looked around. To my left was the gap in the architecture, to my right a flight of stairs.

They were lit by the dawn flooding in through the ruin and at the top was a door. It gave the impression of being solid and it was not locked. Elizabeth was right behind me as I opened it. I stepped into the room she had described. There were the table and chairs, and in the big old fireplace Willi stood, his gun pointing straight at me. There was a very satisfied grin on his face.

CHAPTER 30

My head was at it again, and for an instant I could see two Willis. I was barely able to stop myself rushing at him like a wild animal. Instead I just stood there, feeling very deflated indeed.

'Guten morgen!' he said, waving us into the room with his gun.

'Sit!' he ordered, indicating two chairs in the middle of the room. We sat.

'So, you are thinking to escape. You make me finish my sleep! What a noise you give!' His voice leered at us and he came across to within three feet or so. I measured the distance and wondered about trying a dive at him. He circled out of range and went behind Elizabeth's chair. I watched as he pulled her arms through the back and deftly tied her wrists together with a length of wire, the whole time keeping his gun firmly against her back. I was powerless.

He repeated the same with me. "At least he's not going to kill us," I thought. Not yet.

Back at the fireplace he said, 'And now we wait. To see whether you live or ...' he waved the gun in the air.

I wondered why he had let us go through the pantomime of escaping. Sheer bloody sadism. He certainly was enjoying it. I felt sick. At the same time as fighting off the nausea, I was trying to figure out the situation. He must be waiting for Lansing to come. From making contact with his ... whoever.

When he returned it would either be hostage time for us or ... what was it called? - "The Long Goodbye!" I looked round at Elizabeth. That would be the worst of it. Having to say goodbye ... if I were given the time. She had a face like stone. Keeping my upper arms as still as I could I tried to get my fingers to work on the twisted wire. I might as well have sung "Rule Britannia!"

The sound of a car broke into the silence. A couple of minutes later Hugo Lansing walked in. He looked at the two of us tied in our chairs with surprise, then said to Willi:

'We have one hour. We must make it count.'

Without more ado he walked up to me and slapped me hard across the mouth. All hell was let loose inside my skull. I saw two, three, four Hugo Lansings, then he quivered back to one again and I heard his booming voice asking:

'What is ACME?' The sound echoed round my brain, repeating itself again and again.

Another wave of nausea washed over me, and I turned my head and retched.

'Stop it! Stop it, damn you!' Elizabeth shouted at him, 'Haven't you done enough damage already, you pitiless bastard!'

Hugo took a step towards her then changed his mind.

'Willi.' he said, 'If she interferes again, shoot her. Did you hear that, Lockhart? If you want precious Miss Tasker to go on breathing ... TALK!' I lifted my head and looked into his eyes. He meant it.

'What do you want to know?' My mouth was as dry as a stick of chalk, and I could hardly speak.

'That's better!' He sounded very pleased with himself.

'Now, what comes after Amarillo and Casper?'

I did not know what the hell he was talking about!

'Come on!' he yelled at me, 'Amarillo, then Casper, then where?'

He slapped me again and I felt myself passing out - into a sickening black void. In - and out again. I could just see his threatening face close to mine. I willed myself to go under again to avoid his questions. If I could pass out ... then I remembered Elizabeth and struggled to stay compus mentis. Amarillo, Casper - they must be the initials of place names. That left M and E.

I could think of nowhere that began with these letters! I made a gagging noise - without much difficulty. Hugo gestured to Willi.

'Give him a drink.'

He looked at his watch. Willi came over with a bottle of beer from a few he had in the fireplace. He lifted it to my lips. It tasted like the nectar of the gods. His face was close to mine and I saw that look again. More than that. I remembered the face from somewhere. His eyes met mine and for an instant, fear flickered through them. He hurried away and Hugo stepped towards me again.

'Well, what's the rest?'

'The rest?' I countered, trying to sound puzzled.

'Acme, the rest of Acme. The other two places,' he said quietly.

'You mean after Amarillo and Casper?'

'Stop playing for time, Lockhart. Nobody's coming to your rescue.'

'So why should I tell you? You'll kill us anyway.' Even as I said it, I tried not to believe it.

'No. If you tell me, I'll go away and leave you here. There's a chance someone will happen by in the fullness of time.' He smiled - if you can call it that.

'Go lick your ass!' I said, and tensed myself for another brain swilling blow. It did not come. Instead he leaned forward and whispered in my ear:

'If you don't tell me, Willi will go over to Elizabeth and ...' The threat he uttered was of such obscenity as to make me want to vomit in his face. I tried hard, but could not manage it.

'The other two names!' he said from a safe distance.

I looked at Elizabeth. Her eyes were on Hugo and from their expression I guessed she had heard what he said. How I wished looks really could kill!

But Hugo was not looking in her direction, but at me. I could stall no longer, but I could, with a bit of luck, confuse him.

'You wouldn't believe me if I told you that I didn't know the other names, would you?' I asked with a poor attempt at a smile.

'No, Lockhart, I would not. Now stop these delaying tactics and tell me or I swear I'll let Willi loose!'

Willi stepped towards Elizabeth right on cue.

'Memphis and Encino,' I said in a whisper.

'Louder please, I didn't hear,' said Hugo, his

voice rising in a crescendo. He came towards me. This time, I thought, this time. As he bent towards me I drew back my right foot and measured the distance to his scrotum.

'Don't tell him!' It was Elizabeth, and her interruption made him turn away just as I was about to let him have it!

He struck her with the back of his left hand and she crashed over on the floor. He turned back to me.

'That is positively her last chance, Lockhart. Now give me those names again!'

'Memphis and Encino,' I said, and let my shoulders slump in a gesture of utter defeat.

He smiled triumphantly and went over to Willi at the fireplace. He took a bottle of beer and drank from it, then held a conversation with Willi. Elizabeth lay still on the floor, her eyes closed.

I was working furiously at the wire round my wrists, but with little success. At least if we were not going to get out alive I had given him a couple of names that meant nothing. Whatever Acme was, he wanted a couple of names to complete it, and I had supplied him with the first two that had come into my head. Now, no doubt he would be off hot-foot to his masters with the knowledge.

Then I remembered! Remembered the big guy at the airport. "Tight as a Jew's purse" he had said. So he could not get away with the information! And at midnight - if he was not on the plane - bingo! No Hugo Lansing! I felt like laughing.

He was coming towards me again.

'I think it's time to say goodbye Mister Lockhart,' he said, as though he were leaving a party.

Behind him I could see Willi, gun at the ready.

'Elizabeth first, I think, don't you? Before she wakes up, that would be kindest.'

'So your word's as false as the rest of you?' I said.

He stopped

'You know, then? How very clever of you. Or did she find out? I wonder how ... in any case, it's not going to help you.'

'And where do you think you're going when you've killed us?' I asked.

'Home,' he said, but a slight frown showed on his brow.

Willi was standing over Elizabeth, straining like a hound on the leash. She groaned and opened her eyes.

'You had better tell Willi to wait,' I said, 'Or you won't be going anywhere.'

'Hugo ... please.' She spoke with such feeling I could have wept. He put his hand on Willi's forearm and pushed it down slowly. He looked down at Elizabeth, and I knew he could not do it.

'You better not kill either of us,' I said, 'You see ... '

'Shut up, Lockhart, you interfering bastard,' he snarled.

'I'm trying to save your life, Lansing, you fool. If you kill us there's no way you're going to get away from here.'

At last I had his attention.

'What drivel is this?' he asked.

'I was sent here to take you back alive. If we

don't go out of Rudesheim together - you don't get out alone.'

He looked at Willi.

'Send him to try - if you can trust him, that is,' I threw in.

Willi did not like that. He stepped towards me, but Hugo restrained him and turned to me.

'It's true, Hugo,' Elizabeth spoke.

'What's true, my dear?' he asked as he set her upright again, complete with chair.

'They've orders to ...' I started to speak, but he rounded on me and delivered another of his favourite backhands. My head began again, and I felt myself going under.

'... he said they had the place all sown up and there was no way you could get out.' Elizabeth finished speaking as I came round.

Hugo looked at her for a long moment, then turned to Willi, and took him over to the fireplace. They whispered for a minute or so, then Hugo left.

'Where's your master gone then?' I asked Willi after a couple of minutes. He said nothing, but sat down, drawing a travelling rug round his shoulders. It was the one from my car.

'Will he be long?'

Still no reply.

'Perhaps he's not coming back. Maybe he's already on his way to ... wherever.' I was not sure of how much English he knew, but that got a reaction.

'While you were sleeping here in this cold damp old place he was probably in a nice warm bed somewhere - or in a ...'

'Close your mouth!' he rasped.

'Come now Willi, don't tell me the thought has not occurred to you. I know you're not very clever but ...' That got to him.

He stood up and came towards me. I could see the look in his eye and I tensed myself for the blow that had to come. At the last moment he stepped to one side and struck Elizabeth across the mouth. More blood on her chin - and more gall for me.

I was quiet after that. In silence I mouthed an apology to Elizabeth. Willi sat down again and seemed to doze for a while, but after twenty minutes or so he stole a glance at his watch. I had to risk it again.

'Long time, isn't he? It does take a long time to make arrangements, but ...' I turned to Elizabeth, 'I don't think Hugo is coming back, do you?' She shook her head. I went on. 'You have been left, Willi, had for a sucker.' I searched in my memory for the right word: 'Ein trottel.'

He came across to me and I silently apologised to her again. But no blow fell. Instead he looked at me with a smug grin and said, 'No, he is not going without me. The arrangements he is making. You, too, he will not stay here.'

So - now we were not to be killed. Hugo had other plans for us. Use us as hostages? Not if I could help it.

'Where are you from, Willi? East Berlin? Leipzig?' Small reaction. 'Wouldn't you rather live in the West? Much nicer in the West. Lots of things to spend your money on. Lots of girls, Willi. Or do you prefer boys?'

'Shut your filthy mouth' he said, his face contorting.

'I could arrange it. Think of it, a home in the West. No more shortages while the big guys like him get all the privileges. You help us and I'll help you. A pardon, ein begnadigung. Who knows, I might even be able to get you to America, like Lansing.'

That made him think. He looked at his watch again. I waited. He took a swig from one of the beer bottles in the fireplace.

'Do yourself some good, Willi. Plenty of that in the West. Good beer - for everyone. You're not a Party member, are you? No special privileges for you. No - they keep all the good things for the Gauleiters - and their Russian masters.'

He came towards me, the beginnings of a smile on his face. Trying to decipher that look, I searched around for a telling phrase that would swing it our way. Nothing came. Then Elizaheth spoke.

'I would be most grateful, Willi, really I would.' She smiled at him.

He turned to her - and with a vicious snarl began slapping her face.

'Women! Liars, cheats! ...' With a mouthful of German abuse he rained blows on her face.

I stood up, chair and all, and launched myself bodily at him. My head hit him in the side and he fell with me on top. I tried to smother him and butt him in the face but he got his hands round my throat. Elizabeth scraped along the floor and kicked him in the side of the head. And again. He let go of me and grabbed at her ankles. I brought my knee up into his groin and butted him again, but the pain in my head was awful and I began to go dizzy. He pushed me to one side, but the chair at my back caught on his shoulder. I threw myself backwards and used it to pin him to the ground.

'Get his gun,' I shouted, 'It's on the table!'

She set off towards it, but Wili, with an almighty heave, launched me bodily through the air, and I cannoned into her. We fell in a tangled heap. I tried to trip him up, but Willi made it to the table - and his gun.

He picked it up, cocked it and turned round with a face that was a mixture of pain and fury. He raised it towards me. I could see two of the bloody things. What a way to go!

'Nein,' he said slowly, 'Is too qveek.'

Keeping at a safe distance he circled us and lifted another beer bottle to his lips. He drank the lot.

'Up, UP!' he ordered, and I struggled to my feet and slumped back into the chair, still tied at my back. Elizabeth did the same.

Willi wiped his mouth with the back of his hand and went over to her, his gun pointing at her heart.

He leaned towards her and put his lips to hers. She did not move a muscle.

'So, you will be nice to Willi, yah?' He spat on the floor.

Holding her jaw firmly in his left hand, and with his gun still in her ribs, he bent forward again. He kissed her, horribly. I watched his gun, waiting for it to waver off target before diving at him again. It was difficult because things were not steady in front of my eyes. Elizabeth was moving, he was moving - everything seemed to be ... beyond them I thought I could see the door moving. Willi straightened up, and as he did so, grabbed hold of her blouse. He wrenched at it furiously, tearing most of it off, and looked down at her.

'Yah, you will be ... very nice to Willi.' He laughed - and the gun wavered!

Before I could get to him the door flew open with a crash and he swung round and fired at it. At the same moment Elizabeth's foot struck home at his kneecap. He was half way to the floor when I landed on top of him. Then everything went swimmy again. A shadowy figure did a moon-walk towards me and I passed ... out ... again.

When I came round I felt very sick - and belched - and felt better. I was sitting against the wall with the travelling rug round my shoulders and Elizabeth was holding a bottle of beer to my lips. Someone was bending over Willi and securing his wrists behind his back. The figure straightened up and turned round. It was Paolo Entes!

CHAPTER 31

'We must get you to a hospital, my friend,' he said, a faint smile on his face.

'Never mind hospital,' I protested, 'What the hell are you doing here? Not that you aren't most welcome! Most very bloody welcome!'

Elizabeth started sobbing - again. She was smiling too. Women!

'Here,' he said, 'This is better than beer,' and produced a flask. The brandy tasted heavenly, and I immediately felt better.

'Where's Hugo Lansing?' he asked.

'I don't know, but Willi there was expecting him to return soon, so we had better prepare a welcome,' I said.

'That shouldn't prove too difficult,' said Paolo. 'We'll get him out of the way and ...'

'Except for the bomb,' Elizabeth said quietly.

'My God, I'd forgotten,' I exclaimed.

'What bomb?' Entes asked, already on his way across to Willi.

'There's an unexploded bomb buried in the side of this castle. We tried to dig our way out of the dungeon and exposed it.'

'Unexploded bo ... that'll be from the RAF raid,' he said, nodding sagely.

'How come everybody knows about this place but me?' I asked in mock indignation.

'Homework, my friend, you must do your homework!'

'So you are on a job. I thought it must be that.'

'You've been after Hugo all along, haven't you?' Elizabeth asked. Entes nodded. She smiled and said, 'And I thought ...'

'It was very pleasant research, I assure you,' he replied.

'Look here, you two,' I said, rising to my feet.

'Yes, of course, time for that later,' Entes said. 'Where's the dungeon? We'll put him there ...'

'Next to the bomb,' Elizabeth added, with satisfaction.

'Why not?' I said, grabbing hold of Willi's bonds. Paolo had done a very professional job. Willi could only express himself with his eyes, but they said it all. They held more menace than a cobra's. Leaving Elizabeth to listen in case Hugo returned, we manhandled him down the steps and pushed him into the dungeon. There was light in there now and our demolition work could be seen in the corner - in the middle of which was the dull dark shape of the bomb. I took him by his bonds and dragged him over to the pile of rubble we had made underneath it. Willi did not like that. Not one little bit. His eyes were different now, looking up at the bomb. We left him thus and Paolo closed the door. As an afterthought I hammered home the bolt with a stone and we went back up the stair to rejoin Elizabeth.

She was nowhere to be seen!

The door to the outside lay open. Paolo and I looked at each other, sharing the same awful thought. In the distance we heard a car starting up. We dashed for the door. He got there ahead of me and I bumped into him on the way through. He fell to the ground and I helped him up. Outside I saw the lie of the land for the first time. The castle stood near the top of the steep slope, a path running about twenty-five yards up to the woods. As we raced up I shouted:

'Did you come by car?'

'No, on foot,' Paolo replied, 'Up by the cable car and past the monument.'

When we reached the top we could just see a car receding round a bend in the rough track that ran through the forest.

'Come on,' he yelled, 'Let's try this one,' and made for my car which stood just off the road. He pulled out a set of car keys.

'I took these off Willi,' he said, 'And this.' He threw me a Luger as he got into the car.

For a change it started at the first attempt and the wheels threw up a deluge of leaves and dirt as we took off. The car ahead was going west - towards Assmanshausen along a dirt road used by maintenance vehicles and not intended for fast driving. Paolo handled the car like a rally driver and began to gain ground. After half a mile we rounded a bend and could see clearly the car ahead. I wound down my window and held the gun out, aiming it at their wheels. Before I could get a shot in, our car weaved bumpily out of a rut and I lost aim. Elizabeth appeared at the back window and I hesitated in case I could not keep the bullet low. Then they were screened by trees again.

'There's someone in the back beside her!' Paolo

shouted.

'Yes, holding her at the window. It's not Lansing. He must be driving.'

'D'you know where this road leads?' he asked.

Assmanshausen, a village down on the river. It's not far,' I replied.

We turned a bend after them and the back end of our car swung sideways into a tree with a clunking and tearing. We kept going but lost sight of our quarry. Paolo stood on the gas and we charged off again, skidding and bumping over the rough surface. I thought I could see them up ahead, but was not sure. Then we rounded a bend - and the road divided.

Paolo stood on the brakes and shouted, 'Which way?'

The track was wet now and we went into a skid.

'Left,' I shouted, hoping to keep us moving. Unfortunately the left fork turned out to be a sharper bend than it seemed, and try as he might he could not keep the car on the road. We skidded off and crashed through between two saplings and came to a shuddering halt among the lowest branches of a pine. The steering wheel took Paolo's weight and I held onto the door, banging my side against the dashboard on impact. I had avoided going into the windscreen, but my head did not seem to realise this, for it started its throbbing and spinning again.

'You all right?' asked Paolo.

'Yeah, okay. Can you get this thing going again?'

He restarted the car and put it into reverse, but we were jammed up against the branches on my side and there was not enough traction from the wheels on the soft loamy surface to pull us away. With a muttered Portuguese oath, he gave up. Back at the junction we found their tracks - going to the right, needless to say.

'I'm sorry,' I said, 'But I thought ...'

He waved away my apology and trotted off along the road, gesturing me to follow. I fell into step beside him.

'You never did explain how you came to be here,' I said.

'I've been watching Hugo Lansing for months.'

'You've what?' I asked.

'Just that. We got a tip ...'

'Who's WE?'

'The CIA.'

'You're with the CIA?'

'Don't sound so surprised. We're not all Ivy-leaguers, nor Americans, come to that.'

'I should have been told that you were ...'

'Come, come, you know what Security's like. The right hand doesn't tell the left hand what's going on, never mind the feet!'

I knew what he meant.

The jogging was not helping my head, and I had to slow down. We were nearing the end of the trees and could see a gate ahead. Beyond it was an open space that looked like a car park, but there were no vehicles to be seen. I slowed to a walk and Paolo did likewise.

'You go on,' I said, 'Try to pick up their trail. Get a car if you can. I'll follow and make for the village. There's a cafe overlooking the river. It's called the Rhinegau. Get in touch there if possible. If I'm not there I'll leave a message.'

I must have seemed all-in for he looked at me with concern, but realised my suggestion was the only thing to do.

'OK my friend. Good luck!' he said, and with a quick squeeze of my hand he was off like a middle-distance athlete. He soon reached the gate and swung himself neatly over it.

I followed rather slowly, and cursed myself for not keeping fitter. After a few yards a path crossed the track and I remembered it from the last time I had been there. I turned left off the road towards Assmanshausen, and in a few minutes I saw the top end of the chair-lift down the mountain. The last thing I felt like was another mid-air ride, but it was the quickest way down. It was still early and the morning smell of the trees was very pleasant. For the second time in three days I thought how pleasant it would be to stroll there at leisure. I realised I was doing the same thing as before - looking for Elizabeth ...

I pressed on and reached the top of the chair-lift. There was no-one about as I stood there waiting for the next one round to lift me by the backside and swing me from the ground. I pulled the safety bar across in front of me and tensed myself as I gained height. Then that awful moment when it reached the start of the descent, and lurched out over nothing.

Below me, past the treetops, I could see the river where there were already quite a few boats on the go. Further downstream I could see the tip of an island in midstream. Then the view was cut off as I descended. Although my head ached, it did not seem to mind the height as much as on the first journey down the mountain. I could hardly believe it had been only three days before. It seemed like half a lifetime since I had set out in search of Elizabeth. The thought of her brought me back to the present, and I began to wonder if I would ever see her again.

My only hope was if they had some reason for staying longer in the district. Otherwise ... my thoughts were interrupted by a helicopter which emerged from behind me and rattled its way over the river. I tried to see its insignia, but the sun in my eyes prevented me. At the end of my air-borne journey I hopped off the chair-lift and made my way to the river front. There were a few people about and I received some very queer looks. I wondered why until I realised what a God-awful mess I must have looked!

The Rhinegau cafe was not yet open, and I began to feel the acute discomfort of hunger. I found my way to a bread shop only to discover that I had no money. Paolo had provided me with a gun taken from Willi, but must have been unable to find my wallet. I wondered if he had had any more success in tracking Elizabeth and her captors than I. They did not appear to be in Assmanshausen. My feet led me back down to the river, and I leaned on the railing looking out across the river, wondering what to do next. It was now quite busy with craft of all kinds going in all directions. A smart looking launch came in to the side and tied up at the steps below me.

The only occupant, a man in a leather trench coat, mounted the steps and then saw me. He took out a cigarette and came towards me waving it, looking for a light. I shook my head.

'Sorry,' I said, spreading my empty hands. He came quite close before seeming to understand. He grinned and I could see two rows of teeth.

'Mister Lockhart, I am pointing a gun straight at you,' he said, making a suitable gesture from within his pocket, 'Accompany me - now, without hesitation - or I shall shoot you right here. I would have minimum difficulty in getting away in that boat.'

His eyes bore into mine, and I had minimum difficulty in believing him!

CHAPTER 32

The journey in the launch was short - out to the island in the middle of the river. He did not bother to search me, but I had no chance to get at my gun, far less use it. He made me hold onto a rail at the front, promising to shoot me if I let go with either hand.

The launch took us right into a large boathouse at one end of the island. Once inside he took me ashore at gun-point and up a flight of steps. At the top were two doors. The one straight ahead had a glass top and I could see a path leading to a large house. He opened the other one, on the right, and pushed me into a bare room with a bench running round the walls. It was for all the world like a third class waiting room in an old-fashioned British railway station.

At the far end sat Elizabeth and Hugo. She gave a little gasp as I tumbled in.

'How good of you to join us, Lockhart,' Hugo said without bothering to get up. 'Well done!' he added, in the direction of my captor.

I overbalanced and fell to my knees, trying hard to fumble into my pocket for the gun. My fingers found it and wrapped themselves round the butt. I began to rise, felt for the trigger - then all hell was let loose in my head, as I was struck from behind and I pitched forward into a deep, dark trough.

When I emerged from it I found my self lying

curled up on the floor of the boathouse, my hands tied behind my back. I blinked a few times to focus my eyes, and looked up. Elizabeth knelt beside me, similarly bound. I struggled to a sitting position.

'Are you all right?' she asked, 'I'm sorry, that's a stupid question.'

'Never mind, it's nice to hear your voice. What's been happening?'

'Hugo and the other man are up at the house. I think they're making arrangements ...' she broke off.

'No, our time hasn't come yet. If so, they would have killed us already. They're going to use us as hostages to ensure their own getaway. We're no use to them dead.' I tried to sound convincing - to myself as well as her.

'What happened back at the castle?' I asked.

'While you were downstairs with Willi, I heard a noise outside, went to the door and ...'

'They grabbed you.'

'I'm sorry.'

'Don't apologise. All things considered, you've come through all this with flying colours. After all, it's not your scene. I'm the one who should be putting up a better show, but I'm afraid I'm rather out of my depth. Every time we get anywhere I end up un-bloody-conscious. I've achieved nothing but to prove a minor nuisance to them.'

'What happened to Paolo?' she asked.

'We chased you in my car, but due to my bungling, took the wrong fork and went off the road. We couldn't get the car going again and I was slowing him down on foot so we split up. Then I remembered about the chair-lift and came down to Assmanshausen that way. It doesn't look as though he was able to keep up with them. We made a rendezvous at a cafe, but of course I'm not there, am I?'

I twisted my neck to and fro in a vain attempt to ease the pain in my head, and in so doing noticed for the first time a grubby window high in one wall of the room. I stood up and struggled onto the wooden form that ran round the walls. The window was too high for me to break it by reaching up with my elbow. On tip-toe I could just get my head up to it. I rubbed at it with my hair and wiped away some of the grime. Outside I could see the river, busier now, and the other bank beyond. A helicopter spun towards us and we heard it go on towards Rudesheim. I wondered whether it was the same one I had seen before. There was only one way I was going to break the window. Closing my eyes tightly I drew back my head and banged it against the pane. The result was a clear win for the window. I slumped against the wall and prepared to try again.

'There's someone coming!' Elizabeth croaked.

Before I could get down the door was unlocked and Hugo walked in.

'Brave effort, Lockhart, but I shouldn't think anyone will hear you. Now GET DOWN!' He waved a gun at me. I sat down.

'There's no need to be impatient. Alexei is making one or two last-minute arrangements and we'll be off soon.'

'And us, Hugo, what are you going to do with us?' asked Elizabeth.

'Oh, but you're coming with us, my dear. Wouldn't dream of leaving you behind.' He dropped the gun into a pocket.

'So you think you can get away from here?' I asked, trying to sound confident that he could not.

'Yes, Lockhart. It was good of you to tell me that your colleagues had the place bottled up - or so they thought. But our resources are not so limited.'

'OUR resources?' I asked.

'Yes, the resources of the ...'

'He's a bloody Russian!' Elizabeth put in.

'How very perceptive of you, Elizabeth. Yes, I'm a Russian. There's no harm in you knowing now, Lockhart, for all the good it will do you.'

I wondered why I had never thought of it before. She had. How had they made the switch - and when?

'I can see you're puzzled. Some day, when we've more time, I'll tell you all about it,' he said, condescendingly.

'What's your real name?' asked Elizabeth. 'I never did like Hugo.'

'Rudolf. Rudolf Vorotnikov.'

'I prefer Hugo,' she said, looking him straight in the eye.

'That's typical,' he said, 'That you should prefer the illusion to the real thing.' His voice had gone hard again.

'And how long do you think you could have kept it up?' I asked.

'You fool, you insignificant fool, Lockhart,' he

said, 'Haven't you got the picture yet? There never was a Hugo Lansing. I'M Hugo Lansing, have been for twenty-eight years!'

So that was it! I decided to go on annoying him.

'And now you've blown it! Let a woman find you out! They'll be ever so pleased with you back in the Kremlin!' I said, trying my best to gloat. That got home - and I felt better. Not for long. He came towards me with evil in his eye.

'Hugo, stop, for God's sake, if you've any feelings at all ...' Elizabeth cried out. He looked at her and stopped.

'You know I have feelings,' he said quietly. She looked away. He glanced at his watch.

'Couldn't you just ... leave us here?' Elizabeth asked, her voice barely audible.

'You've got a hell of a nerve, appealing to my better nature. If it wasn't for your snooping and mistrust ...' he barked.

'... You two would have gone on playing happy families back in New York,' I put in.

'Your mouth must get you into an awful lot of trouble, Lockhart.'

'It has been known to happen, Lansi ... sorry, Vorotnikov,' I said.

'And you're the best they can find? Huh!'

'You're hardly in a position to scoff. Blowing your cover to a dame. Now you're on the run. I'd get a move on if I were you, otherwise ...'

'Don't kid yourself, Lockhart, nobody's coming to your rescue. It's only a matter of time and we'll be gone.'

'Couldn't you at least get us something to

drink?' asked Elizabeth.

'Sorry, my dear, you'll just have to wait - both of you.'

He sat down near the door at the other end of the room. There was silence in that strange empty boathouse. Outside there were the sounds of the river, and above them the hooter of a train and the whittering of another helicopter.

'How very cosy!' I said.

'Oh, shut up, Lockhart!' said Elizabeth.

Women!

'How old are you, Hugo? I'm not going to call you anything else,' she asked, looking at him with the faintest trace of a smile.

'You guessed about the age then. I'm fifty this year.' He spoke to her as though I was on another planet, 'What else was it that made you suspect? It couldn't have been just that.'

'There were quite a few small things, none very important on their own. At a movie once you said you remembered an event which must have occurred when you were - at least supposed to be - only two. Then you talked about the Germania monument, you know, Miss Moselle, and later I saw an article about it in National Geographic, and somehow it didn't fit with what you'd said and ...'

'So you came flying over here to take a look-see. If only you'd kept your suspicions to yourself - if only ... we could have ... it was ...'

With my left hand I was pulling the hem of my jacket round behind me, trying to get to the pocket at my back. They had left the gun there! If I could get it and point it at him, even with my hand tied

... They were still talking.

'... and once I got a helluva surprise - it was at that reception for the Leningrad Symphony Orchestra - when my Uncle Boris appeared. He's an Administrator with them. I thought he was going to blow the whole thing.' He gave a sort of stifled laugh.

'You spoke to that Russian cultural guy that night, didn't you?' Elizabeth asked.

'You saw that? I didn't think you would notice.'

He stood up and walked towards her, quite oblivious of me. I curled my fingers round the butt of the Luger, but it had partially fallen through the pocket lining, and I could not disentangle it. Suddenly the door of the boathouse leading to the garden could be heard opening, and immediately afterwards the door of our room rattled. There was a mutter of Russian and Hugo turned and went to the door. As he turned the key in the lock I made a desperate attempt to get my gun pointed at him through the pocket round my left hip.

'Don't open it!' I barked at him. He swung round to look at me. But I was too late and the door flew open.

Paolo Entes walked in!

CHAPTER 33

Paolo thrust a gun into Hugo's ribs and said, 'Keep very still, Lansing, and your hands on your head.'

He took Hugo's gun and threw it out the door. I heard it splash into the water below. He pushed Hugo to the wall and sat him down. Backing up towards me he took out a penknife and cut my bonds.

'What about the other one - up at the house?' I asked.

'He won't give us trouble for a while. I'm sorry for taking so long, but it was some job catching up with you on this island. I thought you must be at the house, so I went there first,' he said, as he freed Elizabeth. He took a length of cord from a pocket and ordered Hugo to turn around. He had difficulty tying the knots while holding the gun, so I said, 'Give me the gun.'

He looked at me for a moment then handed it to me. I trained it on Hugo's head whilst Paolo finished tying him up.

When the job was done I stepped back, and was about to hand Paolo his gun when Elizabeth pushed past me and shoved Hugo onto the seat. He looked up at her and smiled. He opened his mouth to say something, but it never got out because she gave him one helluva smack across the face.

Her grey eyes were on fire and there was a look on her face that I had never seen before. He did not like it, either.

'Come on,' said Paolo, 'Up to the house.' Elizabeth turned away from Hugo.

'Can't we just get away from here?' she pleaded, sounding as if she might start sobbing again.

Paolo waved us out and locked the door of the room, leaving Hugo sitting there with a decidedly deflated look on his face.

'I want to get up to the house to use the phone,' said Paolo.

I put the gun away and took Elizabeth by the arm, saying, 'Hang on just a little longer, and let's make sure we get this lot rounded up. We don't want them getting away ...'

'I don't give a damn!' she said. 'What the hell do I care if they do? I just never want to set eyes on him again. Why don't we just go and let the police take them in?'

'Because they've got diplomatic passports and might be able to talk their way out of it,' Paolo explained.

I pushed her in front of me and we headed up the path towards the house. I blinked in the sunlight and looked around. The island was quite deserted, but the river all around was playing host to numerous craft of all sizes, tiny dinghys, tourist-heavy pleasure boats and long gloomy barges. We were just beyond the bend in the river and could see the outskirts of Assmanshausen on one side and grape green slopes on the other.

The back of the house faced us and we went in

by the kitchen. Elizabeth and I fell about some beer and sausage we found in the fridge, while Paolo went to check on Trench-coat, and make a phone call.

'My contact will not be there for fifteen minutes. We must wait,' he said when he re-appeared.

'Let's go somewhere more comfortable,' I suggested, and we made for the sitting room. On the way there he showed me Trench-coat - neatly trussed up in a cupboard under the stairs.

Elizabeth tapped me on the arm and pointed upstairs. I said, 'Yes and why don't you go somewhere and lie down, you look all in. I'll keep Paolo company.' He nodded in agreement.

'Yes, I was going to do just that,' she replied and gave me a wistful little smile. When she had gone upstairs I took off my jacket and put it over a chair-arm.

'Oh, by the way, here's your gun back,' I said to Paolo, pulled his Luger from a pocket and tossed it to him. I badly needed a drink, and to my delight Paolo had found some. It was the local brandy again and it tasted better than ever. Then I remembered the last time I had drank some, and I made a face.

'Something wrong?' asked Paolo. I grinned.

'No, it's fine,' I replied. I was thinking of Willi next to that bomb. I took another sip of brandy and through the bottom of the glass I could see Paolo. He set his glass down on the table between us and lifted up his gun. Holding it in his hand for a moment, he gave me a funny look and laid it down again.

'Did you know that Hugo Lansing's a Russian?' I asked.

His eyebrows shot up, then he nodded.

'I thought maybe he was,' he said.

'You knew?' How come everyone knew but me, I thought.

'Well, I suspected it for a while,' he said.

'How did you tumble to it?'

'Because of "Peter and the Wolf",' was his cryptic reply.

I did not bother to ask him to elucidate.

'You and Elizabeth got to know each other quite well, I believe,' I said.

'Yes, it was all in the line of duty for me, but very pleasant duty! I'd been nosing around for a while and I thought the best way was to strike up an acquaintanship with her. We went to a few concerts, no more.'

That was rich, I thought, someone had suspected Hugo Lansing all along. Fox would be pleased! I had forgotten about Fox.

'Have some more,' Paolo said, and poured me some brandy He glanced at his watch.

Something at the back of my mind bothered me, but I could not figure out what it was.

'D'you know what A-C-M-E stands for - what it means?' he asked suddenly.

'Where d'you get that from?' I asked, unable to keep the surprise from my voice.

'It's got something to do with all this, I feel sure. I came across it while I was snooping around Hugo's office in New York,' he replied.

'No, I don't know what it means, I really don't,'

I smiled.

'Come on, you must. That's why you followed Hugo here, isn't it?'

'What gave you that idea?'

'Why else did you come chasing across the Atlantic?'

'I simply came after Elizabeth.'

'But you hardly know her!'

For a CIA wallah he was being pretty stupid!

'I was just following orders. Ours not to reason why ... etc.'

'And ACME really doesn't mean anything to you?'

I shook my head. He laughed.

'You're not kidding me, are you?' he asked, looking quite serious again. Before I could answer the phone rang. He mumbled something under his breath and went out.

I sipped my brandy and looked out the window across the river Soon it would be all over and I could sleep. HOW I wanted to sleep! But that would come later. I rose and lifted my jacket from the chair-arm where I had dropped it. I met Paolo in the hall.

'OK, all set,' he said, 'We can go right now.'

'I'll go get Elizabeth, you handle him,' I said, pointing to the cupboard under the stairs.

Upstairs I heard the sound of a toilet flushing.

'Come on, time to be going,' I said through the door.

'Is that you, Lockhart?' Elizabeth called from inside.

'Yes, it's me.'

The door opened and she looked past me. Leaning close to my ear she whispered, 'Go in the bathroom!'

I opened my mouth to make some suitable reply when Paolo shouted up the stair, 'Come on, you two, no sense in hanging about!'

Elizabeth then gave me a violent push and propelled me into the bathroom and shut the door. There, in front of me was the wash-hand basin, and over it a mirror. On the mirror was written, in soap, ENTES IS ONE OF THEM I HEARD HIM ON THE PHONE IN THE BEDROOM.

I had to think - and my head was not clear at all. I splashed my face with water and, as an afterthought, wiped off the soapy message - while trying to think fast. I knew she was right. I knew what had been bothering me.

Entes had never asked me how I had fallen into their hands again after we had separated. He had no need to ask - he knew before I did! He had probably been watching. But why? It could only be because ... He was calling up the stairs again. If I could only manoeuvre ... I opened the door gently ...

Paolo stood on the landing - his gun pointing at my gut!

'Very carefully give me your gun,' he said, 'I know Elizabeth very well, and her eyes gave her away as soon as she looked at me just now,' he explained.

I put my hand in my pocket and removed the Luger, holding it by the barrel. He took it from me, transferred it to his right hand, and dropped the other one in his pocket.

'Thank you,' he said, 'You returned the wrong one earlier, you know, and it was quite empty when I gave it to you up at the castle.'

My head started throbbing again. Held up by an empty gun! He waved me downstairs where I found Elizabeth. She looked like a bereaved spaniel.

Trench-coat was all smiles again, standing by the back door. He looked for all the world like an advert for Pepsodent, gone wrong.

'The situation has somewhat changed,' said Paolo, 'We were going to play out this little charade for a while longer, but now that Big-Ears has listened in once too often, there's no need. Instead my colleague and I - you've not been introduced to Colonel Klutov, have you? - will escort you off this island and I must stress that, although we would be honoured by your continued company, we will have no hesitation in cutting short any misbehaviour in a most decisive manner. Do I make myself clear?'

He did.

We were marched down the path towards the boathouse in two pairs. Elizabeth was followed closely by Klutov, then, a few yards behind, I had Paolo at my back. I lengthened my stride to get nearer the two in front. My head was giving me hell now, and I could feel my temper boiling up. I was getting thoroughly sick of being made a fool.

We trooped through the door into the boathouse, and Entes made his mistake. As the other two went on down the steps he stopped me.

'Wait there,' he ordered, poking me in the ribs with his gun. Behind me he unlocked the door of the room and took a step inside to Hugo. As he did so, I pulled out through the tatty lining of my jacket the iron bar which had been there ever since the dungeon, yelled, 'JUMP ELIZABETH!' and launched myself down the stairs at Klutov. He was turning towards me as I crashed into him, and I caught him round the middle, pinioning his arms to his sides. We went through the guard rail and fell into the launch that had brought me to the island. I hung on for grim death as we landed and was able to roll over, getting him on top of me as a shield for when Entes began shooting.

With my arms still round him and holding the iron bar in both hands across his right wrist, I put a knee in his spine and squeezed until I felt the breaking of bones. He dropped his gun among our legs.

Elizabeth meanwhile, had done what she was told for once and taken an almighty leap for the bottom of the steps. She landed in a heap and rolled sideways off the landing stage into the water. I did not know what kind of a swimmer she was, but I prayed that she could get under and swim out of the boathouse while I kept the others busy.

Entes re-appeared at the top of the steps. I struck Klutov across the windpipe, using the iron bar. He went very limp and made a strange wheezy sound in his throat. Entes pointed his gun down at us, but hesitated. He began to come down the steps while I scrambled for Klutov's gun with one hand

and held him above me with the other. He was a helluva weight and I felt myself getting nowhere rapidly. Paolo was getting nearer. He was coming down the steps with his eyes on me like a cheetah fixed on its prey. The point of his gun waved about as I moved, and he could not get in a clear shot.

Behind him, Hugo had emerged from the room and stood at the top of the stairs, useless, making frantic efforts to untie his wrists. He began rubbing the cord against the rough banister. Paolo decided he would get nowhere shooting at me from above and began to come down more quickly. As he reached the part of the stair from which we had fallen, his foot came down on a broken piece of guard-rail. His leg slid from under him, and with nothing to hold onto, he fell.

His final descent was almost as quick as ours had been and he landed in a heap a few feet away and level with my head.

I rolled away from him and scrambled for the gun in the bottorn of the boat. He had held onto his, and as he came to rest he sat up, shook his head to clear it - and took aim.

Just then the boat gave a lurch as Elizabeth appeared out of the water and pulled on the side. Klutov's gun slid away from me. Entes' gun went off. The bullet passed between Elizabeth and me.

'Get up, Lockhart, or she gets the next bullet!' Entes shouted as he struggled to his feet.

Slowly I did so, and his gun pointed at my belly.

I hoped Elizabeth would disappear under the water again and give me a chance to dive in too. Instead she stayed there, half out of the water, her arms over the side of the boat.

Klutov began to stir and Paolo's gun wavered towards my right side. "Not my other bloody kidney!" I thought. Just then Hugo shouted Paolo's name, making him look up. Suddenly there was a shot from near my feet and Paolo staggered back against the wall, with a black hole where his left eye had been. His mouth gaped, his gun hand, then his whole body sagged and he crumpled in a grotesque heap.

I looked down at Elizabeth.

'Who taught you to shoot?' I asked.

'He did,' she replied and slid back into the water.

Then all hell was let loose. A motor boat chattered its way into the boathouse and the door at the top of the stairs was flung open by a guy in combat gear carrying a carbine. Two others leapt from the motor boat into the launch as Klutov tried to get the gun Elizabeth had dropped.

I stood on his good hand as he reached it, and the newcomers cannoned into me as they leapt aboard. My head struck someone's knee as I fell and then one of them crashed on top of me. I felt myself going under again. I struggled for air, but there seemed to be none available. My head was somewhere else and that big black hole opened up under me again. I tumbled in, wrapped in oblivion.

CHAPTER 34

I came round cradled in Elizabeth's arms, which was very pleasant, especially as her blouse was not doing a very thorough cover-up job after Willi's attentions. She was bathing my face in Rhine water, and as she breathed her breasts rose and fell rhythmically. I looked up at her and could see that she knew what I was thinking about. I grinned - but that leer came out again.

We were still in the launch which was otherwise unoccupied. The Marines - we really had been rescued by marines! - were all around, and at the foot of the steps Paolo's body sat against the wall, his face a horrible imitation of a cubist painting. A captain at the top of the steps was talking into a walkie-talkie. There was no sign of Hugo or Klutov, but I could hear coughing from above.

'They've got them in that little room up there,' Elizabeth said, reading my thoughts.

The captain came down the stairs.

'You OK, bud?' he asked. 'Yuh don't look too pecker to me.'

'I'll be all right,' I said, struggling to my feet. That nausea swept over me again and I willed myself not to throw up. I only just won. The captain was ogling Elizabeth's cleavage or tornage as it was - and I stepped between them, having a gander myself in the process. Then I remembered Willi!

'Did you get Willi?' I asked the captain.

He looked round at his men, mentally doing a role call.

'No, not one of them. The little German guy who was with Lansing and Klutov?'

He looked pretty blank.

'Where did you come from, anyway?' I asked.

'We been buzzin' around up there keepin' an eye on this place all day.'

Of course, the helicopters!

'WE?'

'We's from Frankfurter base. Got called out a few hours ago. A tall guy with bushy eyebrows ...'

'Does he have a mole - here?' I asked, indicating my right cheek.

'Yeah,' he replied.

Fox! "So Fox is here. He'll be more than pleased this time," I said to myself smugly, glancing again in the direction of Elizabeth.

But Willi, where the hell was he? We had left him in the castle, gawping at the bomb and securely tied up - or had we? Paolo had done the tying and I could hardly rely on it. And, although I remembered bolting the cell door before we left, Paolo had had plenty of time to go back and release Willi prior to coming to the island to fake our rescue.

'You got your helicopter here, haven't you?' I asked.

'Yeah, but ...'

'And this launch, plenty of room for all of you. I'm taking the motor boat,' I announced.

'Wait a minute, pal. Your Mister Fox is comin'

and ...'

'I've not time to wait, I've got a rendezvous with a right little bastard,' I said as I clambered into the motor boat alongside. I bent over the controls and started it up.

'Now lookie here, I got my orders.'

'And I'm sure they include giving me every assistance,' I threw at him over my shoulder as the motor started up. I straightened up and felt the boat lurch. Elizabeth had climbed aboard.

'Where the hell d'you think you're going?' I asked.

'With you. You need looking after, you're not well. As I'm sure I can't stop you, I'd better come with you.'

'That is ... ' I began to say, then caught a glance from her eyes, those grey eyes, and I knew I could not stop her, short of physically throwing her back in the launch. And I was not at all sure I could manage that.

'Anyway, you forgot a gun,' she said, waving one at me. It was Klutov's - with which she had shot Paolo. I did not like the look of it.

'Captain, you've been through the house, I take it. You didn't come across my Magnum Special, did you?' I asked.

We were already half way out the boathouse.

'This what you're lookin' for?' asked a sergeant at the foot of the steps, crouching beside Paolo's corpse.

He tossed me my gun, complete with holster. I had not seen it since the night before when Willi had drugged me in the hotel.

'You keep that one,' I said to Elizabeth, 'You seem to be able to shoot.'

She grinned - actually grinned.

The captain was furiously talking into his radio, presumably trying to get instructions to cover the changed situation and I had no intention of hanging around long enough for Fox to tell me not to go after Willi. I had a score to settle. Whatever the local poice might have decided about Klaus' murder being the work of an old lag, I knew better.

I spun the wheel and we headed for shore. Maybe Klutov would be able to worm his way out of this, or at worst have to wait a while to be exchanged for someone we wanted back. Hugo might even get away by that route, after Fox and Co. had bleached out of him all that he knew about Acme - whatever the hell that was.

But I was determined not to let Willi escape from justice, by any route whatsoever.

'Where are we going to look first?' Elizabeth asked, interrupting my thoughts.

'Although it's very unlikely he'll still be there, we'll have to go back to the castle first,' I said.

If he was not there, I reckoned he would have been given the job of organising transport for the next part of the journey that Klutov had planned for us. What that would have been, I had no idea and Klutov certainly would not be telling.

When we reached the landing stage the river bank was much busier. The Rhinegau cafe was doing good business on what was a lovely October morning. The tables outside were full and the sight of all that coffee and brandy was too much.

'I think we've time for a quick pick-me-up, don't you?' I asked.

'As far as I'm concerned, it's essential,' she replied.

She was still very wet. We skirted a big black chauffeur-driven Mercedes and went inside. I would have liked to sit outside, but with Willi still at large we would be sitting targets.

I ordered coffee and brandy - I was very hungry but there was no time to eat anything - while Elizabeth went to the ladies. When she came out she had managed somehow to transform her torn clothes into something quite presentable, but she had been forced to discard her bra. I drank my coffee and looked outside when I could drag my eyes away from her.

Something was niggling at my brain, and I could not figure out what it was. Nor could I understand why my cerebrations had been so slow in the last day or two. I had missed several obvious points - like why had Paolo not informed the authorities about Willi in the castle? If I had asked myself that question it would have been obvious he was not what he pretended to be. I was certainly proving slow on the uptake these days. Maybe it was just because it had been so long since I had been active in the field as opposed to active at the desk or in bed. The thought made me turn to Elizabeth again. As I did so I noticed that the big Mercedes had gone.

That was it! Willi! He was the chauffeur! I had seen only a momentary profile, just a subliminal glance and it had not immediately registered.

'Come on!' I said, 'Finish your drink and pay the man,' and dashed outside.

The second person I asked told me. The Mercedes had turned up the road to Assmannshausen. As Elizabeth emerged I called on her to follow and ran round the corner to where I remembered seeing a taxi stance that morning.

'Go up this road,' I said to the driver of its only occupant, 'I want to catch up with a Mercedes limousine that went up there a few minutes ago.' He got the idea and took off up the hill.

I tried to figure out where Willi was going, but came up with nothing. If he had been parked outside the cafe for some time he was bound to have seen the marines landing on the island. He must have hung around long enough to see if any of his pals were going to get away. Then when he saw us come ashore he would know the game was up. So where would he go then?

He could not get far - the net had been pulled tight around Rudesheim. But if Fox thought they were all on the island, the vigil may have been called off! In which case he might have a free run to Frankfurt. After a mile and a half or so we came to Aulhausen and just into the village the road forked. It did not take us long to find somebody who remembered the Mercedes taking the right fork. Back towards the Niederwald and Germania.

'Where's he going?' Elizabeth asked.

'I dunno, unless he's trying to lose himself in the crowds,' I said.

For once I had come to the right conclusion. We drove round in a semi-circle through the forest and came out at the monument. I glanced up at it ... how long it seemed since I had first seen it on Monday!

There in the car park was the Mercedes limousine. On the front seat lay a chauffeur's cap. I looked around. The place was as busy as Central Park on a Sunday. Where had he gone?

'The cable car!' exclaimed Elizabeth.

We took off at a run and my head began to pound again. Moments later we saw the queue about two hundred yards away waiting to go down. I stopped running and scanned the people standing in line.

He was at the front, and just as I spotted him he got on board a car. But he was not alone. A large fraulein pushed her way in beside him and shut the gate before anyone else could get aboard.

'He hasn't seen us,' I gasped to Elizabeth, 'Come on, we'll have to go down by road and get him at the bottom.'

We raced back to the taxi which still had the meter running, and set off.

'We'll never get down there before him this way,' Elizabeth protested.

'Have you a better suggestion?' I asked in exasperation. She said nothing. But of course she was right. When we reached the bottom end of the cable car we learned that the little guy and the fat woman had been disgorged a couple of minutes before we got there.

'So where to now?' asked Elizabeth and I began to wish she had not come. Then she smiled at me with those grey eyes, and I was not so sure.

'He'll not hang around Rudesheim. Even in these crowds,' I said.

'The railway station?' she suggested.

'It's worth a try, anyway,' I responded, smiling back. I felt better. The taxi took us down there and we paid him off at last.

There were quite a few people standing on the platform. No Willi. Somebody emerged from the crowd and came towards us. It was Edith of the ghastly specs!

'Hello, you two, I see you caught up with her at last, Mister Lockhart.' Her voice faded as she came near and saw the dishevilled mess I was in. Her look asked a question I had no intention of answering. Instead, I asked her:

'You haven't by any chance seen a small German guy wearing ...'

'You don't mean the man who took you out of the hotel when you were ill last night, do you?' she asked, to my surprise.

'Yes, that's him,' said Elizabeth.

'He was asking about trains to somewhere a few minutes ago,' replied Edith. 'He didn't seem to get a satisfactory answer so he went off.'

'Who did he ask?' I asked urgently.

'That official over there,' she said, pointing to a guy in a uniform standing further along the platform. A few questions got me the information that Willi had asked about trains to Koblenz - further down the Rhine. There wasn't another for an hour and he had left.

The only other way there, the station master had told him was by river. I retrieved Elizabeth from

Edith's burning curiosity with difficulty, and we set off for the river only two streets away.

'Wait a minute,' I said as we went, 'There's something wrong.'

'What?'

'Willi must have seen us back at the cafe, so he'll be half expecting us - or someone - to be following. If so, he wouldn't leave such an obvious trail by asking that guy at the station about getting to Koblenz.'

'You think he did that as a blind?'

'Probably. But of course that doesn't help us to find out where he IS going to.'

'In the opposite direction?' she queried.

'I was thinking the same thing,' I said.

Further along the quayside there were a series of billboards advertising the various boat trips available and we made our way towards them.

A few short queues had formed for the different destinations, but he was not in evidence. If he was already on one of the boats he would be able to see us very easily. I turned away, pulling Elizabeth with me. I saw a photographic shop across the road and pointed.

'Over there,' I said.

Inside he had what I was looking for.

'May I try these?' I asked, holding a pair of Zeiss binoculars which were on special display. The man waved me his permission. I stood at the door of the shop scanning the boats at the quayside. They were fairly busy, but I reckoned that if Willi was on any of them going in any direction, he would be bound to look to shore to see if he was being pursued.

No sign of him.

I began to wonder if the whole river idea was a red herring. It was a slow method of transport and would leave him very boxed in if anyone caught up with him. I would not like to be caught on a boat with the only way of escape a jump into the river ...

I cast about with the glasses - and suddenly saw him!

CHAPTER 35

Willi was in a phone booth about half a mile along the road. He was talking earnestly into the phone, then looked at his watch. I lowered the glasses as he glanced around, and stepped back into the shop.

'I've seen him,' I whispered to Elizabeth. I put the glasses down and said, 'Thank you' with the intention of leaving, when I had an idea. On the river or not, the binoculars would be very useful.

'Have you enough to pay for these?' I asked Elizabeth.

'I have my American Express card,' she replied.

I put them back round my neck and stood in the doorway as she made the purchase.

Willi emerged from the phone box and came towards us. I looked intently at the goods in the window and surreptitiously waved at Elizabeth not to come out. A coach passed on the way out of town and he was hidden for a moment. A big American car came towards us from the direction of Wiesbaden, was attracted by a man waving from the sidewalk, drew up to the quayside and stopped. I watched as the driver got out and spoke to the big fellow who had waved. They talked for a minute, the big guy pointing downstream, then at a launch at the foot of the steps where he stood. The rear door of the car opened and a familiar figure got out.

Fox had arrived.

He crossed to the river, and before I could decide whether to hail him or, in view of Willi's nearness, keep mum, he had descended into the launch and it took off, obviously making for the island further downstream. It would have been quicker for him to drive on to Assmannshausen and sail from there, but someone must have bungled his rendezvous.

I had momentarily forgotten Willi and looked back up the road, but he was not in sight. I cursed and Elizabeth asked me what was wrong. I told her what had happened, and that Willi was not to be seen. We scanned the distance and ...

'Look!' said Elizabeth, pointing to a figure on a motorbike.

There he was, coming out of an alley. He glanced from side to side and took off, away from us, towards Wiesbaden.

He had stolen a march on me, and unless we moved fast he was likely to get clean away. I looked around for likely transport, and it was staring me in the face.

'Come on!' I shouted to Elizabeth, and made for the quayside.

Fox had left the driver to pick him up later, and the car was hemmed in by a passing coach disgorging a party of tourists. I raced to it, my head pounding again, and just as I got there the coach moved off. The car was on the wrong side of the road, and as it crossed over I stood in front of it. Elizabeth joined me.

'Stay there,' I whispered, and went round to the

driver's window. I had decided that it would take too long to explain who I was and persuade him to take us, and I had no intention of giving Willi any more time than he already had. The driver was cursing Elizabeth for standing in his way, and gave me a mouthful of Brooklyn expletives when the window was down. While his mouth was still open I stuck the barrel of my Magnum between his teeth.

'Take your weapon out and throw it into the back seat. Then get out - I'm borrowing the department car.'

I must have looked as wild as a warthog because he did exactly as I told him and did not notice that I had not taken off the safety catch of the Magnum.

'Walk into that shop over there,' I ordered when he was out of the car. As he reached it Elizabeth got in and I pulled the car round in a U-turn and we sped away towards Wiesbaden.

'That was a bit risky, wasn't it?' Elizabeth asked, trembling.

'There's no time for pussy-footing around asking for help. Willi's already well ahead. We'll be lucky to catch up with him.'

But our luck was in. About three miles along the road we saw him up ahead. He was not going very fast, either, so as not to draw attention to himself and his stolen mount, or possibly - yes that was it - he was looking for something. He slowed down, glanced up at a sign post and accelerated away again.

As I watched I was thinking about the look on Fox's face when he heard that his car had been hijacked. I laughed as it occurred to me that it would look even worse when he learned that *I* had taken it! Elizabeth looked at me in a funny way - I guess I must have sounded kind of hysterical.

'Don't worry, I haven't flipped my lid,' I said.

'Glad to hear it,' she replied, but did not sound overly convinced.

We were travelling along a valley now, with grape-heavy fields rising up on either side. In the distance to our left I could see a castle with a cluster of buildings round it, partly hidden by trees. At the end of the road leading to it Willi slowed down, looked at the sign and turned in. When we reached the road end the sign said, simply, 'Schloss Fierstenberger.' Next to it was a symbol that looked like a stag's head.

'It's a vineyard,' said Elizabeth.

'Everywhere is around here,' I replied.

'Yes, but I've seen that sign on a wine label. They must make the wine here,' she said.

I turned into the driveway and went very slowly. We turned a bend and I saw the motorbike at the side of the road. Willi had gone ahead on foot. We had reached the edge of the trees and I reversed the car among them, beside the motorbike.

'Come on, this way,' I said, pointing through the trees, 'There's no point in announcing our arrival.'

Five minutes later we had a view of the castle and the winery. The castle stood well back and in front of it was a clutter of buildings of various ages. Using the binoculars, I scanned the place. There seemed to be no-one about. I remember noticing it was two-fifteen or so on the car clock.

'Probably at lunch,' I said. Elizabeth nodded.

Then I saw a smart-looking guy in a tweed sports coat come out of a door, look around quickly and cross the cobbled yard to a wooden stairway on the outside of one of the buildings. He went up and tapped on the door at the top. It opened and Willi stuck his head out, looking around before letting the guy in.

I set off towards the buildings, then turned to Elizabeth.

'You stay here,' I ordered, handing her the glasses.

She was about to protest, but thought better of it, and just nodded. I went between the different structures, keeping out of sight in case they came out again. I got to within twenty feet of the foot of the stairs and there was still no sign of anyone. Drawing my Magnum from its holster, I walked quietly across and went up, two at a time. I listened at the door but there was no sound inside. I opened it. Inside was a fairly large office with the usual sort of furniture, but pretty ancient. On the far side, another door lay open and now I could hear voices beyond. I tip-toed across and poked my head out into a corridor. The sounds had come from a door further along on the other side. As I reached it I recognised Willi's voice, saying the same thing over and over again. I frowned, and just then a floor board creaked - from behind me!

As I turned, something very hard was poked in my back and a voice said:

'Drop the gun, Mister Lockhart. No, don't try anything that would force me to shoot you right here and now ...'

Whoever he was, he meant it!

I dropped the Magnum and he kicked it along the corridor. The door in front of me opened. Willi stood there with a grin on his face, for all the world like a schoolboy who's been given the run of the tuck shop. He stepped back and the gun at my back prodded me into the room.

CHAPTER 36

They sat me down in an office chair, one of the original revolving kind. Willi could not contain his glee. While the other guy kept his gun on me, Willi spun me round and as I came to face him he slapped me across the cheek. Then he did it again in the other direction. I held onto the chair to keep from falling off, I was so dizzy. My brain felt as if it was turning in the opposite direction to the rest of me. All the time I was trying as best I could to figure out how the hell they knew I was coming.

'... so very good of you to drop in on us, Mister Lockhart,' the winery guy was saying, 'And so good of you to come alone. Why, you might have made things very awkward and brought all those funny soldiers who've been flying around the district all day.'

'Well, they certainly made it awkward for your friends ...' I began.

They did not know quite what had happened on the island, and were hoping I would tell them.

'You were saying, Lockhart?' Willi queried. I got the distinct impression he would really rather I said nothing, so that he could have the pleasure of beating it out of me.

Thank God I had left Elizabeth - this way I could string them along, but if she had been there for Willi's pleasure ...

'Well, what happened back there on the island?'

asked Tweed-coat.

'Don't you know? How careless of you to lose contact,' I said.

'Really Lockhart, this sort of cheap wit won't get you anywhere. If we know what happened it might be to your advantage. Otherwise we would be better off with you dead. It would be simple enough to arrange. There are places here where you would never be found.'

I was trying hard to figure out what to tell them.

'You saw what happened,' I said to Willi, 'The "funny soldiers" as you put it, came on the island and rounded up your friends. That's all.'

'And where were you going with the woman?' he asked.

'We just left them to it and went over to the cafe for a drink and some breakfast. I saw you on the way in and left her there to follow you.'

They looked at each other, trying to decide if what I had said was true. It apparently fitted in with what they already believed for they seemed satisfied. Well, Tweed-coat was. Willi was disappointed at being denied another chance to display his sadistic talents.

'It is as well you told us the truth,' said the other, 'If any of our friends had been ... eliminated, it would have been the end for you. As it is, an exchange can no doubt be worked out.'

I kept mum. It was up to them now.

I was trying to figure out how long it would take Fox's man to come after their car. But where I had left it they might not find it. Unless Elizabeth ...

'Come on Lockhart, it's time to prepare you for your journey,' said Tweed-coat.

I did not like the sound of that. Whatever they had in mind, I had had enough.

'Go piss into the wind,' I snarled.

'Is that the best you can do? You are a miserable little man aren't you? Trotting along here after Willi, in a car that can be seen for miles around. Yes, Lockhart, I saw you from the castle. Doing your "I'll-charge-in-and-arrest-him" thing. You are a long way, how do you say it - out of your league. A very long way.'

He spoke like a peevish schoolmaster, his red face coming close to mine to emphasise his point. He shrugged and spread his hands wide - and I kicked him hard in the gut, and went for his gun hand.

It was not very difficult to wrest it from him while keeping him between me and Willi.

I had not noticed, but behind him, Willi had been preparing a dose of his knock-out drops, and had both hands occupied when I made my move. As soon as he realised that I had got hold of the gun he ducked out of the door. The little phial he left on a table. I glanced outside and saw him disappear in the direction of the stairs, but was too late to get in a shot, and was about to follow when Tweed-coat, still on the floor, started to show signs of recovery. I took the phial and went over to him. Standing behind him, I took the dropper and bent down. Before he knew what was happening, I popped two or three drops into his mouth then held it closed for a few seconds. He would be out of it for a while. And now for Willi.

I went along the corridor, retrieved my own gun and looked around for the best way to follow him. It had to be the stair down to the yard, but going that way I would be a sitting target. I took hold of an ancient wooden desk and up-ended it, using it as a shield. I pushed my way out through the door. Thank God for old-fashioned German furniture! The bullets from Willi's gun sank into the wood harmlessly and I fired round the desk in his general direction, then peered round the edge, just in time to see him duck into a doorway across the yard. I could not understand why he had not taken off down the road for the motorbike which would have given him a good chance to get away. The answer came as I dived down the steps. A tractor was coming up the drive, drawing a trailer full of baskets. The grape harvest! I ran towards it, stooping low.

As I neared it Elizabeth emerged from behind a barn and waved it down. The driver was none too bright, but we managed to persuade him to go no further.

My resolve to go in and get Willi was melting. I had no intention of tackling him where he had a distinct advantage, inside those buildings. I asked the guy on the tractor where the phone was. With Willi bottled up in there we could afford to wait for assistance and winkle him out.

'You stay here,' I said to Elizabeth, 'I'm going to call up some help. I might be able to get a message through to Fox. Failing that the local police will have to do. There's nowhere for Willi to go now.'

She looked into my eyes and said, 'Are you all right? Be careful.'

I wanted to say something, but just grinned again. I turned to go. A bullet zinged past my ear and squelched into a basket of grapes. We all dived for cover. It had come from above somewhere.

From behind the trailer I looked up. The only really high point was the tower of the castle set against the background of the hills, and all of two or three hundred yards away. That had been no pistol shot!

Willi had got hold of a rifle. And God knows how much ammunition. It was going to be some job, getting him down from there.

At that moment we heard the chatter of a helicopter coming along the valley. I knew who would be in it. At least I wouldn't need to phone. We turned towards it and waved, but the trees were in the way and it continued past the estate.

'Damn! They must be looking for the car,' I said.

'I'll go and get it and drive it out into the open and ...'

Elizabeth began.

'You'll not get six feet down the road with him up there holding a rifle,' I said, 'But thanks for the try. There's no hurry. They'll be back when they don't see the car up ahead. We can afford to wait.'

But what if they did not see Willi in time and he was able to get a shot at the helicopter!

I decided that I must get after him, but he had us pinned down to good effect. Or maybe not.

I crawled under the trailer to the front and undid the pin that held it to the tractor. It took the three of us all our time to balance the trailer on its two wheels, while hiding behind the tractor, turn it and push it in the direction of the castle. But it was effective.

As Willi saw it move he loosed off a shot or two, but we were well screened by the baskets of grapes. I asked the driver how to get through to the castle, and at last we came within the shadow of the buildings in front of the tower. Willi could no longer see us. I sprinted for the door the man had indicated and made my way through a warehouse. At the other side, the castle was about twenty-five yards away across open space, and I could not be sure I would not be in Willi's sights if I crossed the gap. I peered up at the tower. Round the top there were castellations through which he had been firing. No sign of Willi. Could I get across that distance and avoid getting myself shot?

The sound of the helicopter interrupted my thoughts. I could hear it approach from the valley.

Suddenly, as it got nearer, Willi stood up and fired towards it. I sprinted for the castle, flattened myself against the wall and looked up. The helicopter was turning away and I could see the barrel of Willi's rifle pointing out over the edge of the tower. I had reached the castle's main entrance at the foot of the tower. Before Willi had a chance to look down, I slipped through the open door. It was very gloomy in there and I had to wait a moment to get used to the poor light. The place was mediaeval - a huge hall with heavy black furniture. There were even two suits of armour standing guard on either side of an enormous fireplace you could hold a disco in.

To my right was an open door - into the tower. I wiped my right hand on the seat of my pants to get a sure grip of my gun, and went in. It had a central spiral staircase with rooms opening off every so often, but they had all been boarded up. The topmost room, however, was in use. It appeared to be used by an artist, for paints, canvasses and easels were strewn around. In one corner was a ladder to the roof. As I crept over to it I heard the helicopter again, coming nearer. Then a rifle shot rang out and the chattering blades grew quieter as I went up the ladder. I poked my head out and saw Willi. He had his back to me and was looking down through one of the gaps of the castellations. He seemed satisfied that no-one was below, put the gun down, then turned round to sit down against the stone-work, and looked straight at me.

My gun was pointing at him. I opened my mouth to speak. He went for the rifle and as he grabbed it, I fired. My shot missed him but smashed the stock of the rifle and knocked it out of his grasp. He curled up and sat there shaking as I walked towards him. I fought hard not to shoot him there and then, and could feel my hand trembling. As I got nearer he made such a pathetic sight, cowering and snivelling at my feet that my fury abated and I felt nothing but contempt. I relaxed - and he went for my legs. He came at me with the speed of a striking viper and the shot I fired went harmlessly past him. As he caught me round the legs I went flying and thudded against the lead roof, my gun scuttering from my grasp. He went for my throat, his nails scratching at my neck in the process. I managed to bring a knee up and forced him back with all my might. He let go and seemed to sail through the air like a circus acrobat - unfortunately in the direction of my gun. I dived after him and just managed to grasp hold of his hair as he stretched for the Magnum. I wrenched hard and rolled him away from the gun, but somehow he squirmed round on top of me. He was at my throat again, and as I flailed at his face with my fists he banged my head against the roof.

Things began to go black and he banged my head again. With all that was left of my strength I made a hard flat hand and jabbed repeatedly at his Adam's apple. His grip on my throat loosened and I struggled to my feet, throwing punches as I did so. He still came at me and I found myself with my back to the parapet. I was at one of the gaps with only eighteen inches of wall behind my legs.

Switching his furious attack from my throat, he ducked his head to butt me in the midriff. However, I twisted to one side and his head made glancing contact with my hip. It was not enough to damp his momentum and he carried on past me like a wounded bull past a matador. With a scream he realised he was going over, and his left hand grabbed at me while the rest of him sailed on into space.

Suddenly I found myself with Willi's weight tugging at my coat. I fought hard to stay on my feet, but overbalanced and fell over the edge after him.

CHAPTER 37

It took longer for me to come round this time. The abyss was deeper and darker than ever and the climb back out agonisingly slow.

When I eventually emerged, Elizabeth was by my side and I could see Fox approaching. I lifted my hand to wave to him, but it was bandaged. I couldn't remember injuring it. Then I remembered falling! Looking around, I realised I was in hospital.

I tried hard to think of some clever remark to make, so I said:

'Where am I?'

'American base hospital, Frankfurt,' Elizabeth replied, squeezing my hand. I turned to look at her. She had found the time to make herself up and was wearing something quite stunning I had never seen before. But my head ached and felt all tight and hot, although the ghastly nausea had gone.

Fox looked down at me.

'Howd'ya feel Lockhart?' he asked.

I was pleased that he could not come up with anything very smart either.

'OK boss. What the hell's been happening to me?'

'You've been in surgery. They had to make a hole in your head. You've been bleeding inside, pressure on the brain.'

It sounded to me like a death sentence. It must have shown.

'You'll be fine now, they've done what was needed and it's just a matter of time ... till you get well, I mean,' he added hastily.

Elizabeth nodded and smiled at me. I felt better. A nurse came in and asked me if I would like to sit up a little, and pressed a switch to elevate the top of the bed. The whirring of the motor reminded me of the helicopters and the whole thing came flooding back. I closed my eyes, and the images of the last four days floated in front of me, each one struggling for attention. I opened them again and sighed, and it all seemed like a dream. A bad dream. With good bits. I looked at Elizabeth.

'Come on, out,' ordered the nurse, 'It's time for the patient to rest. You can come back later.'

When they had gone she gave me an injection.

I awoke in the late afternoon and the sunlight through the venetian blind striped the bottom of the bedcover. There were flowers on the window ledge and the room seemed quite different. My right arm was no longer bandaged to an IV infusion and although it ached, it was nice to have the use of it. I sat up and squeezed the bell push. Elizabeth came in.

'Can I help you?' she asked.

'You most certainly can. Pour me a glass of water then tell me what's been happening.'

The water tasted even sweeter than the local brandy. I drank two glassfuls and burped noisily.

She grinned.

'What can you remember? The surgeon said - you do know about the operation? - good. He said you might have some amnesia.'

'I can remember everything quite clearly up to when I fell from the top of the castle tower after Willi.'

'I came after you and arrived on the roof just as you went over. Without you realising it your struggle had taken you to the other side of the tower - where it joins onto the main building. The roof of the castle is only twelve feet below the tower on that side.'

'So that's how I'm still alive!'

'That and the fact that you must have fallen on top of Willi.'

'And him?' I asked.

'A few broken bones, but he survived. He's in prison somewhere, I think.'

'And I got ... all this,' I said, waving at my bandaged skull.

'Not just then. Apparently you had been bleeding ... in your head, for quite some time. Days in fact. They said that with all the bangs on the head you've taken, you're lucky to be ... still with us.'

Funnily enough, I got the distinct impression that she was quite pleased.

'What about Hugo?' I asked, looking at her keenly.

'They took him and the Russian somewhere ... I'm not sure where.'

As she spoke Fox came in - all smiles.

'Well now, Lockhart, you're looking perkier than

a ...'

'Turkey at Thanksgiving!' I said. We all laughed.

'You sure have got your lip back - a sign of recovery no doubt. Although you never did give up on those wisecracks, did you?'

'Now, Boss, you know they brighten up your day!'

'Not for much longer, Lockhart.'

'What does that mean?'

'Just that. I'm on my way Stateside later today.'

'With our Russian friends?' I asked.

'They're no friends of mine,' Elizabeth said decisively.

'What about Lansing, he told you anything yet?' I asked.

'We know some of it. He is Russian, you know,' said Fox.

'We knew that ages ago,' said Elizabeth dismissively.

'Pity you didn't let us in on the secret,' said Fox.

'Now, Boss, don't get bitter. Just because a woman outsmarted you - us, I should say.' He had the good grace to grin.

'When did you realise he is actually a Russian?' I asked Elizabeth.

'Not until you had caught up with me. It was in the car on the way to Rudesheim. You said something about him going to Moscow and it came to me in a flash that he must be ... Russian.'

'Yes, I was pretty slow in cottoning onto that,' I admitted, 'I even thought he had maybe replaced the real Hugo Lansing in the last few years, something like that.'

'You could hardly be expected to guess the truth. He had deceived people close to him for well-nigh thirty years ...' Fox tailed off as he caught Elizabeth's eye.

'Yes, me too,' she admitted.

'How exactly was it done?' I asked.

'Quite simple, really,' explained Fox, 'At the end of the war the Commies were already looking for ways of spying on us. They planted this guy on General Lansing as some sort of long-lost cousin. At first I don't suppose they thought he would get to the States, that was a bonus for them. Having got there he had to go through with it. I reckon they thought he would go a long way. Who knows, he mightta got to the very top - even Secretary General.'

'Who was he, originally?' Elizabeth asked.

'A lieutenant in the Red Army. He was acting on orders.'

'Acting being the operative word,' she said.

'You're taking them both back with you?' I asked.

'Yeah. We'll get as much as we can out of them, then ...'

'We'll hold onto them and maybe do a swop at some time?' I put in.

'That's the idea,' he said.

'Should be quite valuable merchandise,' Elizabeth said.

'Yeah. Two Colonels in the KGB.' Fox nodded sagely.

'Two Colonels?' I asked with surprise.

'Of course, you didn't know. Lansing, that is

Vorotnikov, has been kept on the Moscow payroll all these years. When he went to the States he was transferred to the KGB and they've been paying him ever since. He's now a full Colonel.'

'So he'll have quite a nest egg waiting for him when he does eventually get back,' I said, a trifle bitterly, thinking of my last bank statement.

'He'll have a long time to wait for it, we'll make sure of that. Being a US citizen, technically at least, he'll go down for years before we let him go.'

'And the other - Klutov?'

'He's a bit different. We've not a lot in the way of a concrete charge against him. Poor guy was only doing his job, after all.'

'Some job!' said Elizabeth.

'He was responsible for Klaus's death, wasn't he?' I suggested.

'He claims not,' said Fox.

'Oh, come on!'

'No, he may be telling the truth. He says that he instructed Willi to look out for anyone making inquiries about the town hall records in Rudesheim, and, to destroy them if necessary. BUT he claims he was referring to the records, not the guy doing the looking.'

'But Willi took him to mean ... yes, I suppose it's possible,' I said, 'Anyway, we've got Willi ...' I stopped when I saw the look on Fox's face.

'We have got him, haven't we?' I demanded.

'He's dead,' Fox said.

'DEAD?' Elizabeth and I exclaimed together.

Fox nodded.

'What in hell's name happened?' I asked.

'Don't forget Willi is, WAS, a German citizen,' Fox explained. 'When we got him at the vineyard along with the other guy - I'll tell you about him in a minute - we had to hand him over to the proper authorities. We had caused quite a rumpus in their territory, remember, and we couldn't very well ship them all out, leaving them with nothing to show for it.'

'So what happened?' asked Elizabeth.

'After patching him up they slung him in gaol while making up their minds what to charge him with. He was saying nothing and it wouldda' been difficult to nail him for Klaus. Apparently he had a visitor and ...'

'A visitor!' I exclaimed.

'Yeah. Some mutt felt sorry for him and let this woman in.'

'A woman!'

'You're interrupting again, Lockhart.'

'Sorry.'

'She was only in a few minutes, then after she'd gone they found him half asleep - only it wasn't no lullaby she'd given him. There was an empty brandy miniature in the cell. He never came round.'

'And they got nothing out of him?' I asked.

'The only thing he said before he went under was a name - her name I suppose. HELGA, that's what he said, over and over again. That's all.'

'Who was she?' asked Elizabeth.

'Nobody we know. She sounds like a classy dame. Wearing a red dress and a fur coat. She was in and out in minutes. Sent to do the job, I reckon.'

I nodded in agreement.

'You mean, they killed him?' Elizabeth asked.

'He must have known a lot about their set-up, more than they'd want him to tell. Sooner or later he'da' told what he knew, and they were aware of that.' Fox shrugged and put a match to his pipe.

'So he survived the bomb and the fall from the castle tower only to be killed by a woman,' Elizabeth said, grimly.

'Oh, the bomb - that wouldn't have killed him - or anybody else,' Fox said between puffs at his pipe, 'The owner of the castle had it defused years ago. He left it where you found it only because to dig it out woulda' meant demolishing nearly the whole place, and he couldn't afford to rebuild it.'

I remembered how I had felt on finding the bomb, and could not help smiling.

'Who was the other man?' Elizabeth asked, 'At the vineyard, I mean.'

'Von Lutz is his name. You did a good bit of work tracking Willi there, Lockhart. We found a whole set-up. He was the local Kremlin agent and had got himself damned good cover. He had claimed to have aristocratic connections and wormed his way into the wine business as General Manager to the Count who owns it. He even joined the local branch of the Nazi party - though they call themselves something else nowadays - as cover. He was doing legitimate trade with East Germany - only some of the shipments contained more than wine. We found a half-finished crate that was intended for you Lockhart. He had also figured out a neat way of passing information. He printed the wine labels on an old press at the winery and by varying the design - adding different twirly bits round the edges and so forth - could get messages through to the East with virtually no chance of detection.'

'How come he's been so forthcoming with all this?' I asked.

'Probably something to do with those drops you gave him. Apart from knocking you out most effectively, they make you more pliable when you come round.'

'And he's not had any visitors?' asked Elizabeth.

'No.' Fox laughed.

'To return to Willi for a minute,' I said, 'Has he been positively identified, do you know?'

'Don't think so - why?' asked Fox.

'I had a feeling I had seen him somewhere before, that's all.'

'Maybe from your Interpol days,' suggested Elizabeth.

'Yes, maybe that's it. That might explain why he gave me these knock-out drops almost as soon as we'd found him and Hugo that night. If he remembered me he may have assumed I would recognise him.'

'Funny thing is, Lockhart, he may have saved your life!'

'What!?'

'Yeah. These drops kinda helped to stop the bleeding inside your skull. I don't understand, but the medics tell me that that stuff acts in some way to reduce brain pressure or something. They reckon you was already haemorrhaging that night, and the stuff did some good. You must 'ave gotta helluva bang during the rucus at the farm.'

I shook my head. 'No, it was earlier ... doesn't matter now,' I murmured.

Elizabeth caught my eye and said, 'It was Drummy, wasn't it?'

I nodded, smiling grimly.

'What're you two talking about?' asked Fox.

'Nothing,' I said, 'Just a departed friend. And talking about departed FRIENDS, what about the late, unlamented Paolo Entes? Where exactly does he fit in?'

'Good question, Lockhart. We can only surmise, of course. No-one's gonna come out and tell us.'

'Didn't Klutov ..?' I asked.

'Naw! Aside from claiming he never ordered Klaus's murder, he ain't opening his Moscow jaw.'

'What have you surmised about him? Was he another Russian?' Elizabeth asked.

'Entes? He was genuine Portuguese all right. Well-known in UN circles.'

'So was Hugo-stroke-Rudolf! Hardly a guarantee of rectitude,' Elizabeth said, without a trace of bitterness.

'Yeah, but he had genuine roots, an important family an' all. They have real estate galore in Portugal and even property in New York.'

'An excellent sea-food restaurant, as I recall,' she said.

'I didn't know that,' Fox said, making one of his rare admissions of ignorance.

'Never mind the gastronomic tour, where does he fit in, deception-wise?' I interposed, beginning to feel out of it.

'I think it was a case of the Commies indulging in their well-known habit of not trusting anybody,' Fox began. 'They must have sent him to keep an eye on Lansing to see what he was up to. Maybe also to check on whether or not we were taking an interest. I reckon he came across you, Miss Tasker, and had to find out just what you were up to. There was no way he could be certain you were not planted there to watch your boss. So he strikes up an acquaintance and ...'

'Teaches me to shoot!' Elizabeth added.

'When you think about it, it was quite a clever ploy. If you really had been an agent you would have been a crack shot. It would be difficult to pretend not to know one end of a gun from another in his company unless you stayed away from them. If you had refused to have anything to do with them, he would probably have found some other test. The fact that you were willing to learn - and proved quite good at it - was pretty strong evidence that you were not already a good shot.'

'You mean that a crack shot would find it very difficult to go through the motions of learning it all again from scratch,' Elizabeth said.

'Yes, without giving yourself away. I'll bet he kept an eye on you all the time.'

'He certainly did. And to think I thought it was just because ...'

'Where did you do all this shooting, anyway?' I asked.

'At his Athletic Club. Very proud of his membership, he was. We went riding there too.'

'And you became a damned good shot,' I said with feeling.

'Yes, I got to the final of the Ladies' Novice Cup - the very day I flew out here, last Saturday - only five days ago.'

'I wasn't thinking of last Saturday, so much as yesterday when you saved my life,' I said quietly.

'Yeah, well, it was unfortunate that he died, we could have done with a chat with him. Pity one of the marines had to shoot him.' Fox looked out the window as he spoke. Elizabeth and I exchanged glances.

'What I don't understand,' she said, 'Is the point of all that charade of rescuing us twice when all the time ...'

'The purpose was quite simply to gain your complete confidence,' Fox began.

'So as to get some information out of me,' I added.

'What information?' Elizabeth asked.

I looked at Fox.

'Yes, what about A ...' The look on his face froze the word on my tongue.

Elizabeth looked from one to the other of us.

'I'll leave you two now. There must be things you want to discuss without me.' She stood up and made as if to leave.

I touched her arm.

'You'll come and see me again?' I asked, afraid of what her answer might be.

Fox cleared his throat and looked out of the window again. She looked me straight in the eye with those gorgeous grey peepers and said:

'I'm not going anywhere.'

There was the faintest of smiles on her face as she left the room. After a moment of fantasising I turned to Fox.

'So Entes was after Acme too, was he?'

'I reckon so.'

'Yes, it fits. He must have made contact with Hugo while we were still in the castle. Hugo told him what I had said, and he did his rescue act in order to get me to confide in him. He must have been hellish disappointed when I told him I knew nothing at all.'

'So what had you told Lansing?' Fox asked with a frown.

'He told me that ACME is four initials - place names. At least, he said there is Amarillo, then Casper - then wanted to know the other two. He was quite insistent.'

'And you gave him?'

'Memphis and Encino. They were the first two that came into my head.'

'And you think he believed you?'

'He could have done - he thought he had got it out of me under threat of what he would let Willi do to Elizabeth.'

'The bastard,' said Fox, 'But afterwards you told Entes that you really knew nothing at all about Acme.'

'Which is true. What the hell is ...'

'Just a minute, this is important. Can you tell me if Entes got the chance to tell Lansing that you knew nothing about it?'

'He couldn't have. We were in the house - on the

island when I spoke to him and Lansing was in the boathouse. He only just got to the boathouse to let Hugo out when I jumped Klutov and then Elizabeth shot him.'

'You mean, one of the marines shot him, ..' Fox said blandly.

'Yes, of course,' I nodded in agreement .

'He could have told Klutov - at the house while Elizabeth and I were upstairs.'

'That doesn't matter. It's what Lansing thinks you know that may be important.'

'Now, for God's sake, Boss, will you tell me what this Acme thing is all about? How did it all come into the picture? We started off just chasing after Elizabeth because she had taken off to Frankfurt.'

'Lansing's downfall was dames. Let that be a lesson to you.'

Recalling Mrs Fox, I could understand the sincerity of this advice. I waited as Fox tried to light his pipe again.

'His wife,' he said between gurgly draws, 'Suspected him a long time ago.'

'She WHAT?' I gasped.

'Stop interrupting, Lockhart,' he said, and blew some noxious smoke in my direction. 'She probably suspected for much the same reasons as our Miss Tasker. But, she came to a different conclusion. Realising he wasn't quite what he was supposed to be, she thought he was on our side - a US agent! Her brother the Senator had a little part in Lansing's appointment as head of UNPA and it never occurred to her that someone her brother favoured was working for the other side. That's partly why she never insisted on a divorce after they separated. He occasionally visited her at the ranch in Wyoming. On the last occasion she saw him coming out of her brother's study. She didn't think too much about it at the time, but she mentioned it later. Well, it so happens the Senator ...'

'Of course, Casper, in Wyoming,' I said.

'You're at it again, Lockhart,' Fox said, 'You must be getting better. Anyhow you're right. The Senator had some knowledge of Acme and had been stupid enough to take some papers home. Nothing very top secret of course, he doesn't have access to anything like that. It was just that the folder had A-C-M-E on it and he was playing guessing games with himself as to the sites. He knew Casper, being in his State, and he had jotted Amarillo - he thought that was another. The others he had no idea of. Lansing clearly read his notes and concluded that he had come across something big. Well he was right, although he didn't know just what it was all about. He only knew that something important was to be set up near Casper - and the other places. When Willi had drugged you and taken you to the castle that night, Lansing knew there was no going back. He had to flee to Moscow. Well, he hadn't much to take with him for all his years in the USA - except for Acme.'

'And he thought I had chased him to Germany because of it.'

'Probably. So he tried to get the rest to take home with him to his Kremlin masters.'

Fox set about lighting his pipe again.

'Are you going to tell me, Boss?' I asked quietly.

'I'm not going to tell you the sites. I don't even know them myself. But Acme, A-C-M-E stands for Alternative Congressional and Military Establishments. Four places with those same initials where the US Administration can be set up in the event of a nuclear war. It's been years in the preparation.'

'And are they ...?'

'No more questions, Lockhart. You know too much already. Get some rest now.'

He got up to go. I took a sip of water and closed my eyes.

'Oh, by the way,' he said as he went out the door, 'We've fixed you up with some convalescence. Thought you might like England for a few weeks. Place in the country. King's Ling, or something, it's called. I believe you know that part of the world.'

He grinned.

THE END

BORN ROTTEN.

JOE CANNON.

This bizarre novel is a powerful, gripping and exciting story which tells of the bruitality and violence of London's underworld as it is today.
Joey Bello, the anti-hero described by the title, takes the reader into the criminal haunts of London's Soho, the subculture of Notting Hill where racial tensions fuel sporadic outbreaks of violence, the eerie night-life of the West End, and the strange other world of the expatriate villian basking in the Spanish sun.
As the Bello saga unfolds, the reader is transported into the battle-ground of international crime, where billions of pounds, dollars and other currencies swell the pockets of traffickers in drugs and vice, where conspiracy, extortion corruption and murder are commonplace. Here the Mafia, a criminal octupus, spreads its tentacles worldwide.
BORN ROTTEN throws a searchlight on international crime and in doing so opens up a new era in crime fiction.

Paperback price £4.50 net U.K.

YELLOW BRICK PUBLISHERS. 2, Lonsdale Road, Queens Park. London . NW6 6RD.

ENGLAND'S TOUGHEST VILLIAN.

JOE CANNON.

Gripping, exciting, and often horrifying, this is the story of Joey Bello, an ex-criminal, who wages his own personal war against corruption in the highest places: the untouchable echolons of our own police force and especially the Mafia.
Joey Bello fights on his terms. He meets violence with violence, bruitality with bruitality.
ENGLAND'S TOUGHEST VILLIAN opens a window into the sub-culture of the underworld, introducing the reader to a side of life which he would ordinarily and otherwise not see: a world of theives jargon and evil deeds, where danger lurks in dark corners and where the threat of death is ever-present: a world in which a sawn-off shotgun is no respecter of persons: where a .45 automatic is a great leveller.

Paperback price £4.50 net U.K.

YELLOW BRICK PUBLISHERS. 2, Lonsdale Road, Queens Park, London. NW6 6RD.

JUDGE ME NOT.

JOE CANNON.

In this book, the final volume of the trilogy following BORN ROTTEN and ENGLAND'S TOUGHEST VILLIAN, the saga of Joey Bello continues.
Here the author draws on his considerable knowledge of sophisticated crime to give a picture of computer frauds carried out by Bello and his confederates. While not being a guide to the essential elements of this type of crime, the fiction presented here has a basis in fact, as any computer hacker will know.
A chapter of the book is devoted to a fictionalised account of the probable circumstances surrounding the murder on the Costa del Sol of Great Train Robber Charlie Wilson. Amid a welter of speculation, the author's informed opinion is as good as any and better than most. He opens a window on criminal activity which has hitherto been securely locked and bolted.

CARDBOARD CITY.

JOE CANNON.

Tommy Hutton was a happy man. He had a good job and a comfortable home where he lived with his wife and infant daughter. When wife and child were killed in a train accident, Tommy turned to drink. One day he burned his house to the ground in a drunken rage and set out for London. Now a confirmed alcoholic, he haunted the public houses of Bayswater. When his money ran out, he found refuge among London's homeless beneath the arches of Waterloo Bridge.
The story of his experiences is set against the background of CARDBOARD CITY, a community of the homeless and the hopeless where society's outcasts sleep in cardboard boxes. It is a harrowing story marked by scenes of violence, but in the end he conquers his addiction and dedicates himself to helping the unfortunates who were instrumental in bringing him face to face with reality.

Paperback price £4.95 net U.K.

AUTOBIOGRAPHY

GANGSTER'S LADY

ELLEN CANNON.

The story of ELLEN CANNON'S life tells what it's like being a member of one of Notting Dale's largest families and because of the family tie, the support from the Mafia.
This book is packed with incidents. As her man rose through the ranks of villainy and became a major gangland figure, she was introduced into the society of London's top Jollies of the Underworld. She learned to play the game of the Gangster's Lady in strict accordance with the rules.
Whatever knowledge she had of the secrets of Gangland she kept it to herself-
Now for the first time she's telling all-
She pulls no punches and gives a documented account of the violent life with her husband.
She is a remarkable lady.